PRIEST
PLAY

www.**BarbarianSpy**.com

WARNING: This book is for sale to **ADULT AUDIENCES ONLY**. Contains graphic gay male sex, multiple partners, anal sex, interracial sex, and gay love all of which may be considered offensive by some readers.

All sexually active characters in this work are at least 18 years of age.

BarbarianSpy
Toronto, NSW
Australia

BarbarianSpy

FOR LITERARY HEAT

Priest Play

habu

TABLE OF CONTENTS

Introduction

The subject of priests or ministers as sex partners with other men is one of the more taboo subjects in the writing of erotica. Habu has tackled this theme in gay male writing before, though, so naturally, as a publisher, we urged him to gather some of the stories in a subject-specific anthology, which has resulted in *Priest Play*. We gleaned nearly a dozen previously published stories that included priests at sex play from habu's various anthologies, and, in addition to adding to these, he wrote five new, never-before-published stories to make up a fifteen-story anthology in which the clergy is given dispensation to indulge itself in man sex.

The anthology is split in two sections—stories with historical settings and contemporary stories. Included are works in which a priest is only included among the men engaged in sex, like "24 Exeter Place" and the "Debatables"—and do so without the slightest remorse—and stories that focus on the perplexity of being a priest and still desiring and needing sex with other men, such as the concluding stories "Senegal Surrender," "Fitting In," and "Banishment."

The seven leadoff historical section stories run roughly from most-distant past to more recent time. "Captive Temple Priests" takes us back into the murky ancient history of upper Nile kingdoms and to victory blessing rituals and the intentions of a conquering Assyrian general that get caught up in palace intrigue. "The Brotherhood" is a more brooding and ominous story of sex with young men as a cult ritual in a medieval German monastery. "Inquisitioned" is even more ominous in telling of powerful priests mixing preying on young men sexually with hunting out those with Jewish ancestry in the court at Barcelona during the Spanish Inquisition. Both of these latter stories have never before been published.

"24 Exeter Place" takes us to London and forward in time into the late nineteenth century for a look into the life of the male prostitutes in a "gentlemen's club" male brothel, where a prominent priest is treated as a prominent guest and a local bishop gets in his digs as well. "Carnival at Viareggio" takes the reader to an Italian beach resort in the 1920s to observe the various men, including a prelate, buzzing around a bit of tasty young man bait. In a story set in France leading into the German occupation of the World War Two era there, "Chameleon Love," both the village rabbi and priest are among a village male prostitute's clients as the young man balances the demands of the occupying Germans and the needs of the French Resistance. The last of the historical stories, "Determined Faith," is a period piece from the time of the 1970s Angolan civil war and persecution of Protestant evangelists there.

The eight-story contemporary setting section of the anthology leads off with one not previously published, "Art of the Priest," in which sexual privilege is accorded to a former art thief who has turned priest and become the Vatican's go-to art authenticator. "Jesuit Priest of Goa" is set in the former Portuguese colony of Goa, now incorporated into India, where a monastery has retained its singular kinky rituals, which includes sexual use by all of the monks of a visiting American college student. This is one of habu's early priest stories, which he wrote, he says, just because he wanted to write one about randy priests. An Italian monsignor uses his position to seduce and blackmail a young café singer and to enlist his help in putting together an Italian radio program in "The Songbird and the Philanthropist." "Ruined Pie" is a newly written story of the threat to a male sexual relationship caused by a change in another relationship. Inclusion of a priest among men returning for a college reunion and reminiscing about just how close they were in college is somewhat incidental in "Debatables," but the priest of the story does get male sex.

The concluding three stories of the collection include rumination over the dilemma of being a priest and also a man with desires for and need for sex with other men. In "Senegal Surrender" an American priest, exiled to Senegal for engaging in sex with other priests, gets taken up with the same life in his new post. "Fitting In" is one of a liberal order of Jesuits, who have come to the church because they have sinned but proceed to continue sinning. The story is set at Georgetown University, in Washington, D.C., among the priest sect of the faculty in which fetishes such as frottage and docking are considered permitted release for priests, and a young priest is seduced into loosening up and fitting in by a visiting sexually expert French Jesuit priest. In "Banishment," another newly written story, a priest being elevated to bishop moves to clean up his sexual past with a young priest by sending his lover to South Carolina's remote Daufuskie Island, where there is no discernible parish for the priest to serve.

As with all of his anthologies, with *Priest Play*, habu takes an unusual theme and provides stories for his audience that are varied in setting, inventive in plot, human in characterization, and hot in male-on-male sex. If you are looking for fix on your fetish to have a priest in your bed, this is the anthology for you.

HISTORICAL

Captive Temple Priest

Serquet, the high priest of the temple of the vulture goddess Nekhbet, showed no surprise as the guards of King Min of the upper river Kingdom of Nekhen filed into and along the walls of the temple throne room, a chamber that could be violated by none but the temple's priests during times of ritual. Serquet had already become aware that there would be a ritual. He had been elaborately prepared for the ceremony earlier in the day. As soon as he had seen the approach of the king and his retinue, Serquet summoned the priest of the spear and the priest of the seed to his side from the stone balcony off the ceremonial throne room that overlooked the city.

Out beyond the approaching soldiers and king of Nekhen, beyond the walls of the city of Nekhenian, out on the dusty plain beyond the narrow strip of fertile fields between the mighty river and the desert, Serquet could see the legions of the Assyrian army under the feared monster general, Adamu. And he could hear the beating of their drums as well. The drums had beaten through the night—the death knell of the Kingdom of Nekhen as it once had been. Serquet was a realist. He knew that bestowing of the victory blessing would have little meaning against the legions of the Assyrian monster general, Adamu.

Serquet also knew that King Min no longer could avoid battle; indeed, he should have engaged the enemy long before they arrived on the plain outside the city's gates. King Min's decision to engage in battle meant that he would have to come here for the victory blessing.

The two priests, the one of the spear and the one of the seed, came to his side as Serquet stood at the top of the steps to the vulture throne—a magnificent structure in marble, with its series of foot and hand holds rising up on the wings at each side of the high priest's throne. Serquet held his arms straight out from his body, spread his legs, and planted his bare feet in the foot indentations in front of the throne wings that pointed outward, toward the secular world. The two priests untied the vermillion sash from the waist of the gleaming white robe and pulled it off the magnificent, bronzed, and youthful, pampered, soft-skinned body of the young high priest.

Serquet's body was one of perfection, muscled but not overly muscular—lithe and willowy. It was a young man's body as, indeed, Serquet had barely reached his majority. The hair of his head was black and curly, reaching down to his shoulders. He otherwise, however, was hairless, except for a close-cropped, curly V below his belly pointing down to a thickish, but not overlong, shaft and two pert balls. His robe now stripped, he was clothed only in gold jewelry—a thick yoke of gold on his shoulders; gold bands snaking up his upper arms; gold wristbands, with narrow golden roping down to twist around his middle fingers; and gold bands snaking around his calves, with golden roping down to twist around his middle toes. A ring of gold also surrounded his head, sitting low on his forehead. The root of his cock was set in a gold ring from which gold netting descended to encase his balls.

He was clothed for the ceremony of the victory blessing, having realized in the early morning light, at the sound of distant drums, that the dreaded Assyrian general, Adamu, and his army had arrived outside the gates of the city. The ritual of cleansing, massaging, and oiling his lithe body had lasted into the afternoon.

The king's guard entered the chamber on the half run and poured around the sides of the room. The men were naked except for their gold breastplates, sandals laced up to their knees, gold bicep bands, and helmets with gold flaps descending to protect the bridges of their noses. Each carried a lance, pointed at the ceiling of the chamber. All were magnificently built, as required to be in the king's guard. All also were magnificently equipped in the shafts and balls of men. The two captains of the guard were more magnificently endowed than the others. Most were at least half hard in anticipation of the ritual to come.

Striding into the temple hall in their wake was a tall, muscular man, who was an older, coarser, hairier version of Serquet himself. Adorned—clothed or dressed would not be an accurate description—much like the soldiers of his personal guard—King Min directly approached the throne, mounting the steps and standing, feet in the foot indentions directly in front of and facing the throne—toward the sacred aspect of the kingdom. As King Min presented himself, almost pressing into his high priest, Serquet stepped back, seated himself in the throne, and raised and spread his legs, placing his feet in the foot indentions at the edge of the wings on either side of the throne. King Min leaned over him and took the hand holds in the marble beside and above the high priest's head.

Both symbolically and physically, the sacred aspect of the kingdom, in the form of the high priest, was open, legs raised and spread, pelvis raised, to the mastering of the secular aspect of the kingdom in this time of the need for physical force.

"We must do battle. I have come for the victory blessing," was all the towering, muscular man said, looking down into Serquet's eyes.

"I know," Serquet said. "Begin," he then said, turning, first, to the priest of the spear on his right and then to the priest of the seed on his left. He raised his arms behind his head and grasped the hand holds in the marble there above and closer to his head than the holds King Min was grasping. The marble seat of the throne was in a curve and raised and rolled his pelvis up toward the front of the throne. The leaning angle King Min was naturally placed to thrust his pelvis down to the lap of the high priest, so that the cocks of the two lay on top of each other.

At the "Begin" signal Serquet had given, the two priests at the side reached a hand each over between the high priest and the king, grasped their cocks together and frotted them, stroking them together, causing them both to harden.

All along the side walls, the soldier guards were taking their own cocks in their hands and stroking them to erections. The guards and the two side priests were chanting. The high priest and the king were panting hard.

"Now," the high priest commanded, looking at the priest of the spear, who produced an enamel-covered box from which he extracted a thin gold rod the length on a man's index finger. The priest of the seed held the now-erect cock of King

Min cupped in his hand while the priest of the spear slowly inserted one end of the gold rod into the king's urethra canal, burying half the length of the rod in the king's cock. The priest of the seed then brought the high priest's cock bulb in place and slowly, as Serquet moaned, tensed, and then relaxed, while the priest of the spear caused the exposed end of the gold rod to pierce the high priest's urethra canal, and brought the two bulbs together, making them kiss. The priest of the seed pulled King Min's foreskin over the high priest's bulb and held the two cocks docked and cupped in his hand. The priest of the spear joined the cupping and slight stroking of the two cocks, which were joined together by the piercing gold rod.

With a groan, the sound overlaying the moaning of the high priest, King Min began to tighten his buttocks and move his pelvis, his cock fucking the high priest's cock, moving the gold rod inside the urethra canals of the docked cocks.

Taking the swaying of the king's buttocks as their signal, the guards ringing the chamber began beating their spear butts on the stone floor in the rhythm of the king's thrusts. His thrusts built up speed and intensity, which were accompanied by an increase of the sound of the chanting by the guards and priests in the hall and of the butts of the guards' spears on the floor, and the vigor of their own masturbating of their cocks.

Serquet let out a little cry as he came, his cum burbling out from the rim of King Min's encasing foreskin. King Min came nearly simultaneously, marking his spouting by a victory cry. The guards around the wall each came as closely to that of their king as they could.

The side priests released the docking cocks, each to be pulled away from the king and the high priest by the two captains of the guards, who tore the minor priests' robes from their bodies, pushed them down on their backs on either side of the throne, pushed their knees under the priests' buttocks, thrust inside them, and fucked them hard on the stone floor.

Using the hand and footholds provided on the wings of the throne, King Min climbed up the sides of the marble structure until his cock was at the level of the high priest's mouth. Serquet opened his mouth to the king's shaft, cleaning off the cum from the first taking and sucking the cock to a second ejaculation.

Around the sides of the chamber, the guards had paired off, with one of each set sucking off the cock of his dominant partner.

The king's second ejaculation marked the successful completion of the blessing ceremony. He climbed down from the throne, turned, and marched directly out of the chamber, with his guards following, marching in step. Left in the chamber was the high priest, slumped on his throne, wiping his mouth with the back of his hand, his eyes slitted, the ritual completed but not completely satiating for him.

Panting and moaning on the floor on either side of the throne were the priests of spear and seed. Unlike their high priest, they had been completed and satiated by the monster cocks of the captains of the guard.

Still fidgety and disquieted late in the night, as Serquet lay on his bed, he heard, with joy, the sound of the rustling of the curtains in the doorway to the imperial apartments. He raised his head to see the naked figure of Khafra, the next youngest brother of the king, and the king's chief adviser, approach. He was the spitting image of the king, except that his younger body was more athletic and pleasing than the king's. He shaved his body hair and was not as coarse in movement and habits as the king. He smelled of roses rather than sour sweat, and he moved like a dancer. His kisses were sweeter than King Min's too. There were rituals of the kiss as well, although none of Serquet's anal canal being penetrated. As high priest, that was taboo to all men.

"I wish for your blessings as well," Khafra whispered as he came up on the bed on his knees. He was holding a case with a gold rod in it.

"Yes, yes," Serquet murmured as he arched his back to the surface of the bed and hugged Khafra's hips with his knees. The gold rod was longer and thicker than the one of the ritual. Khafra's cock was longer than that of his older brother, the king. The rod penetrated Serquet's urethra canal deeper than the ritual one had. He moaned deeper and sighed even deeper, as Khafra married their cock bulbs, kissing each other, the gold rod buried inside both of them, and pushed his foreskin over Serquet's bulb. Leaning over Serquet's torso, Khafra captured Serquet's lips with his and held their cocks together with one hand, while both of them moved their pelvises languidly to a mutual ejaculation in the rhythm of the cock fuck.

It was taboo for any man to be inside Serquet's anus, but that didn't hold the other way around. Four hours until the promise of a coming dawn, Serquet lay on his back and Khafra rode his cock to a coming—and then another—and another yet. Serquet was purring from the visit of his lover until it was over all too soon and Khafra had melted away behind the curtain into the imperial apartments.

* * * *

Walking slowly and deliberately in from the stone balcony off the temple throne room, with the priests of the spear and seed in his wake, Serquet, the high priest of the Vulcan goddess Nekhbet of the Kingdom of Nekhen, mounted the steps to his throne and turned and faced the beaten gold-clad outer doors to the chamber. The two minor priests took up positions at either side of the throne.

A mighty thud was sounded on the double doors, they swung open, and a magnificent figure of a man strode into the hall, followed by two lines of his battle-bloodied soldiers, who marched around to positions along the inside walls of the chamber. The tableau was much the same as that of the victory blessing ritual earlier in the day—but with an entirely different, ominous cast.

Adamu, commanding general of the Assyrian army, strode slowly, deliberately, proudly up to the steps of the throne. Serquet looked coolly down into the general's eyes, gleaming with battle lust. The high priest was calm on the outside, but inside he was in turmoil. He had heard much about this monster of a man, taller than any other man, more massive across the chest, albeit solid muscle, than any man Serquet had seen before. Adamu's reputation had come to the land of Nekhen as that of a conquering, vengeful god whose power and wrath could not be escaped. At this moment,

Serquet could well believe in this. It should lodge fear in Serquet's heart—and it surely did—but it made his blood boil as well in arousal.

There was a sensual wildness about the man mountain, with his plaited black beard, his unruly mane flowing down to his shoulder blades, his bulging biceps and chest muscles. His chest, belly, forearms, and thighs were matted with curly black hair. As he had entered the room and strode the length of the hall, he tossed aside a round, black shield worked in a swirling design in silver to one side and a bloodied battle ax to the other. Off came a battle helmet worked in the same metal and tossed aside to one of his soldiers. That he was stripping for action that didn't require weapons of destruction to fulfill his intent was not lost on Serquet.

His torso, scarred and sliced with new cuts was magnificent and made Serquet whimper with need, although he had to fight revealing this to those in the hall. The high priest looked away from him as the sight of the fearsome giant was too much for him to bear and not to melt to. He should not have looked away, though, as then he saw that the soldiers who had entered and ringed the room had their pikes lifted, the points toward the ceiling, and each bore at the top a head of a Nekhen soldier of rank. Serquet could look no further when he saw that of King Min's younger brother and chief adviser—and Serquet's secret lover—Khafra.

When he looked back at the Assyrian general, he gasped and sucked in breath. Adamu was untying his metal-plated skirt and then his linen underskirt and tossing them aside. Other than the black and silver-worked guards on his forearms and calves and his leather sandals, the monster warrior was naked—and in an erection of a length and girth that Serquet had never before seen.

In two bounds the general had mounted the steps to the throne, where he ripped away Serquet's robe and then backhanded the high priest across his mouth, sending Serquet, gasping, stumbling back onto his throne—and onto the curved seat of the throne that thrust the young man's pelvis up, making him vulnerable to the thrust of the Assyrian's throbbing manhood. Adamu grasped Serquet's ankles, cruelly wishboned the young man's legs, crouched down and leaned in, and immediately was into the battle of stuffing the massive bulb of his hard, cruel cock into the virginal anal entrance of the high priest.

Serquet howled in pain, indignation, and fear as Adamu relentlessly pressed his cock inside the channel and began to pump hard and deep. The high priest grabbed the hand holds in the marble throne above his head, and held on for dear life as the Assyrian general rode him hard.

On the floor on either side of the throne, Assyrian soldiers were tearing into the priests of the spear and the seed, fucking them hard—in tandem, not sequentially—fucking them both into the other world.

At first, it appeared that Serquet would join his priests in the beyond—that he could not endure the length, thickness, vigor, and intensity of the Assyrian general's cocking, but slowly, ever so slowly, he found that he could take it. And that he could not only endure it, but could take enjoyment from it. He had grown tired of sexual rituals that aroused him in every way except the ultimate taking. If Khafra had wanted to fuck his anal channel, Serquet would have let him do that and would have kept the secret from the king and the rest of the Nekhen world. He had wanted Khafra to fuck him. But the second in line to the throne was not willing to override Nekhen tradition.

Luckily for Serquet, now that the Assyrian general was riding him with a monstrous cock, the high priest had taken matters into his own hands over the past several months—in the form of a marble penis nearly, but not quite, the size of Adamu. Although there was nothing like the real thing, Serquet's own frustration and willingness to take a risk and some precautions had saved his life. If one were to suggest that the high priest listened to the rumors of both the preferences and the equipment of the Assyrian general and planned for contingencies accordingly months in advance, he would not be wrong. The only error would have been in fully assessing the dimensions and cruelty of the general. From the screams—now having died away—of his minor priests, Serquet could believe that the priests of the spear and the seed had kept to the rituals and had, as a result, been shredded internally.

The conquering Assyrian general had no such qualms as Khafra, his lifeless eyes now looking upon the debauchery of his erstwhile lover from the top of a spike, and had come to Serquet from a bloody battle in which he had vanquished Nekhen. He now was intent on vanquishing Nekhen's religious underpinnings—by fucking the untouchable high priest.

Adamu's soldiers had brought in the quavering remnants of the imperial court to witness the completing of the Assyrians' conquering of the city state. They stood there, in witness, after the Assyrian general had stridden into the chamber, as Adamu did the unthinkable—debauched the untouchable anal canal of the high priest. When Adamu was saddled on Serquet's body on the throne, they could clearly see the bulbous buttocks of the general rear back and then they could see the high priest jerk and hear him cry out in surprise, violation, and pain as the general thrust his hips forward. Pull back, thrust. Pull back, thrust. Serquet cried out again and again, until, as the thrusting continued, his cries subsided into whimpers and his head lolled over to the side of the throne, his eyes glazed over, his mouth open in an O of total surrender.

The assault continued, Adamu fucked on, as the court survivors were herded out of the temple throne room to spread the word that the conquering of Nekhen was now complete.

The man's cock was stretching Serquet's channel to the splitting point and he was thrusting hard and vigorously. Serquet had no doubt that he planned the same fate for him that the Assyrian soldiers were wreaking on the priests of the spear and the seed. So, Serquet did what he had to do. He came back to full consciousness and yielded fully to the assault. He would not surrender so easily. There were battles that could be won on the field and those that could be won in the bed.

Serquet gripped the general's head in his hands and brought Adamu's mouth, first, down to his own for the sweetest kisses he could manage under the circumstances of being stuffed to the limit by a punishing ram, and then down to his nipples. Serquet let the beauty of his body entice and entwine the general. He moved the heels of his feet to the general's buttocks and rubbed them in the rhythm of the fuck, and he began to move his own pelvis to the rhythm as well. He made sounds that the general would understand of enjoying—wanting—the fuck. He enveloped the warrior in the sweet yielding of his body.

And he slowly won the general over so that, when Adamu ejaculated deep in Serquet's channel, Serquet did the same up the man's hairy belly—and then purred for the general and held the man's face into his youthful breast.

Rather than finishing the high priest then, therefore, with a roar of victory, Adamu pulled off him, picked him up, slung him over his shoulder, and strode through the curtain at the side of the temple throne room, into the imperial apartment. Entering the first bed chamber he came to, the Assyrian general threw Serquet down on the bed on his belly; jerked Serquet up to his knees, his buttocks presented for mounting; crouched over the young man's hips; and fucked him again.

They didn't leave the chamber or the bed for a day and a half, and when they did, there was still a victorious general reigning over Nekhen, but it was questionable who was the commander of the couple.

* * * *

Two weeks later and life had settled down in the occupied imperial city of the Kingdom of Nekhen. The rape and pillaging and burning of buildings that followed any conquering and sacking of a city state had died down. The relationship between the Assyrian general, Adamu, and the heretofore high priest, now catamite of the victorious general, Serquet, had also settled down. The two had moved to the king's bed chamber and neither Adamu nor Serquet required the general's hard cock to be throbbing inside Serquet in every waking moment as they both had for that first day and a half of coupling.

Now, for the ease of keeping the surviving Nekhen population subdued if sullen, Serquet sat on the king's throne during the day, with Adamu sitting in a slightly less magnificent throne beside him, with Adamu making the decisions and Serquet proclaiming them. Adamu didn't mind as long as his own soldiers knew he was in charge. Serquet was fine with the arrangement as long as he controlled the hardness of Adamu's cock.

One of the first requests Serquet had made to test his control of the sex-chained Assyrian general was that all of the surviving court that had witnessed his debauchery be surviving no more. Adamu had conceded this to Serquet. Thus, the authority of the high priest, having moved over to the temporal throne, was held pure in the eyes of the populous of the kingdom that still lived.

The nights had become as this night, with Serquet dancing, naked, for Adamu in the king's bed chamber as the general lay in luxury, propped up on the bed pillows and swilling strong wine. Following this, Serquet came up on the bed and charmed Adamu with what had been the victory blessing ritual of frotting their cocks together and introducing the general to the intimacy of the marriage of the cocks with the gold rod and the sheathing of Serquet's cock bulb with Adamu's foreskin until lust overtook the general and he performed a reenactment of the deflowering of the high priest.

Late into the night, Serquet moved from Adamu's encircling embrace, tonguing down the hirsute, hard-muscled body to Adamu's shaft, which Serquet brought to hardness with his mouth before climbing on top of the general, sheathing the shaft, and moving in a variety of ways on the cock until the general awakened enough to grab Serquet's waist and slam him cruelly up and down on the long, thick cock, with Serquet screaming in pain-pleasure until both were spent again.

Adamu liked to conquer by force and Serquet liked the sensation of being taken cruelly without his choice. In later years, it would help him rationalize that he did what he had to do and endured much hardship in the effort.

As sleep overtook Adamu again, Serquet slipped away from him and to the water closet. In the corridor between the two chambers, he was shocked to be pulled into the darkness of a side chamber.

"What? King Min!" he exclaimed in a gasp. "You live."

"Yes, it is I," the king said. "We must be silent, and we must be quick."

"But the battle—"

"Second brother Khafra went in my stead. I did not see the prospect of winning. And there must be a member of the family alive to rule here. I hid myself for the good of the kingdom. You understand that, don't you?"

"Yes. It was just such a shock to see you alive," Serquet whispered. And it *was* a shock. Cowardice was much in the character of Min, but when Serquet had seen Khafra's head on a pike, he'd assumed Min's was on one as well. He just hadn't looked any further down the line of heads. "But what is it you want?"

"Here. Take this dagger. Go back to the general and do what you have to do. The Assyrians will be headless and in disarray. My men will help me retake the palace and we will fight on from here. Can you do what you have to do?"

"Yes, I can," Serquet said, taking the dagger from the king. Just as he believed in Min's basic cowardice, he wasn't the least surprised that he wished Serquet to do the deed and very likely be quickly dispatched afterward by the general's guards.

His decision was instantaneous and not the least difficult to make. Holding his hand over the mouth of King Min, who looked at him with wide, questioning eyes, Serquet plunged the dagger into Min's breast. He pulled it out and plunged it in again.

As the erstwhile king of Nekhen sank to the floor, the next king of Nekhen muttered, "Yes, I know exactly what I have to do. You forget, older brother, that I am the third brother of the imperial line after you and Khafra. I was no less a captive of your court than I am now of the Assyrian general. And I know what you don't know. General Adamu is a military conqueror, not a governor. Soon he will be gone, leaving me on the throne of Nekhen, as its legitimate king."

Leaving the corpse of his older brother there, Serquet returned to the king's bed chamber, stretched out beside the snoring general, nudged Adamu to roll over on top of him, spread his legs, raised his pelvis by bending and pushing up on his knees, and guided the giant's cock head to his entrance. By now Adamu was awake enough to thrust deep inside and begin to pump on his own. Serquet laughed from deep inside his belly, clutched at the general's shoulder blades, started his pelvis in motion, and began once more to weave his own victory charm over what he chose to think of as a pleasant interlude foreign visitor to his, King Serquet's, kingdom—one with a very satisfying cock.

The Brotherhood

Alfons delivered another tankard of beer to the well-dressed gentleman seated at the best table, near the fireplace. It still ranked as the best, with the most substantial chair, even though the table was functionally only the best in the winter, when a fire was going, not now, in high summer. When he set the beer down, the man grabbed Alfons's hand and didn't let it go for the longest moment. Their eyes met, and Alfons shuddered. There was something demanding and controlling in the nearly obsidian eyes of the dark-complexioned, dark-eyed man with the swarthy goatee beard. Beyond that there was an aspect of the fox or wolf about him. He was handsome and not above thirty, but he was a man of darkness and of the shadows—all dressed in black other than the lace at his wrist that denoted a man of importance and wealth. After a moment, though, he released Alfons, the expression on his face changing from a piercing assessing look to a sly smile, almost a sneer, and he slightly bowed his head to the server.

Alfons turned away, finding eye contact difficult to break, but needed elsewhere in the tavern room. The inn's taproom was crowded that evening. The blond, openly sunny, boyish visage of the young man was a sharp contrast to the vulpine aspect of the man sitting in the shadows by the fireplace. The man's eyes followed Alfons around the tavern. The next time Alfons had a moment to locate the man in the room, the seat by the fireplace having been vacated, was when he saw him talking in low tones to the Innkeeper, to whom Alfons was indentured, by the bar. The two men were looking at Alfons as they spoke. Alfons blushed, having a good idea what the discussion was about.

The walled town of Rottenburg am Necker in the fifteenth century was a prosperous German market town, catering to many styles and preferences. A man looking for a tavern or inn accommodating his personal comfort and interests could find one without difficulty. The inn to which Alfons was indentured, having recently been brought into service, was one that catered to men interested in other men. It was Alfons's androgynous beauty and affable disposition that had led to his indenture being sold to Hermann Eberle. Alfons had orally served men before, but it was his virginity to anal penetration that had piqued Eberle's interest in purchasing his indenture and husbanding the young man's initiation.

Eberle wanted his investment back in double, and there were few men capable to paying that in Rottenburg. It would likely have to a rich nobleman or merchant passing through Rottenburg, in high need and of special interests, who would be the first to master Alfons.

Tonight was the night.

Alfons wasn't surprised to see the two men talking earnestly and letting their eyes pick him out as he moved about the tavern, taking orders and serving steins of beer. From the look the man had given him and when the man had held his hand moments longer than was necessary, Alfons had figured he would be in some nook or cranny, on his knees to the man. That could happen once or twice on any given night in the tavern—and he wasn't the only serving man here serving more than beer.

The fox man left by the door out into the stable yard, and Hermann called Alfons over. "The man who was just here is the Count Franz von Türbingen, an important and wealthy man. He wants you to join him in the stable now."

"He wishes me to go on my knees to him?" Alfons asked.

"No. He wishes for you to present your buttocks to him, Alfons. He will mount you. He has paid a high price to be your first."

Alfons began to tremble and lower his face in fear and embarrassment.

"Don't withdraw from it, lad," Eberle hissed, placing a hand on Alfons's arm. "You knew that was what you were indentured here for. You have gone unmounted longer than most. The count has paid a large sum from your chastity. He has bought you for two nights. He has a room at the inn, but he wants to mount you first in the stable. You will stay with him for two days and you will lie under him as he wishes. You will not bring questions on this inn of our reputation from what can be bought here. If you do not give him satisfaction, I will whip you within an inch of your life and give you to the beggars on the street for sport. You should be happy that your first time will be with a clean nobleman. After this, you will take whoever pays a much lower price, I assure you."

The count fucked Alfons over a saddle stand in the stables, Alfons's torso draped over one side, his face staring at the loose hay on the rough-wooden planks of the flooring, his arms hanging down, knuckles dragging on the hay, wrists bound with leather strips, and his mouth gagged with the count's belt fastened around his head to keep the noise down. Alfons still produced muffled cries and huffed and puffed the pain of the first breaching of his sphincter muscle by the slow, but relentless invasion of the count's staff as he crouched over the young man from behind, held Alfons's hips between his hands, and insistently bottomed out with his cock before he plowed and seeded Alfons for the first time. The count wasn't appreciably long or thick—not that Alfons was in the position to have comparisons to gauge—but he was cruel considering it was Alfons's first time, giving the young virgin little time to prepare for and open to him before he was forcing himself inside. This aspect of forcing a virgin ass seemed to be the man's primary interest in paying the extra fee to be able to do so.

Alfons struggled against him initially, which Von Türbingen seemed to enjoy, but as the pain receded and a certain pleasure started to creep in, Alfons settled down, and with a thought to the threats his master had hissed at him, submitted to the plowing. Yes, he'd known this day was coming. Yes, Eberle was right that it was better from a man of position and breeding than from the usual rough workman who came to the tavern. Yes, after this, it *would* be rough workman.

Toward the eventual moment of seeding of the man inside him, his cock steel hard, throbbing, and rapidly digging into Alfons's quick, Alfons succumbed to his own nature and began to move his pelvis, falling into the rhythm of the thrusts of Von Türbingen's shaft. The count laughed, slapped Alfons on the bare buttocks, and released his seed.

The fucking of the next two nights in the privacy of the count's bed in the inn was a time of adjustment by Alfons to the inevitable and learning from the count what a man of refinement wanted from a beautiful young man underneath him, which included Franz holding Alfons in a close embrace and stroking off the young man's cock beyond Alfons's endurance to resist shooting off his own seed. After this, the count would want Alfons to lie between his thighs and make love to his cock—and then to saddle himself on the count's pelvis and ride the staff.

By the time Franz was in the courtyard, mounting his horse, and bidding Alfons farewell, the young man was clinging to the saddle, not wanting his new master to leave him—fearful and anxious about what came after this when he no longer had a single patron.

"Oh, we will meet again, you and I," the count said before he cruelly spurred his horse in the flank and lurched out onto the road in front of the inn.

In the succeeding weeks, Alfons learned just how refined the count had been. He no longer was a valuable commodity, his chastity intact. He was given over to any man willing to pay double the price of a suck, and he lay under a progression of men who smelled, were animals, and took him in every rough way they could imagine.

Thus it was a godsend when the innkeeper, Hermann Eberle, received a letter from the Count Franz Von Türbingen, with a significant amount of money enclosed, engaging Alfons's services in the larger town of Türbingen two day's horse ride to the northeast of Rottenburg to stay for a month's time.

When the innkeeper's wife saw the letter, she said, "A pity the young man cannot go, as it would require a journey through the accursed forest of Höllewald."

"Curse be damned, woman," Eberle answered. "For this amount of money, I would send the lad into hell itself. I will not be giving this money back."

"Sending him into hell—that's what I said you'd be doing if you send him to Türbingen by the route the count demands. He says he's arranged for the lad to overnight at the Monastery of Die Bruderschaft. You've heard the rumors of that place—of the monks living there."

"Prepare yourself, Alfons," Eberle said, ignoring his wife. "You can take the old mare. I wouldn't want to risk the gelding."

But you are willing to risk me, Alfons thought. It was thought without lingering bitterness, though. He welcomed a month in the count's bed opposed to a single night writhing under the rough men Eberle was selling him to. Among other reasons, he now had discovered that the count didn't have the most demanding cock that would challenge Alfons's passageway. He happily went to the stables to prepare the mare for travel.

Eberle's comment on not wanting to risk the gelding hadn't escaped Alfons as an indication that the innkeeper wasn't as contemptuous of his wife's superstition about the forest Alfons would have to ride through as he had let on. The innkeeper's fear that Alfons might not come back, though, became obvious when Eberle trapped him in the wine cellar that night, bent him over a table, and rode his ass hard himself as if the innkeeper might not ever again have a crack at the young man himself.

* * * *

The weather was perfect as Alfons entered the Höllewald forest shortly after passing through the village of Missinger. He heard the gurgling of a stream off to his right, deeper into the trees. He had been sweating hard under the sun before reaching the cover of the trees and decided that he would bathe himself if the creek to his right had any depth. It did have a pool at the bottom of a rock outcropping with a waterfall, which must have been the source of the gurgling noise that had attracted him to the water.

Alfons was stripped and gliding into the pool of water before he realized that he wasn't alone in the water. As he swam to the center of the pool, a head and two arms, connected by a very-well-muscled chest, appeared from behind the base of the waterfall.

"Oh, I didn't realize anyone else was here," Alfons exclaimed.

"You must forgive me," the man said in a pleasing, cultured voice. "I heard you approach and hid myself until I was sure that you were no threat. Then I could not help myself in watching you take off your clothes. You're a beautiful young man. One of God's gifts to the world surely."

Alfons was embarrassed. "Perhaps I should leave. You were here first."

"The pool is big enough for both of us," the man said. "My name is Paul."

"Alfons," the young man instinctively answered.

"And the pool is deep enough too. Where you are swimming is quite deep. You know you can dive in there from the lip of the waterfall and have no danger of hitting bottom. Here, I will show you."

Without waiting for comment from Alfons, the man paddled over to the side of the pool and stood up from the water. He immediately started climbing the rock to the lip of the waterfall and, when he reached it, he stood and posed there. He was naked and his body was magnificent. He was perhaps ten years older than Alfons. His hair was a reddish auburn, showing more red highlights as it descended his body down his chest and into his pubes, the bush of which was curly and a golden red. He was in erection, long and thick. Alfons sucked in his breath as the man dove into the pool, coming up just in front of Alfons, his hands glided up Alfons's legs as he came back up to the surface. One hand went to the young man's waist, but the other one cupped Alfons's cock and balls and remained there.

As Paul's face came up level with Alfons's, he took the young man's mouth into a deep kiss. Alfons hungrily returned the kiss and initially grasped the older man's shoulders in his hands, rubbing their chests together. But then, with a gasp and remembering the circumstance they were in—that he wasn't in the inn now, subject to the desires of any man with money to pay—he broke the kiss, pushed off from Paul and backpeddled to the side of the pond, where he could find footing on the bottom. He had gone to the wrong side of the pool. The man was between him and the bank of the pond where his clothes were. He backed further toward the side of the pond, and the man advanced on him to where he was able to stand on the bottom as well. Alfons was crouched down on his knees, trying to stay under water, trying not to reveal the effect of seeing the man naked and then kissing him had on him.

"Please . . . why . . .?" he sputtered.

"I have been to Rottenburg," Paul said. "I have seen you in Eberle's inn. You work there. You lay under men."

If he'd been in the inn, Alfons realized, the man knew what sort of inn it was. "That doesn't mean—"

"I think it does mean that," the man said. His voice was calming. What he spoke was made to sound so natural, so sensible. "I watched you disrobe. You've seen the effect that had on me. I made sure you saw by leaving the water to say I would dive from the top of the waterfall. I made sure you saw the desire and readiness in me. I have felt the effect that I have on you. You lay under men. We are both in heat. Your response to the kiss told me all I needed to know about your desire for my body to lie on yours. I'm sure that, if you think about it, it told you all you need to know too."

"I don't . . . we can't . . ."

"Yes we can." Paul was right there with him. "I have money I can give you. I will pay you the going rate. You need share none of it with your master. If I were to come into your tavern and pay the innkeeper for your services, you would lay under me there. Your master would give you no choice. What is the difference in doing so here? Am I so unappealing that, given some choice in the matter, you do not want me to cover you?"

Alfons couldn't think of a countering argument to that. And the man *did* have a magnificent body and would be clean. He'd just cleansed himself in the pool. The man took the failure to answer as enough of an answer.

"Rise to me," Paul said, standing in water that reached only to his knees. He reached down and lifted Alfons to his feet. Alfons was shorter then he was, his face only coming to the matting of hair between Pau's pectorals.

"Perhaps you need a reminder," Paul said in a low, cajoling tone. One arm went around Alfons's waist, pulling him into Paul's embrace. With the other hand, Paul raised Alfons's chin and lowered his own face into another kiss that started out tender and flamed into a raging fire of mutual need. Paul moved his free hand to between them and frotted their hard, throbbing cocks together.

Nothing was said between them thereafter. There was no need for anything to be said. Paul pulled them back into the pond to where he could crouch down, creating a lap for Alfons to sit on, facing away from him, with the water coming up to their nipples. Alfons panted and huffed and moaned, as Paul positioned the young man's entrance on the bulb of his cock and then slowly brought Alfons down on the staff, the young man's passage opening to the invading shaft, trained now to taking a man inside him.

Paul moved Alfons up and down on his cock in the water, using the leverage of his arm encasing the young man's waist, as he stroked Alfons off with his other hand. When Alfons didn't have his head turned for a kiss, Paul's lips were buried in the hollow of the young man's throat. At length both men came in a peaceful flow, enhanced by the motion of the water. Then they just held there, kissing, as they both reveled in the feel of Paul, once so long and thick and hard, slowly going flaccid inside Alfons's passage, albeit still long enough to hold deep purchase inside him.

No taking that Alfons had ever experienced at the inn was as pleasurable to him as this was. No man had stayed with him through the mutual pleasure of an afterglow of feeling the once-raging staff inside him go flaccid in satiation—and then, as happened here, stir to life and engorge again.

"Come," Paul said at length, "I want to make love to you on the bank of the pond. As you can feel, I desire to have you again."

The man moved over to the side of the pond—still on the opposite side from where Alfons had stripped and the mare was grazing—and pulled Alfons up onto the bank, laying the young man on a mossy spot next to the man's clothes. Paul was in full and magnificent erection again. He glided his hands up the inner surfaces of Alfons's thighs and the young man opened to him, widening his stance, bending his legs, and placing his feet flat on the moss. Paul hovered over him, on his knees between Alfons's spread thighs. He reached up, grasped the young man's wrists, and held Alfons's arms over his head. Alfons grasped the thin trunks of two trees over his head and raised his pelvis to Paul. He jerked and gave a little cry as Paul slid inside him again, hard and thick and long once more, and began to plow him slowly, but with increasing speed and thrust. The older man lowered his face to Alfons and took him in a kiss that lasted for the time of their coupling, Alfons thrusting his pelvis up to Paul as Paul thrust down, each of them wanting the union to be as deep as possible. Alfons was lost to the man. He'd been fucked before but he'd never been made love to before, like this.

Afterward, the man's payment for Alfons's sex laying on the young man's pile of clothes, Alfons half dozed, as Paul teased his naked body with long blades of grass.

"I don't know where you were going," Paul said with a low, hoarse voice, "but I would like you to come back to my village with me."

"Your village? Which is your village?" Alfons asked. He knew it was impossible—that he had a charge to keep, bound by his indenture—but he didn't want this afternoon to stop.

"I live in Missinger, just outside the edge of the Höllewald."

"Ah, I have just been through there, just now. I am headed into the Höllewald."

"That is not a good idea. Young men like you go into that forest and sometimes don't come out again." He was standing, pulling up his clothes, pulling his black cassock over his head and letting it cascade down to his ankles.

Alfons looked up and his eyes went wide. "You are a priest."

"Yes, I am a priest."

"I can't go with you," Alfons said, rising from the moss. "Priests are celibate. We cannot do this . . . what we just did."

Paul laughed. "Priests obviously aren't always celibate. And the proof of that is that we just did 'this.' We did 'this' twice. If I had the time to be absent from my village, we would do 'this' again. I want you to come back to my village and I will do 'this' to you all night and all week and all month. I am smitten with you."

"You can't. We can't. You belong to the church."

"We all belong to the church, and it is God who made us with the desires we have. I've heard tell that the pope himself has a mistress and enough bastards to fill Rome," Paul said. "Priests have needs. I have needs. You have needs. You can't tell me you don't have needs. You are hard for me again, even now."

Paul pulled his cassock off, pushed Alfons onto the moss on this belly, came down on top of him, entered him strongly, and they were fucking again. Paul grasped Alfons's wrists over his head again, Alfons raised himself slightly on his knees to give Paul deep purchase, and, groaning and whimpering, he moved his pelvis with the rhythm of the fuck.

"We are doing 'this' and 'this' and 'this' again," Paul growled, punctuating every "this" with a thrust. Alfons moaned underneath him. "Tell me you love 'this'—that we *can* be doing 'this.'"

"Yes, yes. It is as you say," Alfons whimpered with a groan.

But when Paul had released his seed again, Alfons rolled out from underneath him with a grunt, dove back into the pond and swam swiftly to the other side. Paul sat on the opposite bank, watching the young man hurriedly put his clothes back on and mount the mare.

"Just ask for Father Paul's church in Missinger," he called out to Alfons as the young man rode away. "Anyone in the village can tell you where to find me. I can offer you a comfortable bed and all of the 'this' that you would want."

* * * *

35

Once Alfons entered the forest of Höllewald the warnings of the innkeeper's wife came back to him and he very well could understand that the forest was haunted and cursed. The old mare he was riding seemed to understand that as well and became more skittish as they moved deeper in the woods, with the gray trees with gnarled trunks and branches blotting out the sky and the air becoming increasingly fetid. He would have missed the monastery of Die Bruderschaft all together if the mare hadn't stopped, laid her ears down, and backed up, with a wild look in her eyes. He slid off her and pulled on her reins to no avail. Looking around to see what could be spooking her, he saw the monastery.

The gray stone walls of what was more a moated fortress than a religious institution blended into the gloomy aspect of the forest. The trail, such as it was, went right past the edge of the moat, giving those inside a clear view of any travelers trying to use this path through the forest, while the traveler, especially when the day was misty as it was today, could pass immediately beside the structure and hardly be aware it was there. This gave the monastery effective control over those who came and went through the forest. Indeed, Alfons thought, there surely could be no other path through the forest, which was more swamp than forest, the path he had been taking running along the top of a rise from the surrounding marshy area under the trees.

He could think of only one way to get the mare to proceed to the monastery, where he had been told to stop for the night, let alone pass it by. He pulled his tunic over his head and wrapped it around the mare's eyes so that she was blinded. Having done that, she became docile and he approached the monastery, looking for an entrance. As he was studying the blank wall with the fetid moat, covered with floating moss, between the wall and the path, he heard the sound of a thump and saw that a drawbridge had been lowered, not in the front wall of the structure, but at the side, near the front edge. A tall, thin, gaunt, and bald-headed man in a brown monk's habit and barefoot walked out of the monastery and across the drawbridge. He turned, looked at Alfons, showing no surprise that there was a visitor, and motioned for the young man to approach.

The young man did so, studying the monk as he came closer—and noticing that the monk was studying him closely also, with a sly look on his face that Alfons recognized in the faces of men who used him in the tavern. Alfons felt naked, having stripped off his tunic, and he flinched when he came up to the monk to receive, in a greeting, not anything spoken nor a hand gesture of any sort, but an intense, hooded gaze from the monk and the monk's hand gliding intimately up the young man's bare chest.

Alfons stepped back, in surprise and embarrassment, released his tunic from the mare's eyes, and slipped it back down over his torso.

"My name is Alfons, from Rottenburg," he said in a nervous voice. "I have been summoned to Türbingen by Count Franz, who said lodging for the night was arranged for me here. This is the monastery of Die Bruderschaft, is it not?"

The monk, not showing any apology for having touched Alfons intimately, merely nodded agreement—agreement of what in the words Alfons had said, the young man wasn't sure—and used hand motions to indicate that Alfons was to bring his horse and enter the monastery. The elaborate signaling the monk provided and the fact that Alfons found he could easily understand what the monk was conveying told Alfons that the monks here must have some sort of vow of silence and had become experts in signaling their messages. The gestures included the admonishment that he was expected to maintain silence as well.

This didn't make Alfons comfortable—and the intimate touch of the monk had made him quite uncomfortable, although it was little different than he was subjected to at the inn—but there was no other choice. After his recent encounter with the priest named Paul, Alfons's understanding of what men dedicated to God did and didn't do. He know knew that they had desires as any man did. He was no longer confident that he would make it through the night here without being in some man's bed. To this, though, he just sighed and continued into the monastery. If he had learned anything over the last few months, it was that he was powerless and at the whims of the desires of men—but that he didn't mind lying with most men he had serviced. He certainly hadn't minded writhing under the priest named Paul.

The night was coming on, and this was where he had been told to break his journey to Türbingen. These were monks. What harm could come to him here that wasn't in his lot already to endure? Still, he shuddered as he was guided over the drawbridge, as the monk walked closely beside him and had a hand on the small of his back. It was almost as if the monk knew that Alfons lay under men for money. Somehow Alfons thought that perhaps his room and board for the night here would be considered a substitute for money.

Inside the monastery compound, he was met by other monks. No questions were asked or signaled about why he was here. He indeed seemed to have been expected. With that, though, Alfons was afraid that they had also been told what he would do for a man, and he briefly wondered if his fears were justified—that he might be expected to lie under a man—or men—this night. Surely not, he thought, though, in his internal struggle. These were religious men. But then, he thought again, so was Paul the priest.

A couple of monks led the mare off to the stable, after having found that they needed to cover her eyes to coax her to move. Alfons, embarrassed, had retrieved and pulled his tunic over his head. The monk who had welcomed him at the gate and another, evidently senior monk, as he was directing the others, ushered Alfons into a guard house just inside the gate, where the tall, gaunt monk handed him a folded monk's habit. The senior monk gestured for Alfons to put the habit on—and to strip himself of everything else he was wearing. Everything. He was to wear just the habit, with nothing underneath it and nothing on his feet. The two monks scrutinized Alfons closely as he stripped and put the habit on.

He was then led up stone stairs set against the wall and into the upper story of a cloister rimming the monastery courtyard on three sides and two tiers. The main monastery building was at one end of the courtyard and the cloisters fanned out on either side of that to form two sides of the courtyard square. As they walked down the passageway, Alfons could see that small, stone-walled rooms were set between the cloister and the outer walls. These evidently were monks' cells.

Alfons was escorted to one of these, shown, with hand gestures the stone platform with the quilt on top of it that was to be his bed and the water jar in one corner and the piss pot in the other. He was left there, and when the two monks backed out of the cell, they closed the wooden door. He heard the sound of the key turning in the lock of the door on the other side. There was a small window in the cell, with bars set in it, and he could see that twilight was setting in. He had made his way to the monastery none too soon.

It wasn't long before the cell door opened and the monk—the first one he'd seen, the gaunt one of indeterminate age, but probably double Alfons's age—who apparently was assigned as Alfons's attendant, entered with a tray of food and a flask of wine. The food was basic, but it was better fare than Alfons was given at the inn unless he was dining with a patron as a foreplay act to being covered by the patron. The wine was particularly delicious—and intoxicating—and the more he drank, the more mellow and sleepy he became until he barely was able to stagger to the stone platform before collapsing onto the quilt into a deep sleep.

* * * *

Alfons slowly came back into consciousness to the sound of far-off chanting. The cell was in total darkness save for slightly less darkness around the barred window. They'd left him a lighted candle, but that had sputtered out. He didn't become fully conscious—just enough to be aware of thoughts. He thought that it must be some time of a daily office or mass in the monastery because he could hear the chanting coming up from the chapel, but he wasn't particularly religious himself, so the chanting was no clue to the time of evening or night. He felt mellow and without worries—just floating along.

It didn't worry him even when he cell door opened and figures filtered into the room. A few of them had torches. They were all humming. They wore black habits tonight whereas in

39

the daylight they had worn brown. They were barefoot. The habits weren't really like normal monks' habits, though, he realized in looking at them. They were spilt in front, down to below the belly, and in the candlelight he realized that they opened at the chest enough to see the men's torsos. They were all lean and muscular. And the openings went down to where Alfons could discern the dark-haired men from the blonds from the strawberry blonds from the color of the men's pubic hair. The monk signaling directions to the others was the same senior monk from earlier in the day. His chest hair and pubic hair was laced with gray. The gaunt monk was there too— black haired below although bald on top—and, although gaunt, he was sinewy with tight muscles.

Believing in his haze that the men had come to use him, as had vaguely happened in the drugged dream he was having when they came into the cell, Alfons sighed in resignation, lifted the hem of his monk's cassock to his waist, and spread and bent his legs, arranging himself for the first of the monks to come in between his thighs. But that didn't happen; one of the monks pulled his cassock back down over his legs and another one was behind him, grasping him under the shoulders.

The gaunt monk and another, younger one, lifted Alfons from the stone platform and carried him between them out into the cloister, down the stairs, and past the chapel, which was open but inexplicably dark—the chanting had not been coming from here—and down circular stairs in a tower. Down, down, down.

Some slight thought deep in Alfons's mind was telling him that he should have a concern about why he was being carried away from his cell and where they were going, to what purpose. But the monks had not used him in his cell, so, in his muddled state, he didn't think he had concerns of that sort. He was still under the influence of the drug that had been in his wine—and, mercifully would be so through the time of the ritual and until sometime after he was returned, moaning, to his cell.

The chamber he was taken to was deep underground. The walls, floor, and vaulted ceiling were of stone block. The chamber was lit, more at the center than in the recesses, by torches hung on the columns holding up the ceiling. The center of the chamber was marked off with a circular pattern of mosaic tiles, with the image of a horned goat in the center. Incense burners were pumping a haze into the air. At one end of the chamber a dais, topped by a large, gold throne, rose up from the floor. Two muscular men, holding spears, butted to the floor, stood on either side of the throne. Their bodies were naked and oiled, gleaming in the torchlight. They wore goat-head masks.

The throne was occupied by another man, obviously the high priest for this ritual. He had a black robe on similar to those of the monks who had come for Alfons, but it was fully open and he was naked underneath. His body was magnificent and he was in erection. He too wore a horned goat mask, but his was gold in contrast to those of the guards, which were painted white.

A second obviously senior figure, also in a black robe open to show a beautiful body with reddish hair and wearing a gold horned goat mask, stood on a platform at a three o'clock position across the circle from the throne platform. He stood there throughout the ceremony, arms folded across his chest, observing all, but remaining above all.

In the center of the chamber, other monks, dressed as Alfons's escorts were, were moving around in a circle, looking to be in a trance. They were the source of the chanting, usually words of no language Alfons knew—or would have known.

His escort carried him to a position across the circle from the throne, at a six o'clock position from that platform. Here there was another platform, with a frame standing on it, and golden chains hanging down from the ceiling in front of it. Still under the influence of the drug in his wine, Alfons showed no concern—although he should have—as the monks' robe he'd been wearing was pulled over his head, leaving him naked. His arms were extended out from his sides and lashed with golden rope to the arms of the frame. His legs then were raised and spread and fastened to the golden chains hanging down from the ceiling. He was trussed now, his torso pinned to the frame and his legs spread and extended to the side, his buttocks parallel to the floor, although slightly raised above his chest so that his pelvis was readily accessible for what every man in the chamber save one was going to do with him over the next two hours.

Now Alfons was getting an inkling of what his function was to be in this primitive ritual—and he understood why he hadn't been sexually taken in his cell.

The high priest on the throne was the first one who fucked Alfons in what was obviously a periodic ritual of the monks of Die Bruderschaft—of the Brotherhood—and when he did, the mystery of why Alfons was here, why he'd been brought here to the monastery in the middle of the foreboding forest where young men entered and were often never were seen again, was revealed to him.

The high priest stood up from his throne, his erection cruelly upturned, his body covered in swirling patterns of curly black hair. He signaled to his two guards, who commenced working their cocks to rock hard too. He descended from the dais and walked across the chamber, through the center of the circle, where monks parted for him but then returned to their shuffling and chanting with renewed vigor and volume. He walked to the platform Alfons was bound on, mounted the steps, moved between Alfons's spread thighs, grabbed Alfons's legs under his knees to spread his legs further, thrust inside Alfons's anus with a cruel, deep upward stroke of his cock, and immediately began plowing him hard. Alfons cried out in pain and violation, but he was trained to the cocks of men, and soon he settled down and took the cock as a trained whore would, without objection and moving his pelvis in rhythm to the stroke.

He also was familiar with this particular cruel cock.

The high priest moved a hand to Alfons's cock and stroked him in synch with the stroking of the cock inside him. At some point he let the horned goat mask drop away and all was answered for Alfons. The high priest of Die Bruderschaft was, of course, Count Franz von Türbingen. Alfons wasn't needed in Türbingen. He was needed right here, to serve a periodic ritual of Die Bruderschaft. And chances were good, since the legend was that young men entered the wood and didn't leave it and there had been no rumors of the ritual at this monastery, that Alfons wouldn't be leaving here either. He could only hope that it was because the sacrifices were turned into monks rather than they were fucked to death and dropped in the moat. Thanks to the drug in the wine, though, Alfons didn't really care. He had been trained to the cocks of men and had come to want them inside him. He had been trained to take *this* cock; *this* cock had claimed his anal virginity.

On this night, in this ritual, he had the cock of every man in the chamber in him save that of the priest standing apart at the side and observing all. Von Türbingen plowed him until he brought Alfons to an ejaculation and then he released his seed deep inside the young man's channel. He stood aside, and Alfonso found that the two guards had taken up position behind Von Türbingen, and each took his piece of Alfons. As they were done, they joined the circle, where the debauchery among the monks commenced. As each monk from the circle climbed the platform, he tossed off his black habit, fucked Alfons, and then joined a group fuck in the circle. As the ritual advanced fewer monks in the circle were wearing black habits and more were writhing around on the floor having at each other. The ritual was over when no one in the chamber save the silent observer was wearing a black habit and all other men were sexually exhausted—Alfons no less than any of the others.

There was some sort of closing ceremony that Alfons was too far gone to follow and then the monks were donning their habits again, Alfons's escort released him from the frame, and he was carried back to his cell.

In the night, Alfons's own moans causing him to slowly awaken, as the drugs wore off and the reality of having taken the cocks of so many men began to catch up with him, Alfons felt the weight of yet another man cover him. Alfons tried to roll from under the man covering him and he did make it to the floor and a step toward the closed cell door, but a strong grip latched onto his wrist and drew him back to the platform, His body completely conquered, Alfons could do nothing but moan his capture. Laying Alfons on his belly on the quilt-covered stone platform, the towering figure tossed off his black habit—but not his mask—stretched out on top of Alfons, skewered him, and covered and fucked the young man until exhaustion and sleep had overtaken Alfons.

* * * *

Alfons had no idea if someone was aiding him for some unknown reason or if this was a game the monks were playing and that he'd be captured and put through the ritual again—possibly fucked to death this time. When he woke, he found he was alone and that the cell door was open a crack. It was still dark out. He scurried down the cloister to the sound of silence throughout the monastery, expecting to be caught and toyed with at any moment.

He had no trouble finding where the old mare was stabled. He had no trouble lowering the drawbridge. The mare was more than happy to be leaving the monastery. Once outside the monastery walls, he mounted the mare. He had escaped—at least for now. The effect of the sudden release of nervous tension combined with the exhausting ordeal he'd been through, though, caused him to collapse into an exhausted coma across the neck of the horse. When he woke again, he was on the edge of the forest but just outside it. He was lying on the ground next to the mare, which was grazing in a meadow.

It took him several minutes to realize that the mare had brought him back out of the forest in the direction of Rottenburg, not on the other side, where he'd been heading—not to Türbingen. There was a moment of panic when he thought that he wasn't where he was supposed to be—that both his master and Count Franz had determined that he would arrive in Türbingen at the count's side today. Then at least snatches of the previous night's events, rising into his consciousness through what had been a drugged haze at the time, alerted him that there had been no intention of him arriving in Türbingen. All along the count, who also was the High Priest of Die Bruderschaft—the Brotherhood—had only meant him to reach as far as the monastery.

What was he to do now? He didn't want to go back to the monastery or even to try to get around it. There was no reason to go to Türbingen. But as far as he knew both the count and his master in Rottenburg would be looking for him—with intent to do him harm. He know now why young men disappeared in the forest of Höllewald. Who was to say that his master hadn't knowingly supplied young men for Die Bruderschaft ritual in the past?

He raised his head and looked around. There, in the near distance, was a small town—Missinger, he realized. And in Missinger was Paul, the priest he'd lain with at the waterfall, the man who had asked him to return to Missinger with him.

Paul would give him shelter—at least until Alfons could decide where to go from here. Paul had told him just to ask for the village priest and he'd be led to Paul. He did that when he rode into Missinger and he was sent to a church, with a cottage next to it—the rectory. No one answered the door at the cottage, but Alfons had nowhere else to go that he could think of at the moment. So he tied the mare to a fence post and let her graze on what little grass there was in the plot in front of the cottage and he wearily lowered himself to the cottage stoop.

Paul, riding into the village on his own horse, saw Alfons from a distance. He pulled his horse to a stop. Alfons hadn't seen him yet. The priest turned to the side to check his saddlebag—to ensure that the black monks' habit and the gold horned goat mask were well hidden in his saddlebag where Alfons wouldn't see them before he could get them hidden in the cottage. Then he formed a beatific smile on his face and resumed riding toward the cottage, ready to heartily welcome his young prey.

Inquisitioned

When Margaret, Countess of Artois, rose from the dinner table in the palace in Barcelona, she motioned for her young bard, Guarin, to attend her and her ladies in waiting. Prince James of Aragon, her new husband, however, motioned Guarin to remain. The young man, small of stature, but perfectly formed, golden blond, fairer of face than a man should be, and with a honey toned voice, had risen at his mistress's bidding from where he'd been playing the lute and singing, and, with a grateful sigh was ready to leave the room with her. His face betrayed a slight fright, though, when the prince had growled that he remain.

In a more reasonable voice, James said, "I find him amusing and we have no other entertainment for ourselves tonight. You have your ladies, Margaret. Can you not let Guarin remain to give me a few more songs? And perhaps you don't have the need for Guarin's attentions for any length of time this evening, because in a short time, I'll be with you to give you my attention."

The countess simpered at the obvious suggestion that the handsome prince would bed her that night. This was the countess's third marriage, all arranged to help keep the disparate parts of the Spanish Hapsburg empire laced together in these early years of the sixteenth century and under the controlling influence of Castile. Castile is where Margaret had been born, a cousin of the current Spanish queen, Isabelle of Castile. Margaret was a dozen years older than her new husband, the prince of Aragon, nephew of Ferdinand of Spain, a former prince of Aragon himself. And he was far more handsome than she was pretty, so he'd been quite a catch for her.

She was still of child-bearing age, but not by much. James was vigorous and virile, though—said to have bastard children peppering the land, or so the rumors had been sown. He was, however, more interested in another direction. But he was duty bound and determined to have a male heir or two on

Margaret. She wasn't exactly ugly, but the bard she'd brought from Artois with her was beautiful—and the prince's inclination was more toward young men than older women.

Guarin's distress with being alone with James if his mistress withdrew without him was founded on the fact that James had already had him three times in the month since James's marriage to Margaret and had expressed full intention to have him again—and again. The prince was a forceful, cruel, and possessive lover.

The young bard looked on with concern as Margaret, smiling now at the thought of James coming to her that night, as indeed, he had done frequently since they'd been wed, bowed her head to her lord and swept out of the dining room with her three attendants in her wake. James was much the best lover and more heavenly endowed of the three husbands—and countless lovers—she had, and at her time of life she reveled in having such a handsome and vigorous man working so hard to fuck a male heir into her. She suspected he already had, but she would say nothing until she started showing, as she didn't want the man's ardor, feigned or otherwise, to decrease.

Guarin wasn't, in fact, alone with the prince in the hall. The prince's confessor, Tomás de Mendoza, was there, and Guarin's lover, the captain of the guard, Miguel de Morillo, was standing over by the door. Guarin was the kind of young man who would not go long wherever he traveled without having a master to lie under, and Morillo, a strapping and well-hung warrior, had scented him out and covered—and then claimed—him within days of the arrival of Margaret's entourage at the court of Barcelona.

The young bard took the presence of these men—especially that of a priest—as some means of protection, but it was a hollow hope. He knew the Miguel could do nothing. He had, in fact, had to stand by as a guard against interruption a week earlier when the prince had fucked Guarin in a summer pavilion in the garden. And the priest would hold counsel on whatever his prince did. Miguel was able to protect Guarin from the randy palace guardsmen, all having been selected by Prince James to assist and sometimes join in the prince's preference for men. But Miguel couldn't protect Guarin from the prince or the men near him.

Indeed, Miguel was being quite circumspect at this time, as he didn't want his family's past delved into too closely. It wasn't long ago that an ancestor of his had converted to the church from Judaism, during an earlier era of Jewish suppression in Spain. Having such a past was a real danger now, in the early sixteenth century, as the work of the Tribunal del Santo de la Inquisition—the Spanish Inquisition—was at its height. Diego de Valera, the archdeacon of Barcelona and a frequent guest and comrade in debauchery of Prince James's, was a particularly diligent agent of the Inquisition.

Although Miguel was more than happy to fuck the sweet young bard whenever he got the chance, there was little prospect of him standing in the way of Prince James and his friends if they wanted to do that too. In fact, although he thought he might be falling in love with Guarin, he wasn't so smitten at this point that he failed to enjoy what now transpired in the room, savoring it to think upon when he next had a crack at the young bard himself and surreptitiously seeing to his own needs to harden and release while the prince lay on top of the small musician and moved his hips as Guarin sighed and moaned under him.

"Please, settle yourself again and play and sing me a sweet love song," the prince said when the ladies were gone. His voice was a rich, honeyed baritone—seductive when he wanted it to be. Of course, seduction wasn't required of him. Aragon was his principality. He could and would take here what he wanted. He liked to think of himself as a champion seducer, though, and those he seduced helped him to think that—for their own good. If they were going to be pinned to the bed with his cock anyway, they might as well curry favor by letting the prince think that it had been accomplished by his charm rather than his authority.

Guarin knew that and, with a sigh, settled back onto the pillowed stool he had been perched on and searched out a song that he knew would please the prince. Perhaps the prince would become so lost in the song that he wouldn't . . .

But, of course he did. He came over and stood very close to Guarin. "Play me a song of a young bard and the prince—of how the bard pines for the prince and begs the prince to cover him and be as one with him."

Dutifully, the young singer sang of the meeting of a prince and his lover in a garden bower. Guarin was resigned enough to refer to the lover as male rather than female. And it wasn't long until the prince, standing very close to Guarin, had the fingers of one hand entwined in Guarin's golden curls and had unlaced his codpiece with his other hand and had his cock out, rubbing it against Guarin's cheek.

"Enough of the strumming and singing," he said in a low voice. "I will hum for both of us." He turned Guarin's head toward his crotch, the young bard dutifully took the cock in his mouth—this would be the fourth time the prince had laid him in a month, so what was expected of and inevitable for him was understood and accepted—and the prince took over the humming of the tune while Guarin sucked his cock to an erection. The prince ran the hand of the arm he was encasing Guarin in down the young man's chest, unlaced the bard's doublet, and gave attention to Guarin's nicely turned out chest and nipples.

James fucked Guarin on the heavy oak dining table, with the priest watching from the end of the table and Miguel from by the door. Guarin, naked, was on his back on the table, with his right ankle hooked on James's shoulder and James holding his left ankle out and up, his crotch pressed into Guarin's ass, and taking the young man cruelly—vigorously, thickly, and deep. He himself was fully clothed except for his dropped codpiece and his doublet flared open to show a muscular chest and hard, flat belly.

Guarin arched his back, panted heavily, and gripped the rim of the table to try to hold himself in place while the prince pounded him hard, his face hovering over Guarin's to take in every nuance of the young man's facial expression in the taking.

The prince laughed when he discerned the transition between pain-pleasure and pleasure-pain in Guarin's face and sensed when the musician no longer was struggling with him, but was going with the fuck—arching his back, counterthrusting with his pelvis, matching the rhythm of the fuck, and moaning deeply, which his tongue hanging out.

"Shall I stop?" the prince asked, with amusement.

"No, please. Don't stop. Seed me. Give me your seed," Guarin murmured breathlessly. It was a two-pronged response. He was telling the prince what he knew the prince wanted to hear. Guarin hadn't risen to playing for the nobility of Europe by not knowing what to praise and when. And beyond that, Guarin worshipped the cock—not just Prince James's cock; any well-turned hard cock. He wanted to be fucked regularly. The only caveats to the prince fucking him were that the prince could be rough and cruel and if the countess learned that James was fucking her minstrel, Guarin most definitely would be tossed out on the paving stones and scrabbling once again for a patron.

But here, now, the action had reached the point that Guarin cared nothing other than that there was a thick cock inside him, setting his channel wall muscles shimmering, and finding every sensitive and tender spot inside him.

"I believe I'll stop," the prince said.

"No, please don't stop," Guarin pleaded. "Make me release."

The prince laughed and fisting Guarin's cock, brought him to a climax. Then, with Guarin nearly sobbing, the prince turned him on to his belly, revolving him on a deeply planted cock, and tested the small man's flexibility. He forced Guarin's legs into the splits along the edge of the table, Guarin grabbed for the opposite table edge with his spread arms, and James pounded him to his own ejaculation.

He made Guarin kneel before him and clean his cock with his mouth. Then Guarin laced up the prince's codpiece and his doublet, stumbling when he tried to stand. The prince laughed at having made Guarin at least temporarily off balance and bowlegged and instructed the priest, Tomás de Mendoza, to help Guarin back to his room. Then he left to attend to the countess when he felt himself recovered enough to plow her. He left Guarin with a compliment.

"You are a sweet lay, Bard. I know you know not to mention this to the countess, but let it be known that all the time I'm moving inside her I'll be thinking of being inside you. And I will be inside you again ere the moon sets and reappears. Compose me a bawdy song you can sing while I am on top of you and plowing you. A new song for each lay until I tire of you."

"Until I tire of you" was ringing in Guarin's mind as Father Mendoza helped him back to his cell. With a shudder, Guarin realized that that was the edge of his existence here at court—dancing between the prince not tiring of him and the countess not knowing that the prince was laying him.

So lost in thought was he when they reached the door of his cell that Mendoza had to repeat what he'd whispered to him.

"What did you say?" Guarin asked.

"I know your secret," the priest repeated. "If you are good to me—as good as you are to the prince—I will not reveal it."

"My secret? What do you mean?"

"That one of your grandmothers was a Hebrew," Mendoza murmured in a low voice while looking up and down the corridor to ensure that no one had heard him. "That is not a fortunate ancestry here in Barcelona—especially with Archdeacon Valera roaming the castle halls. He need not know, though—certainly not from me."

Guarin froze in shock, but then he relaxed and pushed open his cell door. The priest was giving him an obvious choice. He lay on his back on his cot, his legs spread and bent, holding his legs in that position with his hands under the backs of his knees. His feather pillow was lodged under the small of his back, thrusting his pelvis up. Mendoza, his cassock unbuttoned and flared open, was crouched over him between his legs. Where the prince was thick, Mendoza was long. Where James was vigorous and demanding—and cruel—the priest was subtle and attentive, adjusting the depths and rhythm of his long slides to Guarin's groans and moans and the young man's begging for this and more of that. Guarin's receptiveness to the priest's attentions was only halfway gauged to keep the cleric pleased with Guarin. The priest was deeply experienced and, where James just took, took, took, the priest also gave.

After the two plowings, and knowing that both the prince and the priest intended to be there again and frequently, Guarin was exhausted and rolled onto his side when he was alone. But he wasn't alone for long. In the night, the captain of the guard, a tall, muscular man, who was even thicker than the prince and even longer than the priest and who was younger and more virile than either, entered the cell and stretched out behind Guarin. Even though aware that Guarin had already taken a man that evening—he didn't know that the priest had dipped his wick in Guarin as well—Miguel had needs of his own and had watched the prince fuck Guarin. Miguel had a throbbing erection and his own need.

Guarin woke to the sensation of one strong hand cupping his chin, bringing his face into the scratchy chin of the soldier, and the other hand palming his belly and pulling his buttocks into Miguel's crotch and onto his throbbing cock. Miguel took him, first in a side split, and, later in the night in other positions, seeding him again and again and fucking him into the dawn.

By the morning Miguel thought he was in love. By the morning, Guarin thought he was close to having been fucked to death, but he was purring and hadn't tried to push the soldier out of bed.

It was fortunate that the services of a bard came mostly into play in the evening hours. It was unfortunate, though, that the men of the castle—the prince, the priest, and the soldier—were mainly free to play in those same hours.

* * * *

"Where is Miguel? Have you seen Miguel?"

The court priest, Tomás de Mendoza, was holding Guarin bent over the cot in the young bard's cell. It was pitch dark in the night, and Mendoza had stolen into the cell and pulled Guarin, naked, out of his cot.

"I don't know where Miguel is. I haven't seen him for two days." That was the truth and Guarin was jittery as a result.

He hadn't lain under anyone for two days. The prince had promised to plow him almost daily, but now the prince seemed to be avoiding him.

"Has Miguel been covering you? What have you told him? What have you told him about your ancestry? He has Jews in his ancestry. I know that. Has he been covering you and sharing that you both have Hebrew ancestry?" It came out as a hiss. Mendoza had other snake-like aspects, and he was quaking as he held Guarin bent over the bed and close from behind. Guarin could feel the insistence, the excitement, of the man through the cloth of his cassock. The musician was already trembling and moaning. He needed the cock.

"No, I haven't lain with Miguel," he lied. "I want to lie under you." The priest already knew too much. It was dangerous for him to know any more. "I haven't told him anything about my grandmother. He knows nothing about that. He's just a soldier. I don't know him and I don't know where he is. I want you. I want you inside me."

"Something is afoot," Mendoza whispered. "The captain of the guard has gone missing. He has Jews in his background. The archdeacon is strutting around like he knows something, like he's up to something. He's said there are Jews in the background at the court—that members of the court are influencing the prince to lift the Inquisition . . . that the Inquisition will ferret them out and crush them before that can happen . . . that anyone knowing of the Jews in the court and not telling him will be put to the rack. Even the prince is cowering from him."

"Why do you care so much?" Guarin asked. "I thought you were just holding it over my head because you wanted to cover me. But is it more than that? Do you have Jews in your background too, Father Tomás?"

The priest didn't answer that, he just repeated, "Have you told Miguel anything? Have you seen him?"

"I told you I haven't," Guarin whimpered. "But I have need. You are hard. Please, Father Tomás, I need it."

"Very well, but speak to no one about anyone else's background . . . and avoid Archdeacon Valera."

Mendoza was unbuttoning his cassock. He was naked underneath. He embraced Guarin close with an arm around the young man's waist.

"Hurry, please hurry," Guarin whined.

The priest positioned his cock with the other hand, and Guarin let out a groan and a long sigh as the priest entered him with his long, hard cock and pushed it in to the hilt. He held as Guarin panted and adjusted to him and then he began to slow pump the young man. Guarin stretched his hands back and between the flaps of the cassock and the man's slim hips, palmed the priest's buttocks, and help to guide the slides. As they fucked, the tension was drained out of them both and they lost the worries of the present world and entered the realm of sheer sexual pleasure. The priest invoked the name of his god without embarrassment as he released his seed.

Guarin wasn't all that religious, but he couldn't help but think that Mendoza's god might not have appreciated that and would take the priest to task for crying out what he had, in essence exalting the young musician's sweet and talented ass and channel over the throne of God.

* * * *

Prince James saw them coming from a distance—Archdeacon Valera, backed up by a line of priests and soldiers—as he was slumped in a chair in a summer house in the castle gardens and Guarin was sitting, facing him, in his lap and riding his cock. The prince barely had time to push the bard off his lap and exit through the door at the back of the summer house before Valera was there, pointing an accusing finger at a dazed Guarin.

"Take that Jew in for inquisition," he demanded.

The young man was taken to the deep bowels of the castle, where Valera had had an inquisition torture chamber set up in one of the stone walled, floored, and ceilinged dungeons. Other moaning bodies were there on other racks when Guarin was stripped and bound to one. The rack was turned just one notch, to get Guarin's attention and assure him that Valera meant business.

The Inquisitor leaned in close to Guarin's panting face and, running his hand lovingly over the young man's beautiful body, whispered, "It would be a shame to ruin this fine young body of yours. I know that you are of Hebrew ancestry. But I don't care about that. You have only recently come to this court; you are not Spanish. You're French. You can as easily be expelled back to France. It would be a crime to break the bones of a perfect body like this. You just need to tell me who else at court is a hidden Jew. Your mistress, Margaret, perhaps?"

"No, no. I know of no one who is. And I'm not either. I am faithful to the Faith," Guarin cried out in fright. His mind was racing. Miguel? Had Miguel betrayed him? Father Mendoza had interrogated him on what he might have told Miguel. And he said that Miguel had a Jewish background. Could it have been Miguel who . . .?

But then he heard the cough and gag from a nearby rack and looked over at it. He recognized the priest, Tomás de Mendoza. The priest was here, and on a rack, and from observation, it was clear he'd been tortured, been put fully to the rack. Just as Guarin feared *he* was going to be. But he didn't know anything. He looked around madly for Miguel, but didn't see him. There were other men—and a few women—bound to various torture devices, though. But he couldn't see Miguel. He must be here, though. But as much as Guarin thought about it, he couldn't remember having told Miguel about his grandmother—or Miguel telling him anything about his own past, for that matter.

But he must be here.

The Inquisitor's bejeweled hand lingered over Guarin's pelvis and settled on the young man's cock, stroking it for a few moments lovingly. "Ah, perfection," he murmured. "It would be such a pity . . ."

"No, I know nothing about these matters," Guarin murmured, his voice shaking so hard he almost couldn't get the words out. "And, no, God help us, not the countess. She is as devout as they come. Her noble Catholic lineage is known by all."

The Inquisitor released Guarin's cock and ran the fingers of his hand up and down the line of the young bard's body—almost like he was worshipping the perfection that Guarin was, at least for now. The thought entered Guarin's mind at the intimacy of the priest's touch that maybe . . .

"Sir, I'll do anything for you not to put me to this torture. I'm simply a musician. I'm not involved in any scheming against the mother church. Where I come from, we are as Catholic as you are in Spain. I would never . . . and I don't know of anyone else . . . and I would do anything to please you. I have experience in pleasing a man."

"I am aware of that," Valera said dryly. "I know you would please a man who wished to take his pleasures from other men. The prince tells me what you do for him. His court priest has told me, with a bit of persuasion, what you do for him as well."

He stopped there. Guarin saw hope in that. He hadn't mentioned Miguel. Maybe Miguel wasn't here. It must have been Mendoza who denounced him.

"Please, Sir. I will give you pleasure as you have never known before."

"I think you have no idea what pleasures me." Valera gave Guarin a hard look and then stood and called for the guards. "Hang him from that device over there," he commanded, and the soldiers took Guarin off the rack and hung him, with his wrists bound, from the top of a pole that had a cross pieces with restraints on the ends. When Guarin was trussed up to the device, he was hanging from his wrists, but his legs were split in either direction a couple of feet off the ground and tied off at the ankles.

"Now you may go for a rest and not come back for an hour," Valera said to his attendants.

When the guards were gone, Valera stripped off his cassock and underclothes until he was naked. He had a powerful body—thick but not really fat. He also had a colossal erection.

Taking a whip, he laid into Guarin's back and legs, as the young man screamed from the pain—not as painful as if the priest had put the full power of his body behind the lashes, but painful enough to raise red welts on Guarin's tender body. All the time, the priest made the pretense of trying to get Guarin to provide the names of secret Jews at court. But both men knew, really, that the Inquisitor was more interested in his own sexual satisfaction and that his sexual satisfaction hinged on sexual torture.

After whipping Guarin for a short time, he saddled up behind the young man, ran his tongue over the welts on Guarin's back, kissing those and Guarin on the neck and then on the mouth when he'd turned the young man's face to his. He split Guarin's plump, reddened buttocks cheeks with his hard, thick cock and fucked him to a completion.

He was finished before the hour was up, but not really finished. He had his cassock back on when the guards reappeared and instructed them to take Guarin down and to bind him to a series of chains hanging from the ceiling. His wrists were bound over his head to one chain, and his legs were each bound, spread, and stretched parallel to the stone floor on other chains. When the guards were sent away for another hour, Valera stripped, pressed in between Guarin's spread legs, pulled the young man's channel onto his reengorged staff and fucked the musician again interminably to another ejaculation.

The Inquisitor took Guarin a third time that evening, from behind, with Guarin stretched over a saw horse device, with both arms and legs spread and secured at the base of the four legs of the device. By the time the priest was done, Guarin was nearly done as well—unconscious and breathing shallowly, almost not at all.

When the guards returned, Valera declared, "He is close to talking, but I do not have time tonight. Tomorrow he will talk and we will finish with him." They extinguished the torches in the dungeon and left the day's work in the dark. There were moans and groans revolving around the chamber—although there were more bodies on devices in the chamber than were able ever again to moan or groan. Guarin was one who still could.

Guarin regained consciousness in the night to the sensation of being unbound. There was a torch and he looked up and recognized the man freeing him.

"Miguel," he said. "You live."

"For now I do, and so do you," Miguel de Morillo whispered. "But we must be away from here—away from Aragon—away even from Spain if we want to continue to live. I have passage booked for this night on a ship in the harbor bound for France."

"You came for me."

"The booking is for two. I could not leave you. I cannot live without you."

As Guarin was freed and was hobbling away from the torture device, he suddenly said, "The court priest—Father Mendoza—he's here somewhere. He's—"

"Past saving. Past praying for even. He denounced us both. He is somewhere we can't touch him, answering for much. Come, we must go. The ship leaves on the morning tide."

* * * *

Guarin had been aware that the priest had been watching him—had been following him around—since they had cleared the Mediterranean and were sailing up the Atlantic coast. Miguel had booked them on a ship going to France by this route rather than to a French Mediterranean port. He knew that the Church had eyes everywhere and that Archdeacon Valera would not be pleased that they had slipped through his fingers. He would have ships bound for French Mediterranean ports watched carefully.

Was this such a priest, Guarin wondered.

Seeing the priest nearby one day while Miguel was elsewhere on the ship, Guarin gave him a meaningful look and slipped into his cabin, leaving the door open. The ploy worked and the priest followed him in.

"You are Guarin, Countess Margaret's bard," the priest said. "I recognized you."

"Yes, I am," Guarin answered. "Or I was," he added.

"I am Ferdinand de Mena," the priest answered. He was perhaps in the middle of his years, tall and gaunt. His face was not ugly, but it wasn't handsome either. He was giving Guarin an intense look. "I am a friend of the court priest, Tomás de Mendoza. He keeps me well informed of the happenings at court."

He hasn't kept you well informed that he's dead, Guarin thought, but he realized it was a rather hysterical thought. His mind was racing. This man knew. He was going to denounce them. They'd both be taken back and broken on Valera's racks.

Unless Guarin did something. He smiled at the priest and began to unlace his doublet.

"Yes, Mendoza told me he you lay under him—and under the prince as well. He told me that you were a delight to cover. And that's not all he told me. He told me that your grandmother was Hebrew. It's something the Tribunal del Santo de la Inquisition in Barcelona would very much like to know, I'm sure."

"Unless?" Guarin asked, giving the priest a provocative smile and pulling his doublet open to show his bare chest.

"Yes, unless you lay under me too."

Stripping off the doublet, Guarin unfastened his belt, stripped off his breeches, lay back on the bed, and opened his legs and his arms. At the same time, the priest was unbuttoning his cassock. He sank to his knees and attacked Guarin's cock, balls, and hole with his mouth, as Guarin sighed and moaned for him.

The priest was crouched over him, between his legs, feeding a very nice cock in him, as Guarin clutched the man's shoulder blades, content to enjoy the fuck. And the priest was doing very well, not going for broke before pumping him, but going in a few inches, shallow pumping there, as Guarin moved with him, and then sinking in further and pumping some more.

He wasn't all the way in before he stiffened, gave Guarin a surprised look, and slipped over to the side and to the floor. As he slipped away, Miguel came into sight, holding a bloodied dagger in his hand.

"You killed him," Guarin croaked.

"Yes."

"You killed a priest. You'll go to hell."

"As will priests like this. I think you've learned by now that priests are the same as any other man. They lay you just as any other man does. They deceive and betray you as any other man does. And they bleed like any other man does."

Guarin didn't know how to respond to that, so he remained silent.

"Yes, he had to die. It was just Mendoza all over again. It had to be stopped before it began."

"But he wasn't finished. I didn't—"

Miguel laughed. "You are such a little whore," he said. "I can finish you. He can go over the side later."

And, with that, Miguel took up the priest's position, but sank all the way in before he started to pump. Moaning his satisfaction, Guarin clutched at the soldier's shoulder blades and started to move with the fuck.

24 Exeter Place

"Thank you," the monsignor said as I handed him down from the carriage in front of 24 Exeter Place in a quiet pocket garden not far from Victoria Station. I had told him my name was Luke, but he'd managed to go all afternoon without directly addressing me—like I wasn't wholly there. This was the first time he'd thanked me, though, and I thought there was reason enough to be thanked earlier in the day.

"Can we possibly be here?" he asked, looking up at the façade of a brownstone, whose edges blended in with the brownstones of the crescent on either side of it.

"Discretion," Your Eminence, I murmured. "The hallmark of the gentlemen's clubs of London."

"Ah, yes, I do appreciate that," he said, his English good, but with a heavy Spanish accent, as we mounted the steps and I raised and lowered the door knocker. Stewart Brandon, the imposing majordomo met us at the door. "Ah, Your Eminence . . . Luke," he said as he swept aside for us to enter. "I trust everything was satisfactory," he said to the Spanish monsignor, an emissary of the Vatican to the Court of Saint James, who had been introduced to the club by the marquis, Lord Fitzwater of York, one of the club's major patrons.

"Quite satisfactory," the monsignor said. "The young man can see me back to the hotel later?"

"Certainly, as you wish," Brandon said, as he ushered the priest into the drinks parlor, where several members had already gathered. Turning to me, he said, "Mark will need some help with the service; Matthew and John are otherwise occupied."

"Yes, Mr. Brandon," I answered, moving toward the kitchen at the back of the building for a tray of drinks. The four service men of the club were known as Matthew, Mark, Luke, and John no matter what their real names were. It made identifications easier for the members, who barely noticed who was serving them in the public areas of the club, although when we put our trays down, they generally brought us into the orb of their conversations at least long enough to acknowledge our presence, to make small chit chat, and to voice their interests and expectations.

The atmosphere in the drinks parlor was one of boisterous conversation, whiskeys and scotches, and cigars and cigarettes. There were several centers of discussion, focused on the careers and interests of the gentlemen, most in their middle age, all notable beyond the confines of the club walls. I passed by the "courts" group with a tray of drinks. The Right Honorable Peter Bowles, judge of the Appeals Court, was discussing the intricacies of the naval impressment case before him, including the scandalous indignities the press claimed were being imposed on the young sailors, with Admiral Stanley Thornton and the leading barrister of the day, Bradley Thaw.

"Nothing that the noblest of our young men don't encounter in public school," Thaw was saying.

Bowles laid a hand on my forearm and pulled me into the group for a moment. "I looked for you earlier today, Luke," he said. "I believe this was our afternoon." I doubt he'd been to court that day. He was dressed for riding, including having a riding crop in his hand that he kept flicking against his leg.

"Yes, Your Lordship," I answered. "It is, indeed, sir. I'm sorry that we have missed—"

"I don't intend it to be missed. I intend it to be fit in."

"Yes, of course, Your Lordship. I'm sorry. A guest of Lord Fitzwater's was in town and I was sent to him at Grosvenor's for the afternoon."

"Ah, the priest who has just entered then. I didn't recognize him."

"He's Spanish," I said. "Manual Alvarez. Apparently sent here on some diplomatic mission by the pope. Lord Fitzwater was very definite about wanting him to be made comfortable in London and to have someone escort him around."

As we conversed, I saw John come down the stairs behind the Earl, William Yates, and, at Stewart Brandon's beckoning cross to the Spanish priest. I felt the relief that John was seeing to the priest, as I was being torn between my obligations to Alvarez and Lord Peter.

The remainder of the drinks on my tray went to the politics discussion group near the door to the foyer, which included a viscount, Lord Charles Beaumont; the fiery orator in the House of Lords, Sir Travis Compton; and a gentleman so much farther up in the royal house that we never spoke his name or title in this club—just referring to him as "Your Highness."

I passed Mark in the foyer as he was arriving with a fresh drinks tray and I was returning to the kitchen to replenish mine. As I passed the staircase, I caught a glimpse of the Spanish priest's white cassock, denoting his tropical origin, near the top of the stairs. I didn't make it to the kitchen, though, as the door to the music room opened and the baronet, Sir James Stockdale, the club member nearest my age, a reputed ne'er-do-well and dandy the world knew as Dickie, accosted me.

"We are in the need of a singer of a new song Felix has written," he said to me in a slightly slurred voice. "You are the best singer in this establishment, Luke. Get thee in here."

He was a member—and also the one I liked the best—so I entered the music room and he closed the door behind me. This obviously was where the artists were gathering. Among them I marked the current leading man of the theatre, Sir Dennis Winston; and the celebrated novelist, Sir Henry Duwright. Felix, the black musician, who was the toast of Covent Garden underground cafés by night, was at the piano. I didn't escape for the next fifteen minutes while I was forced to warble Felix's new song, with him playing at the piano. Dickie saw to it that I couldn't leave by standing close behind me, holding me close, and giving me sloppy kisses on the neck while I endeavored to make out the crude markings on notes on the score Felix handed me.

Back in the foyer, Peter Bowles caught my eye and nodded and, instead of going to the kitchen, I mounted the stairs to the second floor.

Curious, before I went to my assigned room, I opened a cupboard door between two of the other rooms that led into a narrow secret passage between the rooms and went to the spy holes into the rooms on either side. It was church day on the second floor of 24 Exeter Place. On one side, the bishop of Leeds was on all fours on a bed and Matthew was mounted on his ass and giving him quite a ride. On the other, as I suspected, John was lying belly on the bed, wrists bound to the headboard above him, and the Spanish monsignor, Manual Alvarez, cassock open, flared, and trailing behind his thin body, was plastered to his ass and making like a camel crossing the desert.

The Spaniard had taken me, similarly bound and in the same position, at the Grosvenor that afternoon. There was a hint of the Inquisition in him even when he was fucking a young man.

I came back into the corridor just as the Right Honorable Peter Bowles was reaching the top of the stairs. I regretted the riding crop he was flicking against his leg, but he was a senior member of the club and Stewart Brandon kept pointing out that I should be proud that he scheduled me so often. He paid extra in dues and some of the extra trickled down to the young man who serviced him. That may or may not have made up for the whip, but Stewart Brandon didn't care either way, so the issue was moot.

Today was bothersome, though, as he was a man quick to anger and he'd been made to wait for my services. He was a cruel cocksman when he was angry.

He too made use of the wrist restraints we all had attached to our beds, in addition to the ankle restraints had had me spread-eagled on the bed. He left them loose, however, as he enjoyed my writhing and throwing my body around as he made me rise to my knees under him and he rode me as he'd ridden his horse earlier, my rump between his knees, and his riding crop flogging me on the back, buttocks, and thighs.

Afterward, knowing what the servicing would be, Brandon sent a servant from the kitchen staff—my best friend, the African giant Kwame, to my room to apply unguents to my welts before they could take hold and fester. Kwame was the best of salves himself, taking me in his arms, stretched along my body—he was a good foot taller than me and much meatier—lifting my leg to expose and stretch open my passage, and slowly entering me with a long, long cock as his hand, slathered in the unguent, gently massaged my slight wounds—the judge hadn't got out of control or left much evidence of the exercise of his fetishes—as his staff worked my passage to a mutual ejaculation.

The Right Honorable Peter Bowles never was concerned for whether I came in his use of my body—today, despite having been made to wait, having been far less demanding than the days when his cases weren't going as he liked and he used his fists. It was only his own pleasure that he paid the extra dues for. On his bad days, the next day or two were bad for me too, causing me to lose sessions. We were paid by the session—and for each client ejaculation in a session—having to keep and report a tally of each release by way of discreet chalk marks on the inner walls of the night stand top drawers.

As I was descending the staircase, ready to take up my first-floor service duties again, the baronet, James Stockdale, was standing at the bottom of the stairs, looking up expectantly, and barring my way.

Stockdale was young, hung, athletic, and inventive. Usually I welcomed his approach as being a fresh break from the older members, whose repertoires were largely limited to the missionary and doggy positions and whose ejaculations, generally, were weak and rapid and their erection incomplete. Even the weak ejaculations were recorded and paid for, though.

There was nothing incomplete about Stockdale's erections or weak and rapid about his ejaculations. And he was a master of the male Kama Sutra.

But coming so soon after being worked over by the judge . . .

He walked up two steps of the stairs, his gaze still expectantly boring into my face, and, with a sigh, I turned and preceded him to my room.

No restraints with Stockdale. He fucked me all over the room, manipulating my body into various inventive positions. During the hour-long process, in which he showed he could make me come twice but save himself for one, long, prolonged gush, I, first, watched the dust motes build up under my bed as he fucked me like a dog on the floor, and then all four walls, as he took me in a standing fuck, me draped on his chest, my knees gripping his waist, as he walked around the room slamming me up and down on his cock. Then it was the ceiling I viewed as he put my weight on my shoulders, jackknifed my legs, and hammered down inside me from above. He saved his coming for tenderly embracing me on the bed, taking me in a side split, and capturing my eyes with his as we kissed deeply and he pumped my ass full of cum.

Stewart Brandon found me some minutes after Stockdale had dressed and left, on my back on my bed, my legs bent and spread to provide relief to my throbbing ass channel, Stockdale's cum dribbling out of my hole, and still moaning over the athletic man's attentions.

"The Spanish priest is ready to go back to the Grosvenor," he said, making no remark on my state of exhaustion as I lay on my bed. "Give him an hour there, but be back by dinner. You are accompanying the marquis to the theatre. I don't expect you back on duty before morning."

I groaned and rolled over to the side of the bed and searched for the floor with my bare feet. How could he consider a night with the marquis, Lord Charles Beaumont, not being on duty? Why were there only four of us to service these men? The members were a randy bunch. The club should hire two more prostitutes.

Monsignor Manuel, well serviced before, including two torturous fuckings of me in his Grosvenor hotel room earlier than afternoon, didn't need the whole hour. He was done and ready to bathe, take confession from Spanish residents of London, and attend a mass after no more than twenty minutes of plowing my ass, as I lay on my back at the foot of the bed, bending and pulling my legs up toward my chest and spreading them wide myself, while he crouched between my thighs, his cassock open and flaring behind him, and slammed me hard with a thin, upcurved cock rising out of an unruly black, curly thatch. He only managed a trickle of cum, but there was no way they could claim that the 24 Exeter Place gentleman's club hadn't fully met his expectations and needs.

I arrived back at the club in time for an early dinner, which I enjoyed with John and Kwame in the servants' hall off the kitchen. It was my habit to go out for a long walk after dinner, not only to settle my meal but also to have a few moments to myself and to exercise the limbs that kept my body in trim and supple rather than the muscles I more frequently used to grasp a gentleman's cock with to make shimmering love to it.

However, today that was not to be realized. Stewart Brandon came to me at the door as I was about to leave the club. His demeanor was one of excitement rather than regret to interrupt the time of the day I enjoyed the most—other than those nights that Kwame crept into my room and worked me over with an impossibly thick and long cock and stamina that no members of the club other than the baronet Sir James Stockdale could equal.

"His Highness is on the third floor, the Swan Suite. He's asked explicitly for you."

"Matthew?"

"It doesn't matter. His Highness has asked for you to attend him. Matthew is pouting, but that isn't your concern; I will knock him together."

With a sigh, I turned and mounted the stairs—first to my own room, as a call to serve such a royal required some special preparations—and then to the third floor. Till now Matthew had been the sole server for the man. But he'd asked for me, so there was nothing else to consider.

Afterward I was plied with questions on the encounter. Who topped? What positions? Is he hung . . . thick . . . long? Does he have a Prince Albert? (This last question bring twitters all around.)

Like Matthew, I kept the details to myself, as Stewart Brandon expected and would find out if I didn't, only responding to one of the questions. "Aren't all of the royals thick?" I asked, which was met with appreciative laughter.

First, we weren't alone. The guy in the corner was much too small and cute to be a bodyguard, I thought. And I was informed he was a dresser. His Highness couldn't undress himself by himself? OK, the extra man's cute, I thought, I can go with that—imagine myself with him rather than this walrus. It wasn't unknown for one club member to want to watch while another club member—or two, although doubles were John's specialty more than mine—fucked me.

The imperial walrus indeed was thick—as thick as I'd had—and, surprisingly and appropriately, he did have a thick Prince Albert ring in the head of the cock. Otherwise, he was quite royal. He laid on his back, his arms crossed behind his neck, and viewed me with a somewhat distant and amused look in his eyes as I straddled his hips and did all of the work for the first ten minutes, which wasn't easy considering the thickness of him; it took nearly the full ten minutes to bottom him out— all this until he engaged and decided that I had something he wanted to take from me, and then he swiftly turned our bodies, slapped my legs apart, thrust inside me, and completely dominated and pulled every ounce of value out of me for his own pleasure. In other words, the British Empire in a nutshell.

All of this within the span of thirteen or fourteen minutes. It was a blitzkrieg, and it was all about him—which was no surprise to me—once he took full control, it was wham, bang, five strokes and an ejaculation. And a world-record ejaculation to boot, itself a production of a good twenty seconds, multiple eruptions, and a tidal wave of cum.

As I lay on my side, his cock still inside me, and panting, he patted me on the rump and said, "Good show. I will want you again in a few days."

In the end, he said he wasn't in the mood for seconds, just a cock sucking. The gold of his Prince Albert clicked against my teeth as he forced his royalty down my throat and creamed my tonsils with his regal nectar.

Again, Steward Brandon found me laying all akimbo on the bed and panting hard in the suite after His Highness' dresser moved from the corner of the room and draped and smoothed the man out. The dresser was young and cute. I could only imagine what His Highness did with him. He gave me a shy, sympathetic smile, and I felt my cock harden. As with most of the rest, His Highness did nothing about any needs I might have and he'd fired off and gone soft just when I was beginning to get revved up. I still had a need after this onslaught. The dresser seemed to understand that. We shared smiles and I winked at him, moving my hand to my cock, which was half erect and unsatisfied. Brandon was all smiles too when he entered the room as the dresser left.

"He is very pleased," Brandon said. "He will ask for you again."

"That's what he said to me," I answered, not trying to make my voice sound flat, but I'm sure it did. All hail the gods, I thought, but rather than say anything else, I just tiredly waved my hand in an imperial salute.

As I had intended, the dresser slithered back into the room after Brandon left.

"Excuse me, sir. Is there anything I can do for you?"

"There certainly is," I murmured, taking my cock in my hand and shaking it at him.

In no time, he was kneeling between my legs and taking my staff in his mouth. When I was fully erect, I pulled him up to me, turned him, fumbled a bit in getting his ass bare, and then split his cheeks with my cock. He sighed and moaned as I pumped him slow and deep. There were club members who wished to be bottoms, but never enough for my tastes. I had built up a lot of cum over the day, and I gave it all to the dresser as he gasped and fell over himself in telling me how good I was.

"Better than . . .?"

"Yes, much better."

I dropped my idea of having a Prince Albert added to my equipment.

I made another, unsuccessful stab at getting out of the club for a walk on my own. The encounter with His Highness had taken practically no time at all. Once more Stewart Brandon was waiting for me at the front door in the foyer.

"The marquis is in the library and is asking for you," he said.

"But it's too early for us to leave for the theatre," I said.

"He says he is tense now."

"Ah. And I suppose he'll be tense after the theatre too," I couldn't resist saying.

"I have no opinion on that," Brandon said, and leveling his eyes on me, "and neither to you."

I got the message.

"I hear that you are a bit tense, Your Lordship," I said as I entered the library. Other than the marquis sitting in a wing back chair with a scotch and a lit cigar on the table next to him, the library was deserted. I left Brandon standing at the door, and assumed he was on guard. It was against the club rules to engage in sex on the public floor. The marquis didn't care much about other people's rules, though.

"Yes, Luke, I am. Kindly service me."

With a sigh, I went down on my knees between his spread legs, unbuttoned his fly, fished out his erect cock, took it in my mouth, and, looking up into his eyes as I knew he liked, gave him a slow, deep-throating blow job that had me sputtering to capture and swallow his prodigious load. The marquis could build up cum like no other member of the club in my experience—and I had experienced nearly all of the members. All members of this club were interested in the services that I and Matthew, Mark, and John provided—that's why they joined and paid the exorbitant fees here.

On the carriage ride to the theatre, the marquis returned the service, although it didn't have anything to do with what I would want. He enjoyed giving head as much as he did taking it. In the darkness of the back of the carriage, he leaned over, took my lips in his, murmured about how handsome I was in evening wear, unbuttoned my fly, and lowered his face to my lap. He was wearing gloves and inserted a hand under my balls, running a gloved finger into my channel, and found my prostate. Rubbing there enhanced the rise of cum up from my ball sac. I pulled out the handkerchief I had brought with me for this contingency, and held it nearby as his head bobbed up and down on my cock. At least he was permitting me to come. I couldn't always count on that, even in circumstances like this. I warned him when I was coming and he pulled his mouth away, keeping his hand fisting the base of my cock and stroking and watched the expression on my face, as I folded the handkerchief over the bulb of my cock and spasmed my release three times.

As the carriage pulled up to the front of the theatre, I was reminded of the major reason I had taken the position I had—the position of lying under powerful men. The courtyard was lined with beggars. The economic situation was terrible. Without my handsome looks and sleek body and the ability to take cock after cock, I could well be one of these beggars myself. It was something to think about when I was tempted to complain about days like today. I was well paid, especially given that I had little opportunity to spend money, I was well fed and had a roof over my head. The men who fucked me were clean and wealthy. A few of them were generous. A couple had offered to set me up in my own apartment just to await their visits. I was saving that option for a few years when I felt I might be losing my charms. But I was not inclined to open my legs for only one man.

Even if I had taken another type of job altogether, I would still crave the cock. A variety of men and a variety of cocks. Even penetration by a cock as soon as one had pulled out of me. I was addicted to being fucked. "Whore" was a term of release for me, not a dirty word. All in all, it was the perfect job for me—as long as I could keep my looks and my channel was able to take a cock.

I had been given no idea what we were seeing at the theatre, nor did I care. It was time not spent on my back with a cock up my ass on a taxing day. It gave me the respite I had wanted to get by taking a walk and nothing was required of me. I sat in the last row in the box. The marchioness was there, sitting by the marquis, the two of them putting on a display for the world. She didn't ask who I was and obviously didn't care.

At the interval, they went to wherever the important people go and I went to the men's cloak room.

"Luke. You've come to the theatre." It was said in surprise. I turned to see the baronet, Sir James Stockdale, standing there, licking his chops like he'd like to eat me—which, in fact, he'd already done that day. Standing behind him was the novelist, Sir Henry Duwright. He hadn't eaten me out today, but did so on alternate days. Was this an even or odd

71

day? I wondered. I'd lost count. Today was the type of day that I lost count of cocks as well.

"Great seeing you here," Stockdale continued. "Henry and I were just discussing what we wanted to do after the theatre. If you're free and would like to earn a little extra, we would love sharing you."

I knew what he meant by sharing me. A double—both of their cocks in me at the same time, the two of them making love with each other while having sex in me. It was a pity they both were tops; they would have made a lovely couple. They'd pay me a pound or two for that, at least. They loved taking me that way. I didn't mind it myself. But it had been a taxing day and I wasn't really free. "I'm here with the marquis," I said. "I'll be with him the whole night."

"Pity," Stockdale said, sounding like he meant it. "Another time, then. I'd book you at Exeter Place, but I know you wouldn't get much out of that for yourself."

"No, I wouldn't," I answered. I bit my tongue from pointing out right then that I always could be tipped directly at the Exeter, although I'd never known the baronet to do that.

"Perhaps on your day off."

"I don't have days off," I answered. And then I went for it. "Of course, there can be a bit extra under the sheets at the Exeter. You and Sir Henry could always—"

"Yes, that's always a possibility," he said. But his eyes were already roaming. I had little doubt that, as handsome as he was and with his reputation for prowess and startling equipment, that he and Sir Henry would be able to find some fellow to accommodate them this evening for free and for the bragging rights of having had the cocks of two such notable men in him at the same time.

When I returned to the box, the Bishop of Leeds was there, insinuating himself into joining the marquis' party of two for the rest of the evening. I could tell that Lord Fitzwater wasn't entirely pleased, but I could also tell that the Bishop of Leeds had some sort of control over him. I'd heard something about a land dispute that the bishop had come down on the side of the marquis in, but I couldn't remember any details.

After the theatre, we went to dinner—or rather the marquis and the bishop went to dinner and I was just along for the ride—and to be ridden. I wasn't asked if I had eaten—and thank goodness I had. I only was asked if I'd heard of the new men's dinner club, the Tombs, which, indeed, was in a subterranean chamber entered from an alley and was not the type of place that could advertise publicly.

I also didn't know that the entertainment included a young man engaged to periodically swing on a trapeze over the diners. Tonight I was volunteered to be that man. It was all part of a game. The orchestra played and I swung. When the orchestra stopped playing abruptly, I had to take off an article of clothing and toss it down into the crowd—not any part of the tuxedo I'd walked in with but a costume of billowy white silken shirt under a velvet vest; long, silken hose attached to a garter belt; and two layers of skimpy underdrawers. The man who caught the last article of clothing—my inner set of underdrawers—was given twenty minutes with me beyond a doorway covered with a beaded curtain beside the orchestra stand.

I was paid, but not nearly on the scale of the 24 Exeter Club.

My man was a burly thug who dressed like a gentleman but wasn't one. It took him less than fifteen minutes to slam me, belly against the wall, against the stones in the corridor behind the stage, release a thick slug of a cock and low-hanging hairy balls, skewer me from behind, and unload his ball sac.

When I returned to the table where the marquis and bishop were sitting, they didn't bother to ask me anything about the experience—and they were ready to leave for the drive back to the club. The bishop said he was quite happy to go to the club too, and what could the marquis say? The bishop was a member.

Neither of them asked me what I thought about it.

"You were so arousing swinging on the trapeze that I wanted to be the one to catch your underdrawers," the marquis said. "I'm not sure I can wait until we arrive back at Exeter Place."

"Why make the effort to?" the bishop helpfully said.

"Why, indeed?" Lord Fitzwater answered.

The bishop helped strip me of my trousers and underdrawers and to set me on the marquis' cock as he sat on the plush carriage seat. Helping to hold me there as I took the responsibility to rise and fall on the staff, the bishop lowered his head into my lap and took my cock in his mouth.

The bishop doggedly followed us into the club and up the stairs to the third floor, where the visitor suites were kept in readiness for the club members who decided to stay the night. The marquis had booked a room. I could tell that the marquis wasn't pleased that the bishop stayed with us, but it wasn't up to me to voice an opinion or do anything to hold the bishop back.

The bishop watched for some time as Lord Fitzwater started out by fucking me missionary style at the foot of the bed, but he soon tired and laid himself out on the bed on his back and bid me mount the cock and do the riding. It was at this point that the bishop decided he wanted to be included. He approached the bed from behind me as I was facing the marquis's head and rocking back and forth on the cock. He had stripped. He muttered something about permission, but didn't wait for an answer. In short order the bishop had nestled in behind me; pushed my torso forward, causing my hips to roll up; and was forcing his cock in above Lord Fitzwater's.

So, after having negotiated with the baronet and the novelist over this very activity this night, here I was being double penetrated by a marquis and a bishop. I closed my eyes, relaxed as best I could, and went with the flow of the members' preferences.

The bishop didn't stay with us past his ejaculation, and both the marquis and I were tired enough that we just went to sleep in each other's arms.

The next morning we both woke to the sound of a knock on the door. Ever the servant, I rose and went to the door to fetch the tray of coffee and croissants that had been sent up for the marquis. I brought them back to the bed, sat, and placed the tray where the marquis could reach it. I hadn't had the least bit of a problem in discerning from his naked body stretched out on his back that he was erect and in need of attention.

As I twisted around and took the cock in my mouth, the marquis reached out for the coffee with one hand and for my head with the other, running his fingers through my unruly blond curls.

"Even in the morning, you are a beautiful young man," he murmured. "I hope that you had an enjoyable day yesterday."

"It was much as any day here at the club," I said, momentarily pulling my mouth off his cock to respond to his question.

"I wish for your day today to start with me," he said. "Please take this tray away, come into the bed, and open your legs to me."

Yes, just another day like any other here at 24 Exeter Place, I thought, with a sigh of resignation, as I lifted the tray and moved it to the top of the bureau.

The marquis was on his back, covers off, holding his cock erect and steady, patiently waiting for me to sit on it. All so civilized and gentlemanly here at the 24 Exeter Gentlemen's Club.

Carnival at Viareggio

"I've never looked out on the Tyrrhenian Sea before. All in all, the beaches of Viareggio surpass those we have visited in Venice. Perhaps we should just stay here longer."

"I couldn't help but overhear you, sir," a well-dressed young gentleman, complete with white suit, vest, and white bowler hat and shoes called over from under a nearby beach umbrella. "You said Tyrrhenian Sea. That, I am afraid is a common misconception of the tourist to Italy. That's actually the Ligurian Sea out there. But it's just a natural mistake. I would agree that the beaches here are better than those in Venice, though."

Hugo Von Stoben had been talking to a different, younger man sitting with him under a beach umbrella, who stood as Von Stoben's attention went to the nattily dressed—and quite incongruently attired for the beach, he thought—young man who had just corrected him on the body of water they were facing. The younger man stretched and sauntered down to the sea.

He was dressed for the seaside as any well-formed young man of the 1920s would be—in a one-piece, form-fitting, short-legged woolen costume topped by an athletic shirt adhering to the young man's muscular chest and with deep arm slits and neckline. Such bathing suits apparently had been meant for modesty but had neglected to provide anything that hid the obvious line of the young man's left-dressed cock and the curve of his balls. To most young women and a certain kind of man, the young man was breathtaking in his innocent beauty.

Both Von Stoben and the formally attired young man watched him walk down to the surf—the view from behind of the pert, but bulbous buttocks being as interesting as the frontal view—and start stretching his body. Within minutes he walked into the surf up to his knees, executed a beautifully arced surface dive into an approaching rolling wave, and started swimming out to sea in strong, sure strokes.

"You have a handsome son, sir," the young man said. "You should be proud of him."

"I am quite proud of Eric, yes," Von Stoben answered. "He's a strong, elegant swimmer."

The young man had swum out some distance from the beach and was swimming laps parallel to the beach between the wave-breaking rock walls at either end of the beach. He kept his curly mop of platinum blond hair above the water, as he did the pert bulbs of his buttocks, and his arm strokes were regular and pulled him a long distance with each stroke. In the water, he looked much taller than he did on land.

On the beach, Von Stoben and the young man he was talking with weren't the only ones watching Eric swim. On the other side of Von Stoben, a canvas chair under an umbrella was just now being occupied by a German doctor, Gerhard Mueller, from Hamburg, who was large-boned, a bit on the heavy side, and had a florid, redheaded complexion. He was perhaps in his forties. He, and the man sitting on the other side of him, an older French Catholic priest, fully clothed in black clerical garb and a high, white collar, Father Jacques, had met the Von Stobens here on the beach the previous day.

"Not the Von Stobens of Munich?" Mueller had asked when they were introduced, and when they allowed as how they were, indeed, those Von Stobens, Mueller had attached himself to them like glue.

To that point he had been staying close to the fifth man in the little bunch in canvas chairs under five beach umbrellas. The Englishman, Sir Reginald Chamberlain, a man appearing to be in his fifties, was tall and rugged looking, almost cadaverous in appearance, but with piercing black eyes that were very much alive. There had been a hint at the introductions that he was in Tuscany convalescing from some wasting disease, but the discussion had not yet delved deeper into that topic. Nor had it explored the depths of what the French priest, a professor at the Faculté Notre-Dame Catholic seminary, in Paris, was doing on the western coast of Italy in March of 1924 beyond that his order had determined he needed to take a sabbatical.

All four men sitting with Von Stoben, even Dr. Mueller, as he arrived on the beach, being the only one of the group who said he came to the beaches on Tuscany's Riviera della Versilia every spring, were scrutinizing the young man swimming in the sea. Only Von Stoben was looking at the men he was talking to during their disjointed chatting.

The only one of the group who wasn't watching the swimmer, and the only woman present, was Ingrid, who sat immediately to Hugo Von Stoben's left, but set back behind him under a separate umbrella. Like the young gentleman in the white suit, she was fully dressed in a somber, long-sleeved dress that ran up to a choke collar, pinned with a large cameo broach, and down to the ground, with the points of black leather boots peeking out from under her multiple petticoats. She paid little attention to the men, keeping her nose in a series of Victorian Romance novels. The impression given was that vacationing at a Mediterranean beach hadn't been her idea, and that she didn't wish for Hugo to forget that.

"We've been in Viareggio for three days now, and the architecture hasn't ceased to amaze me," Hugo said to the young man sitting to his right. "I was led to believe it was an ancient town, but I don't think I've ever seen a larger collection of Art Noveau-style buildings."

"Ah, that would be explained by the fire we had seven years ago that leveled much of this area of the city. Only the Grand Hotel Principé di Piemonte survived. Perhaps you've seen the hotel?"

"We are staying there."

"A good choice." The young man raised his eyebrows. Only the very rich stayed there. "I have one of the Art Noveau buildings myself."

"You? You live here? I took you for a fellow tourist," Hugo said. "Your accent. I thought—"

"That I was an American, right?"

"Yes, I confess I did think that."

"I am, as a matter of fact. But a displaced one. I am Martin Biddle, and I have an antique store here on the Piazza Puccini, not far from the Grand Hotel." He briefly looked away from Eric swimming in the sea to shake Hugo's hand and then looked back. "My family thought it safer for their reputation for me to live abroad," he added.

Hugo didn't pursue this point, but he did register it in his mind. He turned his head and took another look at the young man. He was quite handsome. Trim, but with good musculature. And obviously sophisticated and refined—and well to do, as he was expensively dressed, if overdressed for the seaside. And perhaps knowing now that he lived in Viareggio explained why he was fully dressed. It was unusually warm for the beginning of March in Tuscany, but that was all relative. It was warm enough for bathing wear for the likes of Hugo and Dr. Mueller and the English nobleman at this time of year— and even for the sixty-year-old, gaunt French priest, who was, to use a pun, sticking to his habit—but it likely would still be too cold for the beach for a local inhabitant.

Eric came out of the water but remained on the hard sand at the water's edge. He was, indeed, a beautiful young man. Short, but trim with a boyish body that, nonetheless, had good torso definition and strong looking arms and legs, as he would have to have to have been swimming as strongly and expertly as he had been. He was Germanic, light blond, with striking blue eyes, and a dazzling smile when he wasn't looking shy and withdrawn into himself—or aloof to the scrutiny he obviously knew he was being given from the line of umbrellas.

A sigh went up from the cluster of men sitting around the Von Stobens as Eric unbuttoned the straps on the shoulder of his form-fitting one-piece swim suit and let the top of the suit drop to reveal his smooth, both boyish and well-muscled torso. Seemingly entirely blind to the multiple sets of eyes capturing and mentally caressing his form from the line of umbrellas, he reached down and readjusted his genitals inside his swim suit—to the intake of breath by more than one man under the umbrellas—the priest's sigh was audible—and started doing stretch exercises again to step down from the vigorous swim in the sea—and then a few mild calisthenics.

"Did I overhear right, that this is your first visit to the Riviera della Versilia?" Biddle asked Hugo—although his eyes were glued to Eric.

"Yes, we are doing the rounds of beach resorts this year. January was the Turkish beaches, the island of Cyprus in February. Italy was reserved for March and April. We will go to Venice, where we have gone before, after our visit here. And later in the spring we'll take in the French Riviera. Eric wants to swim in the sea, and I love to spoil Eric."

"I can well see why," Biddle murmured. In fact he could only wonder at the effort Von Stoben must have to make to keep men's hands off the young man. His own hands were twitching at the prospect, which he hoped to be able to pursue. The young man must know the effect he was having here on the beach. In a louder voice, though, he said, "But how can your young son be out of school for such a long time?"

"He's not as young as he looks," Hugo said, with a small laugh. "He finished his basic schooling last year. He wanted to take this year off to perfect his swimming skills. He enters the Universitat at Heidelberg in the fall—a year older than most entering students—but the difference certainly won't be seen in his visage; he still look years younger than the others. He wants to swim competitively for the Universitat, but he believes, because of his size, that he will have to convince the coaches with his skill. They invariably will say he is too small just from looking at him."

"Ah, I see," Biddle said, giving a little smile and slitting his eyes as he peered at the young man. His interest was diminished in one respect, the matter of age, but the lessening of the risk involved compensated—almost. And the young man *did* look quite young. The sensation would be of covering someone younger. "He does swim like a fish, and so elegantly."

Eric returned to the chairs, with the eyes of at least four men following him, but only long enough to gather a towel, which he took out to the sand between the watchers and the sea, and then reclined, his torso raised a bit by the set of his elbows in the sand—his beautiful small body pointed at the line of umbrellas—and flopped his curly haired blond head back so that his face and torso and legs were exposed to the best advantage to the rays of the sun.

"Do you and your family plan to join with the Carnival of Viareggio festivities tomorrow, Herr Von Stoben?" Biddle asked in a low, gravelly voice.

"The carnival? They have a carnival here?"

"Yes, of course. Tomorrow is Shrove Tuesday—we also have a Mardi Gras parade. It's been celebrated for nearly fifty years here every year and rivals the one in Venice in enthusiasm if not in expense. It's a time for our people to let loose and show their true selves. There's a parade and dancing in the streets and partying in the wine shops. Partying in the streets too, for that matter, before the celebration is finished."

"Show their true selves?" Hugo asked. "That's an interesting way to put it."

"Yes, it's a time that they can wear real masks but act as themselves, rather than showing their faces and masking their needs, desires, and deepest sins."

Hugo looked at Biddle with interest, but Biddle was looking at Eric.

"I hadn't known about the carnival. And we have no costumes or masks."

"I could quickly fix that," Biddle said, turning a dazzling smile on Hugo. "There are many Mardi Gras costumes in my antique store. And masks aplenty. I would be happy to let you and your wife and son borrow what you need. Your family really must not lose out on our carnival."

Hugo laughed. "I'm afraid that Ingrid would rather walk on burning coals than go out into the street in a mask and a gaudy costume."

"Then you and your son. You must visit my shop this afternoon and pick something out. Here, here's my card. I won't take no for an answer."

* * * *

Hugo explored Biddle's antique store with fascination after Biddle had picked out costumes and masks for them. Hugo would go as a Roman senator.

"I think perhaps a young sailor—or cabin boy—for young Eric here," Biddle had said, carefully helping the young

81

man try out several costumes. He certainly did look arresting in the sailor suit, with a white tunic that came down only to his midriff and tight, white trousers with a square buttoned codpiece. A blue and white scarf tied around his neck and a sailor's hat set at a jaunty angle on his blond curls completed a look that, yes, was arresting, although sensual might have been a better term for it. It also, to Biddle's arousal, brought the aspects of youth and vulnerability out of the young man. The shy smile Eric gave him made Biddle tremble in anticipation of possibilities.

The choices completed and Eric changed back into his clothes, the young man joined Hugo at a case that had drawn Von Stoben's admiring attention. The showcase gleamed with gold and contained an array of expensive-looking gold chains and watch fobs. Von Stoben pointed to a fob with three deep-red rubies inlaid in it that he particularly admired.

"Let me show you something over here," Martin Biddle said, as he put an arm around Eric's shoulders and guided him to another part of the shop. They had their heads together in conversation as they leaned over another case. Hugo was aware of them but devoted most of his attention to admiring the gold chains and watch fobs in the case in front of him.

All three men were smiling when Eric and Hugo left the shop.

* * * *

The parade and the Carnival of Viareggio raucous celebration in the streets lived up to its billing. The Torre di Via Regia seaside promenade and Viareggio Avenue and the blocks off this parade-route were teeming with boisterous, mostly drunken revelers in every conceivable costume and, as the festivities chugged on, lack of costume that one could imagine.

Hugo and Eric were parted by a stream of revelers meeting a counterstream of revelers, all shoulder to shoulder and hip to hip, moving in no discernible direction in the streets as the last of the parade floated by. The serious partying was starting now and wine was flowing on the promenade.

Eric could hear the noise of the celebration from only a short distance away from where he was suspended off the ground and pressed up against the wall of a shop in an alley off Viareggio Avenue behind a stack of wine casks. The sounds closer to hand were the grunts and heavy breathing of the devil pressing him to the wall and his own moans and groans as the buried cock of the man in the devil suit slid Eric's back up and down on the rough shop wall with the strength of the cruel upward thrusts in Eric's channel. The front flap of Eric's sailor trousers was open and slapping back against the wall between his raised and parted legs. His knees were hooked on the devil's hips, and his hands tightly grasped and then released their grip on the devil's biceps through the red velvet of the devil's suit, matching the rhythm of thrusts of the devil's cock up into his channel.

His head was thrown back against the rough bricks of the wall, and his mouth was open as he gulped for breath and moaned deeply.

The devil's hands were under the half tunic of the white sailor shirt and gripping the sides of Eric's torso as he lifted the small body and slammed it down on the up-thrusting cock. Lifted and slammed down. Lifted and slammed down, giving greater depth of the invading cock with each thrust.

The devil was muttering what a nice little piece Eric was, how tight his passage was, while Eric whimpered, "Yes, deeper, harder. Fuck me hard."

The noise of the crowd beyond the alley ebbed and flowed, but the pace of the cock thrusts steadily increased as did the intensity of the two coupling bodies in a mutual effort to explode, which Eric did first, with a little scream in unintelligible German, whereupon he collapsed in sighs and groans as the devil fucked on for several more minutes before realizing his own shuddered release.

When he was finished, the devil swirled away, leaving Eric in a sighing heap at the base of the wall, where two nearly drunk Italian fishermen revelers found him and each took their turn with him before staggering off, surprised as the fine little piece of tail had held his own with them rather than struggling.

When Hugo and Eric somehow managed to reunite in the milling crowd, slowly wearing down from the height of its partying, nothing was said about the short interval they had been parted.

Late in the night, when Martin Biddle had finished his inventory and redisplaying in the antique store downstairs, locked the front door to the shop, and mounted the stairs to his flat above the shop, he found Eric standing at the open wardrobe in his bedroom, fingering the velvet material of the devil's costume hanging therein.

"Where? How?" a shocked and confused Biddle asked.

"You were in the back of the shop and I just walked in and came up here without you seeing me," Eric said. "But do you really want to have a discussion at this moment?" He opened his other hand to reveal that he had found Biddle's stash of Sheik lambskins.

Biddle didn't see the need to discuss anything. He enveloped Eric in his arms, and while they were kissing deeply, he unbuckled Eric's belt, unbuttoned his fly, and pushed the young man's trousers down to his ankles. He went down on his knees and buried his face in Eric's belly, kissing and tonguing the young man's navel.

Eric placed his hands on the back of Biddle's head to hold the man, not much older than he was, to his belly. He gave a little laugh and murmured, "Eat me out, suck me. Fuck me."

With a low moan, Biddle palmed Eric's buttocks and closed his mouth over the small blond's cock. After a while, he turned Eric and stroked Eric's cock with both of his hands, encircling the young man's hips with his arms, and snaked his tongue into Eric's asshole.

The first fucking was on the bed, with Biddle sitting on the foot of the bed and holding Eric's wrists, as Eric's legs streamed out around and behind Biddle's hips, and his torso cantilevered out over the floor beyond the foot of the bed, giving him the aspect of a thrusting figurehead on the prow of a boat. Eric used the leverage of his feet to fuck himself on Biddle's cock, remarking that it was just like barebacking.

Biddle used lambskins precisely for that effect, but he wondered—with wonder—how the young man knew what barebacking felt like.

After a rest, their bodies entwined on the bed, Biddle pushed Eric over on his belly, wrapped an arm around his waist to bring him up onto his knees, mounted his hips from above, and fucked him deep and rapidly like a dog.

Eric demonstrated in no uncertain terms that he was getting exactly the attention he wanted.

As they cooled down afterward, Eric said, "I'd better go before I'm missed."

"How can you not have been missed?" Biddle asked.

"I have a separate room at the Grand," he said.

"Ah, then, it's still early," Biddle murmured, as he pulled Eric's rump into his groin, raised Eric's leg to give himself a better angle, and entered him strongly and deeply again.

* * * *

The little group fell into a set pattern over the next several days. They would all be out on the beach in the late morning, with Eric doing his swimming exercise ritual, and four sets of eyes—those of Biddle, of course; Sir Reginald; Dr. Mueller; and Father Jacques—watching Eric closely and somewhat greedily, if guardedly. Both Hugo and Ingrid were buried in books most of the time.

All would go back to their respective abodes in the mid afternoon for siestas but would be back on the beach for a second round of swimming exercises and sighing gawking in the late afternoon.

Then during the night, Eric would slip out of the hotel and lie under the young, sexy American antique dealer in the flat above his shop, expending lambskins at an alarming rate.

On the fourth afternoon, though, Eric came out of the surf holding his arm and nearly close to tears. Hugo rose from his canvas chair and came down to the surf to meet him.

"He's scraped his arm on rocks," Hugo explained to the others when the two came back to the line of umbrellas. "He swam too close to the rock breaker wall out there to the north of the beach."

Dr. Mueller, full of concern, rose from his chair and went to Eric and examined the arm. "It doesn't look too bad, but it's easy to get infection from such cuts in this circumstance," he said.

Hugo turned to Biddle. "Is there a clinic nearby?"

"No need," Dr. Mueller interjected. "I had disinfectant in my room at the Grand. The boy can come back with me. What do you say to that, Eric? I will take you for an ice cream afterward, before we come back to the beach, if you promise not to cry at the sting of the disinfectant."

It was obvious that the doctor wanted to see Eric as a small boy.

An hour later, after listening briefly at the door of the doctor's room at the hotel, Hugo used a skeleton key to quietly open the door and slip into the room.

Dr. Mueller didn't see or hear him at the beginning. He was otherwise energetically occupied.

Eric was lying on his back at the foot of the bed, his legs raised and spread—his ankles in the grip of Dr. Mueller, as the doctor, naked, as was Eric, huffed and puffed at the effort of pumping Eric's channel with his hard cock. A box of the newly marketed rubber Trojans lay at his feet, packets of them strewn out on the floor.

Hugo cleared his throat, and the doctor whipped his head around in shock and fright, although he couldn't stop himself from continuing to pump. He was about to come and wouldn't be denied. He gave Hugo a panicked but greedy look and fucked on. Eric was gripping his hips on both sides with his hands and crying out for the doctor to finish him.

When he had, the doctor pulled out of Eric's ass and turned to the side, hunching in on himself and covering his genitals with his hands.

"I don't mean . . . I wouldn't . . . the boy was egging me on . . . I was just . . ." Mueller muttered incomprehensibly. His face was as red as a beet and the flush had spread over the rest of his pudgy torso.

He really looked pathetic. Eric raised his torso on his elbows and turned his gaze on Hugo.

"You were just introducing the lad to a new brand of French Letters? To disinfect a cut on his arm? But I think we can fix this. I think we can make an accommodation," Hugo said.

* * * *

Hugo heard the two enter Eric's room next door. He waited patiently until he heard the sound he was listening for—the knocking on the wall on the other side of the headboard of the bed in his room. The bed in Eric's room was set against that wall too. They had set it so that distinctive motion on the bed would knock the headboard against the wall, as all the signal Hugo would need.

Taking his skeleton keys, he quietly left his room and went to the door of Eric's room. As quietly as he could, Hugo used the key to open the door, stepped into the room, and closed the door behind him. They were on the bed. Father Jacques, naked was on his back. Eric, wearing the priest's cassock loosely on his back, flared open and flowing down off his back and onto the priest's lower legs, was saddled on the priest's cock, facing his face, and slowly riding him. Eric was bent over the priest's prone body and the two were locked in a kiss when Hugo entered.

"Ahem," Hugo voiced, and the faces turned to him, Eric, with a knowing smile, and Father Jacques in deathly consternation. Eric raised his hips again and thrust down—once, twice, three times—and, having already been on the edge of the ejaculation, Father Jacques made his sin complete.

* * * *

"I guess that gets them all except the young American, and we can move on to Venice soon," Horst, who was not really named Hugo Von Stoben, said later that evening. "It was a good haul here—nearly enough to cover the expenses of the entire season. The priest paid as much as the other two put together. I guess this is what his seminary sent him here to avoid and he doesn't want them to know he can't kick the habit."

Both of them gave a little laugh at that.

"The priest should have paid double. He was the cruelest of all," Eric said. "He had taken a riding crop to me in a laundry closet before I managed to get him to my room." But then Eric, who was really named Kurt, added, "We can move on now, if you wish, Horst. I've taken care of the American."

"He's already fucked you?"

"Repeatedly." Kurt was smiling.

"So, that's where you went at night?"

"Yes."

"I'm not surprised. He is the youngest and sexiest of the group. I rather thought he would be fucking you by now. I don't begrudge you having it off with a muscular man nearer your age. But you gave it to him for free? Is that what you're saying?"

"No, go look in the pocket of my trousers."

Horst rose off the bed and padded over to the chair where Kurt's clothes were neatly folded. He fished around in the pockets, and a big smile was planted on his face when he came up with a gold chain and watch fob with three deep-red rubies embedded on the fob. "You noticed that I liked this."

"Yes. I lifted that the first night I let him fuck me." Kurt saw no reason to mention the elaborate assignation between Biddle and him for the fuck in the alley during the carnival—nor to mention the two muscular, hung fisherman afterward. He did wonder, with some amusement, though, when those men realized that they were missing their money clips. "He's either never noticed or has written it off as being owed to me for the cocking. I have a few other trinkets that should be worth a bit too."

Horst gave the young man an admonishing look. "I believe I told you it was dangerous to mix your pickpocket skills with our other scheme. But, no matter, just don't do it in our next outing. Tomorrow morning, then," he said, "We'll leave tomorrow morning before the others have stirred," as he returned to the bed, gently pushed the stretched-out naked body of the son who wasn't his son onto his belly, mounted the young blond's buttocks, and began a slow, deep, bareback fuck. Kurt moaned deeply—but not deeply enough to disturb the reading of the woman in the adjoining room, who was Katie, not Ingrid, and wasn't related to—or particularly interested in—either of the men as long as they paid her regularly for her easy pretense.

Chameleon Love

June, 1940, Blaye-et-Sainte-Luce, France

Henri noticed how quiet the square was as he left the bakery shop with the piles of baguettes under his arm to be delivered around the village. Was this the day, he wondered. The Germans would enter the town to occupy it any day now. Their month-long movement was just about to reach the Bordeaux region, arriving in his own village on the southwest coast at the Gironde Estuary before the push into Bordeaux. The only saving grace was that they wouldn't billet many troops here, saving the bulk of them to occupy the far larger and better strategically placed Bordeaux.

Many of the villagers had already left, so he had just two deliveries to make—to the large, but deteriorating villa directly across the square and then to the house of the teacher, Samuel Levin, in the smaller house at the edge of the square. He would dither at the teacher's house until it was time to scrum with the village's rugby team out in the field to the west of the village. The first delivery was to his own house, where he lived with his grandfather, Ansel, a former, greatly revered town mayor, now almost immobilized by gout, and his maiden aunts, Suzanne and Marie. The Ballard family, once the richest and most prominent in the village, had fallen on bad times financially, with the deaths of Henri's parents in one of the plague-like influenza outbreaks that had passed through the village a decade earlier. The bread he was bringing to them from the baker was part of Henri's wages from working in the bakery in the morning.

What else Henri did to earn money for his family's keep was what he had to do—and what he did basically because he enjoyed doing it.

After the delivery to his relatives, Henri crossed the still-ominously and atypically silent square to the house of the teacher to deliver his daily bread as recompense for the tuition for the baker's four children. As usual, the door to the small house was ajar, the first floor of the building being two schoolrooms. Henri mounted the stairs to the dwelling of the teacher above, and knocked on the door.

"Is that you, Henri? You alone?"

"Yes, teacher. As always."

"Enter."

Henri did so, leaving the bread on the counter in the kitchen, living, dining and nearly everything else room and then moved to the doorway to the back room—Samuel's bedroom.

Samuel, a Jewish rabbi as well as the village teacher, dark, hirsute, forties, and bearded, was Orthodox in appearance, other than the fact that he was naked and sitting on the side of his bed in full erection. He motioned Henri to come forward and kneel before him, which the young, perfectly formed and handsome man in his early twenties did, without hesitation. Henri knelt between Samuel's spread thighs, took the teacher's erect staff in his mouth, and gave it suck.

Later Henri became as naked as Samuel. Samuel was still sitting on the side of his bed. Henri's body was reclined toward the floor, supported by Samuel's legs, with Henri's legs wrapped around Samuel's gaunt torso, ankles crossed behind his back, while, gripping Henri's wrists, the strong Jew pulled Henri off and on his cock.

When ejaculation was achieved by them both, Henri was belly down on the arm of Samuel's reading chair in the corner of the bedroom, with Henri looking down on the side table where Samuel's wire-frame glasses rested on student papers he was correcting, and Samuel crouched over Henri's back and fucked him from behind and above.

When both were dressed, Samuel, as usual, walked Henri down to the front door to the house after Henri picked up the coins representing his payment from the kitchen counter where he had laid the baguettes. After surveying the supposedly empty square—but not too well—the teacher and village male prostitute kissed inside the shadows of the hallway—although not far enough inside. After drawing away from the kiss, Henri looked down, laughed, and pointed out that Samuel's trousers were not buttoned. Henri did the service for him.

What neither had noticed was that there was an open-roofed German military command car sitting at idle across the square, where the Wehrmacht Hauptmann—captain—sat in back waiting for the column of foot soldiers to arrive for the formal occupation of the village. Hauptmann Gerhard Rein watched the farewell of Samuel and Henri in Samuel's doorway, the buttoning of Henri's fly by Samuel not the least, with great interest and with pleasure that it would not require much effort to set up his routine while in this village.

It was known to only a small segment of the population of Blaye-et-Sainte-Luce—mostly those connected with the activity—that Henri, the greatly attractive young heir to the declining Ballard fortunes, was also the village male-on-male prostitute. All villages had them, of course. In many villages they were barely tolerated—but tolerated nonetheless because they were a necessity of life. Henri was from a tragic prominent family and was so likable—and of such a handsome countenance and sweet disposition—that even those who knew of his nefarious function in the village and who were not connected with it tolerated it and accepted him. Those who would publicly disapprove were simply kept in the dark to ensure village stability.

For his part, Henri enjoyed doing what men wanted him to do, and he needed the extra money and services to keep his family fed. His grandfather could do nothing any more but dispense wisdom and affection. His aunts took in sewing, but that was hardly enough to keep the roof of the large villa from caving in on them. So Henri had his arrangements—the morning work at the baker and bread for the family for an occasional side fuck by the variety-loving baker. The coins from the teacher. Select meats from the village butcher. And so forth.

From the teacher's house Henri walked west of the village to the field where the town team practiced its rugby. Henri was a popular player there because, though smaller than most of the rest, he was strong, fast, clever on his feet. And he was good with his hands in finding and holding the ball. Even a few of the rugby players could attest to how good he was with his hands—and with holding balls. The village butcher,

92

Giles, a huge, muscular man, was both the team goalkeeper and its captain/coach. He was the power player on the team, defending the goal fiercely and well.

Following the practice, while the other teammates, muddied but highly pleased with the practice and each other, headed east toward the village, Giles placed an arm around Henri's shoulder, with the excuse of pulling him aside to give him some strategy pointers. The others looking in the direction they were headed, Giles marched Henri into a grove of trees next to the field. Neither noticed the military staff car that had been parked near the field, with Hauptmann Reins watching the practice—both the play and the obvious after play.

In the grove of trees, Henri lay on his back between the roots of a tree with his soccer shorts and cup off, his legs raised and spread, as Giles, shirt off and soccer shorts pinned down under his balls, knelt between Henri's thighs. Henri arched his back, panted, and cried out at the initial penetration as Giles's oversized cock entered his ass channel. As the bigger man began to pump Henri's ass, the younger, blond beauty slitted his eyes, licked his lips, and ran his hands over the bulges of the butcher's chest and biceps. There would be a fine cut of meat on the Ballard dining table tonight in exchange for the fine cut of meat the butcher was now receiving from Henri. And Henri wasn't the least bit embarrassed at how he was providing for his family. He enjoyed the attentions of men, and it was a precarious life for all in the village, especially with the uncertainty of the now-arrived German occupation.

Henri loved the fucking. He didn't have to love all of the men who provided it. But if he had to be a chameleon about showing his love for what they did to him, a chameleon he would be.

After Giles left him, Henri lay there for several more minutes, his legs spread, calming his breathing. Giles had the biggest, cruelest cock by far of all the men Henri took in the village. It took Henri a few minutes to recover.

In those few minutes, however, Hauptmann Reins appeared at the edge of the trees, and the eyes of the two met. Henri defensively reached for his soccer shorts to cover his privates, but neither of them was fooled about what had transpired there.

Henri's first response was feeling a chill of fear run up his spine. The Germans were reputed to be highly puritanical—to persecute any variant activity. Would Henri be sent to the camps he'd heard about on the first day of the German occupation?

But then Hauptmann Reins smiled broadly at Henri, and Henri understood that that was not to be his fate. He smiled back, tossed the soccer shorts off to the side again, spread his bent legs farther apart, rolled his hips up, fisted his cock with a hand, and gave the German captain a provocative look. If a chameleon he had to be a chameleon he would be.

The German army officer unbuttoned his trousers, pulled out a long, thin, erect cock, and approached and sank between Henri's thighs. As the cock made a long, cruel thrust up into Henri's channel and Reins closed his hands around Henri's throat and began to pump his ass, Henri, the chameleon, arched his back; gagged, gasped, and groaned, as he knew the German would want to hear; and began to move his hips in the rhythm of the fuck. There must be some way he could gain advantage from this for himself and his family in the German occupation, he mused.

When Reins had ejaculated and was holding Henri close and breathing hard, his cock still buried deep inside Henri's channel, Henri whispered in the almost adequate German he'd learned thanks to his liaison with Samuel Levin, words to try to bind the German to him—words of loving the fuck, of wanting it again. Of how handsome and masterful the German officer was. Of how he melted to the attentions of a man in uniform.

Beaming not only because of how sweet and willing Henri's body had been, or even that the young man knew some German, but mostly because the sweet piece wanted to be fucked again immediately, seeming eager to have Reins plowing him again, Reins took as little time as he needed to comply.

He'd been of two minds—whether to use the public humiliation of this young man and the resulting punishment as an example to cow the people of this village into subjugation, or to use him and hold the vilification for later. The Frenchmen's succulence and willingness had determined that he would live his life of service to men a little longer.

* * * *

Henri's premonition of what was to come and an understanding of the high-stakes risks that now existed propelled him into motion as soon as he returned to the villa. Luckily, he got no argument from Suzanne and Marie and stalwart support from Grandfather Ansell. Of course he didn't tell them the real reason this had to be—but they weren't stupid. They'd heard about other French villages the German had occupied. They could discern what some of the safer options were.

On his way back into the village, Henri had stopped at the stablery and hired a buggy, horses, and driver to appear at the back gate of the villa grounds. He had no trouble doing so, as the stable master, Pierre, was one of his men. He only had to promise two free lays, which he considered cheap, considering the short notice and how far up the coast the farm of the Ballard cousins was. The deal was struck on the spot, with Henri giving the stable master a quick blow job, which he made clear was in addition to the lays he had promised.

While Marie packed trunks for herself and Suzanne, Henri and Suzanne scoured the house for valuables the absence of which wouldn't be noticed by first-time visitors and hid them away in the recess in the chimney in Suzanne's room that had been used for similar emergencies in the two hundred years the villa had stood here. There were more secrets in the house than just this hiding place.

The women had been gone none too soon when the knock on the door that Henri had anticipated came. Standing on the landing in front of the door, backed by two soldiers— one older and grizzly and one almost as young as Henri and wide-eyed and full of unspoken questions—was Hauptmann Gerhard Reins, eyes aglow from the servicing he'd received earlier in the day. Henri didn't regret having given into the man. He was maybe in his late thirties; ramrod straight, not just in his spine; and tall, on the thin side, but muscular, hair even blonder than Henri's—nearly pure white—and piercing, cruel pale-blue eyes. The mouth was set in a superior-attitude near-sneer, which contrasted with the older soldier behind him, whose sneer was knowing and demanding. When he was honest, Henri had to admit to himself that he preferred a demanding—and, yes, even a bit cruel—man. This soldier, at least, had been told of Reins's earlier tryst with Henri, Henri was certain. And it was just as likely that he wanted to claim a share.

"We require billets," Reins declared. "Your house has been identified as the most appropriate one in the village. And I expect it to provide full amenities." The captain gave Henri a meaningful look.

Henri knew there were houses in better shape, but he had to admit that this villa was the most imposing one and with the most furnished bedrooms. This had been his premonition—that the German captain would come straight here for housing—and other benefits. The "other benefits" fit in with Henri's desperate plans, though.

Henri merely inclined his head in assent and acquiescence.

"This is Obersoldat Johan Mueller," Reins said, gesturing to the older solder, "and this is Soldat Hans Kant," he said, pointing to the younger and obviously junior—and certainly only nervous one—of the trio.

And then Reins said what Henri had been hoping for. "We do not pay for the use of the house, but we pay for the food, enough for everyone under the roof—and who will that be?"

"Just my grandfather and me," Henri answered. "He is old and hard of hearing and won't be in your way."

"Ah, good. And for the bad hearing when it comes for us to need that." He gave Henry a meaningful look, which Henri fully understood, "and do you have servants?" he continued.

"Just the cook and a day maid," Henri responded.

"And because of the special circumstances, I will pay extra for your exclusive services—for me and these two soldiers who will billet with me. Am I right that you receive payment for your services? That this is a function you serve in this village? For men? I have seen you with the rabbi and the butcher."

The look was piercing. The younger soldier didn't seem to understand what was being said, but the older one certainly did. And now Henri was certain he knew the real reason his house had been chosen by the captain for billeting.

"Yes," he answered demurely, eyes downcast. "These are the services I provide. For men." He didn't add, which you well know, but he could have. Of course the captain hadn't know that Henri got paid for his services in the village. Henri didn't expect the captain to pay for them, if he didn't want to.

"And to my two adjuncts too?"

"Yes, of course."

Then Henri looked up—his smile went behind the captain to the Obersoldat, Mueller, conveying his particular interest in the rougher of the three. "If you'll come upstairs with me, I'll show you to bedrooms. All are prepared"—and, indeed, part of the work of Suzanne and Marie's departure was to remake their rooms, both quite comfortable rooms dominated by four-poster beds with heavy, durable canopies and strong corner pillars. They would withstand the moving weight of two men—or more—in them. There also were thick draperies on the windows and thick, sound-proof walls. To be sure they understood, Henri noted, as they mounted the sturdy staircase from the front foyer, "There are four bedrooms on the second level. The bedrooms on the third floor are not in use. Both the cook and my grandfather have rooms on the first floor in a wing beyond the kitchen, well away from the main house. The rooms on the second floor are for you, your two soldiers, and me. My room connects to yours, Captain. I hope this meets your needs."

The German captain quite explicitly said that it did. Perversely, Henri had assigned Reins to Suzanne's room, the one with the fireplace that hid the family's most precious possessions.

That night Reins showed his fetish streak. He had his two soldiers tie Henri's wrists to a corner of the frame of the canopy bed in his room, with him, naked, stretched below. The grizzly and wiry older solder, Mueller, held Henri on one side by pulling Henri's leg up toward the headboard, his heels on top of the headboard, while the younger, magnificently built private, Kant, did the same on the other. Kant wasn't just the one in the best muscular shape; he also was the lowest hung of the three. Reins knelt below Henri's buttocks, ramrod straight other than the forward jut of his pelvis, with his long, hard cock thrust upward, while, his two soldiers maneuvered Henri's rolled up hips in position and then, screwing his ass channel on Reins' cock, moved Henri back and forth on the shaft.

Knowing what he had to do and sensing even then that he needed to enlist the sympathy of at least one of the three, and the choice being obvious to him, as he could tell there would be no sympathy in any kind to expect from Mueller, Henri turned his face to that of the youngest soldier, and the two kissed deeply.

Later, as Mueller cruelly pistoned Henri from behind, bent over the side of the bed, Kant knelt in front of the reclining Reins—by his own choice—and sucked Reins to an ejaculation.

Before dismissing his attendants, Reins had them tie Henri, wrist and ankle, to the four strong posts of the bed. They tied him high off the bed, so that the droop in his buttocks surpassed six inches off the surface of the bed. Bursting one of the feather pillows open, the captain poured the feathers over Henri's body and blew and delicately pushed them along the surface of Henri's delicate skin to take pleasure in Henri's moans and begging for relief and in watching him struggle against his bonds and writhe in midair. When Henri was whimpering from exhaustion, Reins moved onto the bed, knelt between Henri's suspended thighs, grasped and spread Henri's buttocks with his hands, pulled Henri's puckered entrance onto the bulb of his cock. With a vicious pull and an accompanying gasp from Henri, Reins pulled Henri's channel on the shaft and then deeper and deeper on the cock, as Henri writhed, arched his head back and marveled in words he knew the German wanted to hear of how deep the cock was reaching. Reins pulled Henri on and off his buried cock to a mutual ejaculation, and Henri's murmurs of maximum pleasure.

Guarding the tone of his voice and pulling a wan smile across his face, Henri told the sadist German captain that this masterful sex made him love Reins and wish for all of the inventive ways his body could be used to stimulate and serve the German's needs. He hoped that Reins' inventiveness would last him for some days to come.

That seemed to be enough for Reins's wants for the night, although in days and nights to come he was to devise many more unusual and decadent fetishes in the taking of Henri, much of which entailed the bondage of Henri and the use of the strength of the bed pillars and overhead canopy. All four men retired to their respective bedrooms.

To further Henri's own plans, he crept into Hans Kant's bedroom in the middle of the night; climbed under the covers with the young, hung, magnificently built German soldier; assured him his captain need never know that Henri came to him; coaxed him to the hardest of woods with mouth play; straddled the young soldier's pelvis; and rode him for an hour, leaving the young soldier glassy-eyed and murmuring of awe, love, and devotion. It also left the young soldier with a secret from the captain that he and Henri shared—including that Henri enjoyed Kant's cock far more than he enjoyed the captain's.

Hans' hands on Henri's waist were strong and calloused. He was a young stud, new enough to sex with men to be surprised and jerk and tremble when Henri, thoroughly experienced in the pleasures of men, surprised him with intimate touches—eating out Hans' ass as he writhed and luxuriated in the first such intimate service, taking the young man's balls in his mouth and humming, taking Hans almost to ejaculation by deep-throating the whimpering warrior's throbbing staff before mounting him, kissing and pinching Hans' nipples while rising and falling on the cock, nipping his nipples and his neck for the feel of his flinching and driving his cock deeper, begging constantly in broken German for the cock to dig deeper, reaching back and entering the young stud with a finger at the conclusion and rubbing Hans' prostate to make him explode deep in Henri's ass.

Other than one of the village priests, who was delicate and almost effeminate in sex even though he was on top, Henri was mostly fucked by older men. It was a thrill to have a younger, perfectly cut, vigorous, and virile man between his thighs—and he told Kant so. And even after an hour, it wasn't just the one fuck, with Henri riding Hans' thick cock. The young German soldier lost his shyness and, after a short recovery, took control and rode Henri—and then rode Henri again—and again.

The German was fast and furious with fire-off power; Henri more controlled. Hans was kneeling over Henri's prone body, his knees separating Henri's bent legs as he released a bucket of cum across Henri's heaving chest. Learning fast, the blond god rubbed the bulb of his bubbling cock over and over again on one of Henri's cum-slicked nipples while taking Henri's cock in his other hand and pumping him. Seeing through the slit in the draperies that it nearly was dawn, Henri gave the German his seed, arcing it up to mingle his cum with the young soldier's on his chest.

Hans' breathy whispers of devotions, in which Henri discerned the word *Liebchen*—lover—assured Henri that he had won one ally in the cruel triumvirate—and that he driven a wedge between Kant and his superior officer.

* * * *

The days stretched into weeks, and it wasn't hard for Henri to make clear to the men he normally serviced and received favors from that he now was exclusively taken—and by the enemy. This had ominous results, though, even though it was out of his control and the men had gone with in the village should have understood that. It wasn't just the attitude of the village men that became ominous, though. The first thing he noticed was that the house of the Jewish teacher, Samuel Levin, was closed up, the windows boarded up, but with scorch marks on the bricks around them to indicate that there had been a fire.

It was Ansel who told Henri of the village gossip that Samuel had been taken away in the night and torches thrown through his windows that caused fires that the neighbors put out after Samuel had been dragged away. Henri had known nothing of it even though it had occurred just across the square from his family villa, because he was being strung up facing a pillar of Suzanne's bed at the time, in her room with the thick walls and noise-dampening draperies and having his legs held up and stretched out at either side by Mueller and Kant, while Reins fucked him from behind.

He did recall afterward that Reins kept going to the window on the front of the villa and peeking through the curtain, so it was highly possible that the captain had prior knowledge of what would happen with Samuel that night.

The next day, Henri found there was no need to make excuses about not going to the bakery, as the bakery was closed up tight. So was the butchery. And so were the stables, the stable manager, Pierre, having melted away without calling in the two fuck sessions Henri had promised him. The baker, butcher, and stable manager, as well as more than half of Henri's rugby team had taken to the countryside to form a resistance group, Henri's grandfather was told in a whisper by the day and maid, and Henri's father had passed the information on to his grandson.

As tough a choice as it was, Henri's giving in so readily and easily to the wants of Hauptmann Reins had worked in the Ballard men's favor. If the soldiers had not billeted in the Ballard villa, the family's source of bread and meat would have evaporated. Instead, Reins had forced both businesses to remain open with new proprietors and more than sufficient food was being supplied to the Ballard villa kitchen.

The secret of the totality of Henri's collaboration with the enemy came out full blown in the village gossip stream not too long afterward when the captain decided he wanted to treat his unit of men to an evening of debauchery.

He commandeered the local maison close—brothel— on the edge of the village, complete with the two women prostitutes who worked the two rooms above the barroom, and put on a lavish party. Henri didn't have a head for liquor

101

and probably didn't know fully what he was doing when he was coaxed to stand on top of a table with the two women prostitutes, all naked, and danced a sensuous dance until each was pulled down by the eager hands of soldiers, laid out on separate tables, and gang fucked by a succession of randy and drunk German soldiers, all the time with their captain looking on, laughing and egging them on.

The brothel's staff—other than the two unfortunate prostitutes—fled the bedlam early in the evening. But they looked on from safe positions and all later attested to the willing wantonness and fraternization of Henri with the Germans when, long after the two prostitutes had curled up into bruised, whimpering balls of withdrawal, Henri was sitting on Hauptmann Reins' lap, riding his cock, and waving his arms like he was an American rodeo star.

After that, all doors in the village were closed to Henri—with the exception of the village church. The next afternoon, when Father Christophe entered the main sanctuary, it was to find Henri lying, belly down, arms outstretched in front of the altar and murmuring prayers of confession. In the day's light he fully understood what his drunken behavior the previous night had revealed to the village. His ability to be a chameleon was abruptly being compromised.

At the soft voice of the priest, Henri looked up. He groaned. He had hoped it would be old Father Marc who would be there to hear his confession, but it wasn't. It was the younger Father Christophe.

"Come. Rise. Come through with me and we will discuss this," Father Christophe said. In the father's spare cell behind the church kitchens, Father Christophe gently pressed on Henri's shoulders to make the young man sit down on the side of his bed, raised his cassock to reveal he was naked underneath and in erection, and, cupping Henri's chin, guided Henri's mouth to his cock.

Of all the men in the village, it was the young priest who was willing to continue sinning with the village male prostitute.

An hour later, when Father Christophe, one of Henri's regular hookups in the village, had fucked Henri in a side split from behind in a spoon position on the cot to ejaculations by both, Father Christophe said, "I can hear your confession now."

Henri dutifully confessed his sins in trying to be the chameleon and to the best he could for his family under the conditions of the German occupation. Christophe took the confession, named the penance, which was mild, but added the word of advice, "The resistance here will become violent, I'm afraid, son. It would be in your best interests to withdraw to somewhere else considering what the village is saying about you."

It hadn't been a full confession, as Henri had heard that he wasn't the only one cooperating with the French—that Christophe was falling into their line too and was fraternizing with the enemy as much as Henri was. Indeed, as the priest led Henri back to his sleeping cell, Henri caught a glimpse of a young German soldier withdrawing down a corridor.

Henri didn't think really that he needed to be told that he should leave the village—and he wondered who heard Father Christophe's confession and suspected that much of the melancholy in the priest's voice in giving him this advice came from the regret the advice would end these occasional trysts in the priest's bed. He was trapped, though. He knew the priest was right, but there was Grand-Père Ansel to think of. What would befall him if Henri just left? It was Henri's responsibility to put the well-being of his family first.

Oh what a pickle his attempt to play chameleon to solve problems that were insolvable had placed him in.

* * * *

By listening to the Hauptmann and his two attendants converse, Henri was able to discern that the occupation of the village was in trouble, both because the resistance here was threatening to swamp the resources the Hauptmann had been given and because the resistance in nearby Bordeaux was necessitating the retrenchment of forces there. Bordeaux was, by far, a higher priority for occupation than this small village was.

Increasingly, Reins was showing his worry and concern—and his fear. The soldiers he had under his command were drawn closer to the Ballard villa, strengthening the defenses here, but acknowledging the weakness to the activities of the resistance elsewhere in the village and surrounding countryside. His worry was shown also in the frenzied way he and his attendants were using Henri's services throughout the day—like each fuck might be their last.

As active as Henri had been before, although he'd never been involved in threesomes before now nor been put in the positions of bondage and cruelty before as now, he had never been double penetrated. Now that was happening routinely, with the third usually using his mouth at the same time. Henri had no idea how much crueler Gerhard and Johan could get, with regularly now riding him on all fours on the floor while digging the heels of their boots into his calves and beating every exposed surface with a riding crop. Only the young soldier, Hans, held back from this—satisfied, no doubt by Henri's nightly visits to his bed for more intimate and loving fucking.

Having the Germans comfortable with his presence, though, helped Henri in the timing of what he knew needed be done. This was brought to a head by Hauptmann Reins himself one night over dinner.

"I'm afraid we pull out tomorrow," he informed Henri. "We have been called to pull back to Bordeaux to strengthen the defenses there."

"I . . . I will miss you," Henri answered, halfway believing it himself. He had not done much self-analysis of his response to the captain's form of lovemaking—halfway in fear of what he had to admit his response was—arousal, and to a high degree, pleasure at the cruel use of his body, especially now by the gaunt and grizzly Obersoldat Mueller, who made no bones about testing Henri to the limit. Catholic that he was, despite the light penance Father Christophe had given him, Henri knew that he deserved what Mueller was doing to him. And, to his embarrassment, he longed to have more of what Mueller did to him.

"You don't have to miss me. You are coming with me," Reins said. "I am comfortable with your services. I don't see the need to find a new young man who will serve my needs as well as you do. I'm sure you realize—and appreciate—that I could have you thrown into a camp at any moment for deviant behavior and have not done so."

This was the way Henri realized it would go with Reins and it was the direction in which Henri had tried to develop the relationship. It wasn't a final answer, he knew. He no longer believed there was a final answer that would save him. But this could save his family and help his country.

He crept away to Grand-Père Ansel to tell him in as limited way as he could what he must do and why—although he was sure that the old man had known all along and hadn't seen any better choices for Henri and the family than the one Henri had made.

"You must go now, Grand-Père, by the secret door in the fence to the neighboring lot." The villa was guarded front and back by German soldiers and the two adjacent house had been commandeered and vacated. But there was access across the lots through hidden doors in fences that had long been devised and maintained by the residents.

"You must find the resisters. I know that the butcher, Giles, is leading them. You must call me out as a German collaborator and say that you and the aunties have managed to escape me. And then, after the Germans have pulled out—I am going with them—you must live as quietly as possible. You and aunties must learn to be chameleons. The Germans may return, and, when they do, it may be for all time."

Understanding, Ansel hugged his grandson, and, with tears in his eyes, shuffled away to the secret door into the neighboring lot.

Before returning to Reins and his attendants for a last frenzied night of demanding sex in the Ballard villa, Henri told the cook to put out a breakfast on the buffet in the dining room early in the morning and then, herself, to use the secret door to escape—and to assure Giles, in the function she had been serving of slipping messages to the resistance from Henri, that he would continue to do all he could to get whatever information on German plans and movements back to the resistance as he had done all the time he was with the captain.

"Ahh, you should not be taking all of this on yourself, Monsieur Henri," she objected. "You have been the best of patriots yourself, sacrificing yourself like this—letting the villagers, and now, even your own grandfather, believe you are a collaborator. When you are not."

"I am whatever I have to be, Lisle," Henri responded, knowing that the safest way to continue life as a chameleon was to maintain pretenses as much as possible. "Grandfather is too infirm to be expected to keep the secret. So he must not know yet. And you must denounce me in public after I'm gone, as well. If justice prevails, Giles and the others will vindicate me someday when the Germans have been expunged from France. For now my collaboration must be believable."

The next day Henri rode out of the village of Blaye-et-Sainte-Luce in Hauptmann Gerhard Reins's open staff car, not knowing what the future held, but continually looking for the opportunity to use chameleon love to survive.

Reins sat close to him on his right and Mueller on his left, and they were barely on the road when both began to fondle his body and put upon him—with Mueller even managing to reach into the folds of his clothes, grasp his balls, and squeeze to the point of making Henri gasp and want to faint. It would have been so much better to be able to sit next to the young golden god, Hans Kant, now in the front seat of the vehicle, who was so besotted with Henri now that he would do anything—including passing on plans of German troop movements and intentions.

Still, the chameleon in Henri made him work up all options. The last thing he wanted to have happen to him was to be exposed as a male-on-male prostitute and sent to a camp. He'd rather die than that. When the car was stopped on the road for Reins to confer with a group of soldiers, Henri turned his face to Mueller and whispered, "It is my hope that someday you and I can be alone and I can enjoy the full attentions of your specialties."

Mueller glowered at him, his mouth twisting into a cruel leer. "Trust me, if I get you alone, I'll break you for all time."

It was an ultimate option for Henri. Something to keep in reserve in case his attempt at patriotism came to a dead end.

Determined Faith

It was just a moment in time. At least David thought it had been no longer than that, but every time he thought back on it, it seemed like it had rolled on forever, long enough for him to see the look in everyone's eyes and to analyze what they were thinking. Paolo Flores, the mixed Portuguese-Bantu Mestico young man who was his assistant in translating the Bible into Bantu had pointed to a word in a translation. "I think there's a better Bantu word to convey this," he'd said.

"Which word? Show me," David Proctor had said as he stood behind Paolo, seated at a table in the rudimentary conference and classroom of the four-room school in the compound of the church's orphanage at the edge of Calai, Angola. Leaning over Paolo, he'd placed his hands on Paolo's shoulders. He would have thought nothing of it any time after that if he hadn't heard the snort and intake of breath behind him and looked up, first out of the paneless window out onto the front porch and then, turning, at the door to the hallway leading to the other three rooms.

His wife, Hope, younger than he by fifteen years and with the delicate porcelain breakability look about her of blonde hair and alabaster-skin, was standing on the porch, framed by the window, her arms raised, as if paralyzed, in the air. Pastor Thomas Sears, also blond, handsome, and robust, ten years David's junior, was in the other half of the frame. He and Hope had been conversing, but sound from in back of David had suspended their conversation and caused both of them to swivel their eyes to where David leaned over Paolo— and to hold them there, motionless, for what seemed to be forever.

When David tore his eyes from them and looked around, he saw the orphanage's handyman, the young Bantu, Faro Jamba, staring at him. It had been Faro who had snorted and sucked in his breath.

Instinctively, David pulled his hands away, rose, and took a step away from Paolo. The original movement had all been so natural, though. He had just been checking a word that his assistant had been pointing out to him.

The moment was broken and, rather than return to his conversation with Hope, Thomas Sears spoke to David. "The shipment of Bibles have arrived from the States, Brother David," he said. "I thought that Sister Hope and I could drive the ones for the school over in Kongola. Do you want to come along, or . . . ?"

He left that hanging. "Is there something else you'd prefer I did, Pastor Thomas?" David responded. Kongola was a long, dusty drive from here—and no longer in Angola. It was in the South African mandated territory of South-West Africa, across an uncertain border from the desolate outpost the Assembly of God enclave occupied in the far lower, southeast quadrant of Angola. They could not return until after dark—or perhaps they'd have to spend the night in Kongola if there was any trouble from roadblocks or with the Jeep. This was a relatively safe area of Angola, which had been in a state of civil war for the four years since the Proctors had been assigned here in 1960—indeed it was so remote and desolate that the rebels tended not to be interested in expending forces to occupy it. But the government troops were nearly as lawless and threatening as the rebels were. It was a Catholic country that some powerful forces in the country wanted to be a communist country allied with Cuba. There was minimal tolerance for Protestant Evangelists like the Assembly of God orphanages and schools that the Proctors worked and lived in.

"Well, considering that the government confiscated the last shipment of Bibles, I'd like to get these distributed as quickly as possible," Thomas said. "If you stayed, you and Paolo could unpack and divide them for distribution tomorrow. Sister Hope and I'd best assume that we might have to stay in Kongola for the night."

"Yes, yes, of course. We'll tend to the Bibles here," David said. Paolo had looked up at him, all trust and innocence, which caused David to turn and look to where Faro had been standing. Faro was a worry to them—always looking around suspiciously, seemingly critical of the work the Protestants were doing here and disapproving whenever work with the orphans moved into speaking of the Bible and its teachings. When Pastor Thomas had arrived earlier in the year to take over management of the orphanage and school, David had tried to suggest that maybe Faro should be replaced—that maybe he was spying on them for the government, but Thomas, while not dismissing David's views, had not made a change.

"No doubt the government is watching us closely," he said. "If it is Faro who is watching us for them, at least we'll know who to be careful around. I do understand that we must be ever observant and not give the government any reason to close us down."

Any reason to close us down, David thought, as he looked to where Faro had been standing, watching him. But Faro wasn't there anymore.

"Now the word I was thinking of—" Paolo said, returning to his translation.

"We should leave that for now," David said, as he moved to the window out onto the porch. Pastor Thomas was helping Hope into the Jeep. David admired the musculature of the young man, who was not nearly as intense in his mission, David knew, as he was, but was more charismatic and imbued with life than David was. The young pastor moved around the Jeep with grace, like a dancer, a sparkling smile on his face. David, feeling a tightness in his body and a longing to be more Thomas and less David, followed the movement of the young man until he had settled behind the wheel of the Jeep and backed it out onto the road.

Hope had an overnight bag with her. She looked so delicate, vulnerable, and out of place in this setting, small and willowy, dressed, as usual, in a stark white cotton dress that David had no idea how she could keep so clean in this hot, dusty climate. She had been almost a child when he'd married her, the daughter of one of his professors at the seminary. He had wanted to refuse the assignment to Angola, worrying that she couldn't survive it. But she had managed it a lot better than he had. He felt too deeply—both about his religion and about the economic and intellectual poverty of the Angolans of this region—he thought. He was always agonizing over what there still was to do, while Hope just took one issue, one Angolan, at a time, serving them but not trying to change—or save—them, and, in the end, the orphans all worshipped her and used her as an example. They were saved by good works, not by indoctrination alone. He had to keep telling himself that.

Even when, two months earlier, it looked like the civil war was coming closer to them, and David had asked, worried for Hope's safekeeping, that they be transferred elsewhere, Pastor Thomas's response had been that Hope could not be spared from the mission here. David couldn't claim that that hadn't stung. This was his, David's, posting, but it was Hope who could not be spared. Hope had shamed him by agreeing with Thomas.

What could be more important than bringing Angolans—including the Catholics—to the right way of it or of the work that he and Paolo were doing with the Bible translations?

He had really wanted to suggest that Hope be sent home, but he hadn't gotten that far before Pastor Thomas had decided that she was the indispensable one here. It probably was the fifteen-year difference in their ages as much as the difficult conditions here, but everything had gone cool between David and Hope. It never had been red hot. Marrying and bringing people to God in far-off places had been romantic at the time, but the reality hadn't been as fulfilling as either of them had wanted. And the age difference seemed to have settled in to put the two of them in different worlds. It had come to David feeling he was always being watched for some reason, in a cage, not as free as he liked—like when the moment in time had suddenly been suspended with three pairs of eyes on him when he was just checking a word translation Paolo was pointing out to him.

David hadn't hesitated at all when Pastor Thomas suggested what would surely be an overnight trip that Hope would accompany him on. It would be two fewer pairs of eyes on David for a night and much of the next day. And he could find some mission away from the compound to send Faro on.

111

"We should go to the shed and sort out the Bibles that just arrived," he said to Paolo, as he looked around to see if he could see Faro—and if Faro was watching him.

* * * *

Late in the night, David came suddenly awake, without knowing why. He was alone in his bed and had to take a moment to wonder why. But that's not what had awakened him. He realized that there was light at the window—and not the burning light of a southeast Angolan sunbeam, but a flicker, crackling, dance light of a fire. Putting his feet on the floor, he quickly pulled on his trousers and raced for the front door of his bungalow. There wasn't anything there that should be burning. Pastor Thomas and Hope hadn't returned. They had the Jeep.

He was brought up short at the door. The flames were coming from a pile of books that had been torched—the Bibles that had just arrived. Scattered about the courtyard were soldiers, with rifles—Angolan government soldiers.

"What is this?" he exclaimed, his eyes fighting to pick out the officer in command, and in the scan seeing, first, Paolo, clad only in a loincloth, being held between two soldiers, hunched over as if he'd been beaten, and, then, Faro Jamba, standing beside the older man who obviously was the soldier in charge.

"Him. That is the man—the proselytizer—the violator," Faro called out, pointing at David.

"What is the meaning of this?" David asked. He thought he knew the meaning of it, though. The last Bible order had been intercepted and burned. Faro obviously had told the authorities about this new shipment. He most likely had told them about the earlier shipment too.

But David was wrong about the meaning of this.

"Him. He's the man who has been lying with Paolo Flores here, leading him astray, forcing him into man sex."

"David Proctor," the soldier in authority said, "I am arresting you for the crime of homosexuality."

* * * *

Thomas Sears sat in the living room of the Kongola compound guest bungalow until nearly midnight, reading the Bible. It had been more than an hour since the Bantu woman had departed, the hem of her floor-length orange and red sari brushing the wooden floor and her bare feet slapping, making a hollow sound on the raised floor, as she finished tidying up. They rarely had overnight guests at Kongola, and the man sitting and reading his Bible so diligently not only was a handsome devil, for a white man, but he also was the head man at the orphanage over in Calai, in the troubled land of the Angolans.

The young miss looked too weak and breakable to be wandering around the desert. No wonder she had retired hours ago. She was not long for this desolate region, the Bantu housekeeper didn't think. There was no substance to her, the small, mousey thing.

With a sigh, as the clock on the sideboard chimed midnight, Pastor Thomas laid the Bible aside, stood, stretched, and, after taking an inspection walk around the outside of the bungalow, reentered the building and walked back down the hallway of the four-room building, built as far as he could see on the same plans as the classroom building in the Calai orphanage compound.

He thought of knocking on Hope's door to see if she was still awake but then decided against making any noise whatsoever. He opened the door and stood in the doorway, leaning up against the frame and looking at her as she lay on the bed.

Of course she was awake. They had already decided that he could come at midnight. She was wearing a white cotton nightgown. But when she saw him in the doorway, his frame picked out by the strong beam of moonlight penetrating the room through a window, she reached down, pulled the hem of the nightgown up above her breasts, spread and bent her legs, and reached down to touch her sex with the tip of a finger.

Overly dramatic, Thomas thought, but he'd take her anyway he could get her.

She was about to speak when she saw him put his finger to his mouth, signaling that they should remain, for protection, in silence. Having conveyed that instruction, he ran the finger around his lips, parted his lips, and pushed the finger inside. With a smile, her eyes glued to him, Hope did the same with her sex, rimming it with her finger and then, as she arched her back and gave the slightest of moans, penetrated herself with the finger.

She watched as Thomas brushed the suspenders off his shoulders, unbuttoned his fly, and pushed his trousers and underdrawers to the floor. For the longest minute they remained in place, watching each other. She moved her finger in and out of herself as he stroked his thick cock.

Then, like a panther, he was on her, lacing his arms through her thighs, raising and spreading them, burying his face in the folds of her vulva, and penetrating her with his tongue as she gave deep sighs, arched her back, and moved her hands to work her taut nipples.

His hand went to covering her mouth to stifle her cries, as his body moved up hers, he pressed inside her with his hard cock. She embraced his legs, rubbing the meat of his calves with her heels, as he began to move deep inside her. She sucked in air when he thrust inside her and exhaled as he withdrew, only to thrust again. Thrust and suck in air; withdraw and exhale. Thrust and suck. She clutched his buttocks with her hands, trying to pull his entire body inside her.

"Fuck me. Fuck me deep," she murmured.

"I'm afraid that I'll—" he whispered, his voice hoarse, clogged with lust.

"I won't break. Surely by now you know I won't break," she answered. "Harder, faster, deeper. Take me away from here. You know where. You know how."

Unsatisfied with the pace at which he was taking her, she pushed him to the side, causing him to roll over onto his back. Straddling his chest with her knees, she impaled herself on his cock and rode him with wild gyrations of lust and wantonness.

* * * *

"No, no, don't come near me. Stay over there. They must see that you've stayed over there."

"But you're hurt, Paolo. They've beaten you. You need help."

"No, Brother David. There's no help you can give. Stay on your side of the cell."

David, who had raised himself up from a sitting position, legs pulled up into his chest, at the base of the wall at one side of the cell below the wooden plank serving as a bed, took one step toward the other side of the cell, where there was another platform bed, when Paolo stretched out a hand and stopped him. David had been dozing on this, the second day of his incarceration in the Calai jail, when the steel door had been opened and Paolo, still only in a loincloth, was propelled inside. Paolo clearly had been beaten at least once again since David had last seen him held between two soldiers at the orphanage compound.

"Why won't you let me help you?" David asked.

"They want you to," Paolo answered in sotto voce so that David had to strain to hear him. "They want you to come to me. They want you to embrace me. They will take photos. They need proof of your crime."

"My crime?"

"The crime they have accused you of. They won't prosecute me, they say. They say it could not be my fault. That it would be you, the foreigner, who forced me. They don't want to acknowledge that an Angolan would . . . anything of that nature. I'm supposed to give them proof."

"But just tending you wounds . . ."

"Me almost naked like this. An Angolan court. They would see what they wanted to see in the photos. They want all Protestant Evangelists out of the country. Just . . . stay over on that side—for your own good; for the good of both of us."

David sank back down on the wall and folded himself into himself. He could have been thinking. He probably was praying. Several minutes later, he spoke, his voice strong.

115

"Determination. And faith. Determined faith. That is what we need here. I understand. I stay over here and you stay over there. All we need is determined faith."

"You have nothing to dress my wounds with anyway," Paolo murmured. "And I have family here with some influence. They will send someone to attend me."

"And my wife and Pastor Thomas. They won't let me remain here long. Not if there is no proof of anything, and there won't be."

Paolo didn't answer this. Paolo was more observant of the dynamics among the Americans at the Calai Assembly of God orphanage and school than David was.

But, sure enough, within hours a visible irritated and disappointed military officer came to take Paolo out of the cell and to announce that David had a visitor.

Pastor Thomas was concerned, naturally, but a little standoffish.

"These charges . . . ," he said.

"They are just trying to get rid of us," David answered. "They will resort to any means now to do so. That Baptist minister they have put in prison in Cunjamba. I'm sure he had no contact with the revolutionaries. But they can't claim we all have. They have to come up with something else."

"Of course," Thomas answered. "I will go into Luanda when I can. We'll get the embassy on this. You'll be free very soon."

"And Paolo?"

"Perhaps we need to separate efforts for you from those for Paolo, but I'll see what can be done."

David started to say something about that, but then he changed course. "Hope. She didn't come with you."

"This isn't a place where Hope should be coming. She's not up to this, I'm sure."

"But about the charge . . . has she said anything?"

"We haven't discussed it. I'm sure she has faith in you. Her physical constitution might be delicate, but her faith is determined. She's a woman of determined faith."

"Yes, of course," David said. "But you will tell her . . . ?"

"Yes, of course I will. Now there are some issues I have to get settled before I go, but as soon as I take care of those, it's off to Luanda."

"Luanda is so far away."

"Yes, but we must do something to get you out of these . . . conditions."

After Thomas left, Paolo was brought back in, his wounds attended to and a pair of low-hanging shorts on his frame. The military officer gave him a meaningful look and a head gesture toward David, but Paolo went immediately to his side of the cell and remained there. David sank back down to his "hiding from the world" crouch on the floor against the wall at the end of his platform bed.

Hope Proctor was standing in the doorway of Pastor Thomas' bungalow when Thomas returned.

"Did they let you see him?" she asked as Thomas climbed the stairs to the porch.

"Yes."

"I wish I could have gone with you. Despite everything, he's my husband."

"The jail in Calai is no place for an American woman to be," David answered.

"The charges. Did he—?"

"He didn't deny them. And they've put Paolo in the cell with him."

Hope shuddered and crossed her arms tightly across her breasts, as if shielding herself from something she didn't want to hear—that she didn't want to believe or know. "What can we do for him?"

"Not much. I'll call the church's central office in Luanda. But you know what this can mean for us?"

"I've thought of little else all day," Hope answered.

"So?"

"Yes. I can't wait."

He didn't make her wait. He bent her over the arm of the sofa in his living room, pushing the back of her white cotton dress up to the small of her back, exposing her bare buttocks. He laughed at the discovery that she wasn't wearing panties. She cried out when he thrust inside her, needing no buildup time, as he'd gone hard on the drive back to the compound from the mere thought of them not needing to meet in secret now.

"Is it . . . ? Am I . . . ?" he murmured.

"Give it to me hard. Harder; deeper," she gasped as she grasped the edge of a sofa cushion with her hands and began to bang him back hard with her rump, meeting his thrusts with counterthrusts of her own. He grabbed her hips with his hands and began to piston her hard. She took it like a champ, and later that night, when he was stretched on his back and she was riding his cock like a bull rider with a steel rod up the back, there was no hint of delicacy or weakness about her either.

* * * *

Three weeks later, a visibly irritated and disappointed military officer came to the cell to free Paolo. His family had finally brought their clout to bear, and in the absence of anything but innuendo from one witness, the shifty-eyed Faro Jamba, there was insufficient proof to hold him. There had, however, been additional charges of spying that were being lodged against David Proctor.

Another week later, Thomas appeared again.

"The wheels are spinning in Luanda," he assured David. He didn't however, tell David that he hadn't gone to Luanda himself. "There's some bad news I must tell you, however."

"Hope?" David asked. He'd yet to have received so much as a message from her. It's not that she hadn't sent any, but that she'd sent them through Thomas and they weren't being delivered.

"Yes, Hope. It's the original charge thing, I'm afraid. She can't stop thinking about it. And, as you know, this isn't really the place for a woman as delicate as she is. And it's not getting any safer. The rebels have expanding their areas of operation. I'm afraid she's going home—and she's starting proceedings."

"A divorce?"

"Yes, I'm sorry to say. But the embassy should have you out of here soon. And you can then come back to the States, and I'm sure she'll come around when you're there."

"You said 'come back to the States,'" David said.

"Yes. I'm being reassigned back to the States too. I'll probably be going back on the same plane as Hope is—so you need not worry about her traveling alone. But the embassy in Luanda is on it. This spying charge, of course, is ludicrous. It won't stand."

"That Baptist minister in Cunjamba? He's been freed?" David asked, his voice showing some sign of hopefulness.

"Well, no. He's still in prison. But we're not the Baptists. The Assembly of God is in better stead with the Angolans than the Baptists are."

When Thomas left, David, now alone in his cell, sank back down into the near-fetal position against the wall that had become his habitual retreat from reality.

The trials of Job, he was thinking, his mind dredging up and repeating some of the passages from the Bible on that. Faith. He knew he had to keep faith. Determined faith.

* * * *

"We need to leave now, in a hurry. And keep your voice down."

David had been surprised to look up when the door to his cell opened and there, instead of the jailer, one of the few people he'd seen in the last seven months, stood Paolo Flores, dressed in dark colors. The young man had motioned him and said, "Come on out. You're free. But keep it quiet."

Almost like he was swimming underwater, David dumbly responded to Paolo's call, not asking any questions, but standing up from his crouch at the end of his bed and shuffling toward the door. When he got to the door, though, he said, in a hoarse, rarely used voice, "Free? Charges dropped?"

Paolo didn't answer that. Just, while looking up and down the corridor outside the cell door, he gently took David by the arm and guided him out of the cell and down the corridor.

119

Outside, in the Jeep—in the Calai Assembly of God orphanage and school Jeep—Paolo had handed over a pair of trousers and a shirt and instructed David, still whispering, to put them on.

"These look like mine."

"They are," Paolo said. "I took them from your bungalow at the orphanage. There's a suitcase in back with more of your clothes and belongings in it."

"Is that where we're going? To the church compound?" David asked as he started to change while sitting in the passenger seat.

"No, we're not going back there. It's the first place they'll go to look for you."

"I haven't really been released, have I?" David asked, interrupting the buttoning of his shirt.

"I released you. I got tired of the red tape. I have friends who helped make the guards look the other way tonight. I went directly to Luanda when they let me out, only to find that neither the church office there nor the American embassy had any idea you were in jail and didn't seem to want to take my word for it. They called, but Pastor Thomas told them nothing was wrong."

"The compound. Thomas . . . and my wife."

"They've gone back to the States . . . together. I'm sorry, David. There's nothing at the compound for you anymore."

"I . . . I guess I knew all along," David said. "So, where are we . . . ?"

"We're going across the border into South-West Africa. The church compound at Kongola there. You can call the office in Luanda and the embassy yourself from there. But you'll be safer across the border. And Kongola is so remote and the South Africans so disinterested in their mandate over South-West Africa and no one will bother us there."

"Us?"

"I'm going with you. It will be safer for me across the border too now . . . with you."

They drove across the desolate land, under the stars, in silence, arriving in the early morning hours at the Kongola compound guesthouse. Paolo immediately went back into one of the bedrooms, but David sat in the living room and reached for a Bible. He hadn't had a Bible in his hand for seven months and he needed to settle his jangled nerves. After seven months of isolation and inactivity, he suddenly had been hit with a flurry of activity and a charge of adrenaline.

An hour later, David rose, calm, from the chair in the living room and walked back to the bedrooms. Opening one of the doors, he stood framed in the moonlight streaming in through the window. Paolo was lying on his back on the bed, naked, his legs spread and bent, his hand encasing his cock, his eyes turned toward the doorway, a little smile on his face.

David sucked in his breath. The light chocolate of the young man's well-defined, muscular body gleamed in the available light. David's eyes went to the jet-black cock and balls of the beautiful mixed Portuguese and Bantu young man, whose body had taken on the best features of each of his heritages. The skin tone for most of his body was Mediterranean, but the eyes were drawn to the blackness of the Bantu cock and balls. The hair on his head and pubes was jet black, but curly.

He was slowly masturbating his cock, which was erect. David felt himself going erect as well, as he slipped the suspenders off his shoulders, unbuttoned his fly, and let his trousers and underdrawers cascade to the floor. As he was unbuttoning and shucking off his shirt, Paolo was sitting up on the end of the bed so that when David, naked now himself, reached the bed, Paolo need only move his hands around to grasp David's buttocks and pull the older man into him, open his mouth, and let David's cock slide to the back of his throat.

Paolo was moaning and sighing, grasping David's head between his hands, and resting his legs on David's shoulders, when David was knelt on the floor below the foot of the bed and giving Paolo head. Then David was standing, grasping Paolo's hips, and pulling him to and onto David's cock, while Paolo cried out in pleasure-pain at the penetration and possession of his channel by the older, larger man's cock. He raised his arms and grasped the rungs of the brass headboard, as David, putting all of the frustration and fury of going seven months without sex with Paulo into his thrusts, fucked Paolo hard and deep.

Afterward, the two of them lay in a close embrace. David was still inside Paolo, not hard but not soft either, just resting, an interlude before they would be fucking again. Paolo whispered, "I've missed you so. I've missed this." He was fingering Paolo's ass entrance. Paulo moved his buttocks so that the finger entered him. His muscles there drew the finger inside him. The mutual sigh was in harmony—David's baritone to Paulo's tenor.

"Seven months. Seven months without this. The last time we made love was on the night they arrested us," David murmured.

"Yes, I thought I'd go mad," Paolo murmured. "Wanting so much to be doing exactly what the jailers wanted us to be doing in the cell, but knowing we had to stay away from each other, pretending that the truth wasn't true."

"It's faith," David whispered. "I kept telling you that determined faith would pull us through. It even solved the problem of Hope. I could not bring myself to abandon her, and fate intervened to make her leave me willingly. All it took was determined faith."

"Yes, and I have faith that you . . . and just like that you're getting hard again," Paolo whispered with a sigh.

"Yes, I am," David answered as his hips began to move again, his cock engorging and beginning to stroke again—Paolo sighing and groaning for him as his pelvis started to respond as well, the two of them sinking into the rewards of having been capable of sustained, determined faith that their love would win through.

CONTEMPORARY

Art of the Priest

"No, I will have them with me," Monsignor Roman Scarlotti almost bleated as he held the parcels closer to his chest. And then, realizing that the driver was only trying to be helpful, he added in a calmer voice, "Thank you, my son, but these I must keep close to me."

The driver shrugged and opened the back door of the all-terrain vehicle that had seen its best days. The monsignor hesitated to enter the backseat of vehicle, a maneuver that was made difficult by the bundles he carried in his arm but would not let anyone else hold.

Waiting for the monsignor to struggle into the vehicle, I looked up the cliff face above the small Swiss town of Flüelen, nestled on the shore of Lake Lucerne between the water and a towering cliff that rose to the alps behind. The driver had said that our destination, the Ettal Monastery, was up at the top of the cliff somewhere and had waved his hand in that direction. He said it could be seen from here, but I couldn't discern the monastery's stone walls from the cliff rocks. I suspect that this had been the plan when the monastery was first built in the sixteenth century—that many a plundering enemy had just not seen it and had passed it by. I was sure that you had to know what you were looking for to pick the form of the monastery out from here.

"Here, let me hold them while you get in, Monsignor, and I will hand them to you." I tried to sound soothing. He'd been holding onto my forearm tight with his free hand. "I'll be right here with them," I added.

Looking relieved, he said, "Thank you, Father John," but he still gave the parcels a nervous look after he'd handed them to me, gathered his cassock about him, and folded himself in the seat. I was probably the only one Scarlotti would trust in this way, and I could sympathize with that. He was the assistant art curator of the Vatican, and I was *his* assistant. The parcels he clutched were four art works that either were priceless or forgeries. He suspected forgeries, but that wasn't his call, and so the two works claimed to be by Hieronymus Bosch and those of Pieter Bruegel and Fra Angelico had to be given full respect and protection until they were shown not to be worth it.

Scarlotti was usually a man who was fully in command of himself and of those around him. He was tall, slim, handsome, and aristocratic, having descended from the counts of Lombardy. Age—he was in his early fifties—had only added to his dignity. At the same time he was a secretive, remote man, considered to be cold as ice. I worked closely and amicably enough with him, though, to know that he was holding himself in reserve—that he was a man of deep emotion and passion who, because of his obligations, had to continually hold himself in check. I was quite sure that I had been chosen as his assistant because he wanted me near him—that he wanted to touch me; that, in fact, he wanted to fuck me.

I knew, intimately, what he had to hold himself in check from, because I could see his need and desires in his eyes. It was the same look that other priests at the Vatican gave me and that some of them had built on. If they were important enough and could advance me, I opened my legs to them. Scarlotti was an important figure in the Vatican. Any time he wanted, I would let him fuck me.

The paintings, as well wrapped as they were, were not unmanageably large, and, when Scarlotti held the bottom edges of them on his lap, they extended outward almost to his knees but didn't rise as far as his chin. As the vehicle lurched off for what was going to be an unseemingly steep incline drive up the road to the top of the cliff, one of Scarlotti's arms embraced the paintings but his other hand rested again on my forearm. He had been wearing gloves, but he had stripped the glove of that hand off and had pushed the sleeve of my cassock up so that he was laying flesh on flesh. He'd never had the courage to do that before, although I knew that he wanted that and more, but he was so concerned with the situation that I don't think he was aware of the connection. But maybe he was and was exhibiting that strength of reserve he was notable for.

The connection was electric, though. I could feel him trembling, and I felt the sensuality of the long, slim fingers kneading the flesh of my forearm. The driver was in the front seat of the vehicle, with a glass window separating the passenger compartment from him. He wouldn't know if I unbuttoned my cassock at the crotch and moved Scarlotti's hand to where I knew he longed to put it. But I wouldn't do that. Scarlotti would have to make the first move. It wasn't a case where I would be unwilling or had not done it before. I would not have made my way to the Vatican and within the walls of the Vatican as young as I was, not yet twenty-five, if I had not lain under priests who could advance my standing. And I knew from the moment that Scarlotti had asked for me to be made his assistant that he wanted more than a secretary. But he had made no move—at least not yet.

"Thank you for offering to help me, Father John," he murmured. "You are such a help to me."

"You know I would do anything you wished of me," I answered. "Anything." I could feel him trembling through his hand on my forearm, but yet he didn't make the move I was sure he wanted to make.

It was quite possible, I thought, that he had arranged for me to come with him to Switzerland to declare and act on his desires. Perhaps he was intimidated by being in the Vatican and always in contention for advancement and always under scrutiny. I could have told him that fucking young priests wouldn't be counted against him in the Vatican—oh how I could speak to that—but perhaps being an Italian from an old noble family had been holding him in check in Italy. Perhaps here in Switzerland, away from the center of the church . . .

I wasn't especially anxious to get his cock inside me— other than after that had happened, I will have gained control over him—but I was getting anxious to have it done and his name added to my list of supporters in the Vatican.

* * * *

The Ettal Monastery was bleak and foreboding, not a place where I would normally have thought that one of the world's leading experts in medieval church art would reside.

But Brother Otto Kepler wasn't the usual sort of art expert. He wasn't even the usual sort of monk.

The cold, stone edifice was like a medieval fortress, complete with moat on the side away from the edge of the cliff, where the lower stories of the monastery cascaded down, and the only entry I saw was by way of a wooden drawbridge and under a nasty-looking, spike-bottomed portcullis. It seemed more a bastion or a prison to keep the monks in and separate from the world than the residence of a major light of the art world.

We were taken to Brother Kepler in silence by a young monk who was fully as young, blond, and fair of visage as I was myself but who kept his face looking at his bare feet in his sandals and his eyes cast down. Kepler wasn't the abbot, nor did he hold any other office in the monastery, but, as a valuable resource of the Vatican itself, he had a commodious office that was well appointed and, in keeping with his avocation, that overrode his monkhood, the walls of the chamber were hung with priceless art. Both the monsignor and I sucked in our breath as we entered the room, as it was a shock to come from the passages of austere and cold stone and enter into such beauty.

The appointments other than the art work were also sumptuous. The monk obviously was a man who appreciated and was accustomed to having the finer comforts of life.

The man himself, though, looked the part of a monk, of one whose function in the monastery was more the crude peasant role of hard labor working in the fields and with animal husbandry. He was big and robust, more muscular than fat. He was bald and bullet headed with a thick neck. The man had steel-blue eyes that bored into whoever he was giving attention to and a cruel-looking mouth. He was coarse looking, almost like a thug, which, as I knew his background, was in keeping with what he'd been before he had taken the vows. Even the prison-like atmosphere of the monastery was in keeping with what Otto Kepler once had been, and it was likely that the man felt comfortable here in this fortress that gave the feeling of being locked in—as much protected from as separated from the outside world—but that still gave him every personal luxury he coveted.

Kepler's reputation as a specialist in medieval church art stemmed from the fact that he had been a major and highly successful art thief, stealing only the best and having become an expert in what was the best to steal. He specialized in medieval church art depicting sin, damnation, and hell. The four pieces of art Monsignor Scarlotti was bringing to him here—the presumed Bosches, the Bruegel, and the Fra Angelico—for examination and authentication were just such works of art—views from the church of sin, damnation, and hell.

"This is my assistant, Father John Sands. He comes to the Vatican from the United States," the monsignor said to Kepler as he stared, with mixed concern and interest, at the young monk Kepler had given the paintings over to when Scarlotti had reluctantly handed them to Kepler, and who was expertly unwrapping them. As he did so, though, the young monk gave me a shy smile of comradery—both of us being seconded to a much more exalted and demanding man. I wondered what Kepler demanded of this young monk.

I knew what Kepler had once demanded of me—and gotten.

"Father Sands and I have already met," Kepler said, giving me a curt, cold look, "in the Vatican last summer when I spoke at the art consortium."

And indeed we had met. I shuddered at the thought of that meeting and the power, danger, brutality—yet sensuality—that the man exuded. He was not a man to cross. He was best avoided altogether if you didn't want to experience the effects of that hell he was such an expert in assessing.

He stood, looking at the four paintings for nearly a half hour, focusing on them as if we weren't even in the room. At length, though, he turned and said, "It's nearly the dinner hour and you'll be wanting to attend the mass afterward. I must contemplate these paintings late into the night, as you have said you wish to leave again tomorrow. All arrangements for the night have been made. You will be fed in a private dining room and Brother Müeller here will show you to your rooms and will guide you to dinner and mass. I will give you my assessment in the morning. Brother Müeller will be at your complete disposal, Monsignor—to meet whatever need you have."

And that was that. We sucked in breath again as we were led out into the stone cloister by the young monk and to rooms that were not much more than cells but that had the convenience of private water closets and barely adequate beds—more iron-frame cots than beds. I found there was no electricity, though, and although candles were provided, I turned in early after the end of the mass, being weary from the plane and lurching vehicle trip from Rome to this remote monastery and not being in the mood to read the biblical theory book I had brought with me by weak light.

The truth was, though, that I wanted to be prepared in case the monsignor had brought me here with him for the opportunity to declare himself and to cover me. I knew what I owed him for taking me as his assistant, and I'm sure he was aware of how I'd shown gratitude to other pillars of the church who had shown me favoritism by lying on my back and opening my legs for them. Thus, I didn't lock my cell door and I slipped under the covers in the nude. I had no compulsion to giving Scarlotti what I knew he ached for. I had lain under many a priest in the last three years and my only complaint was that they uniformly were so timid and guilt ridden about finding release with another priest, which I thought was so much more sensible than laying with a lay person and revealing that most priests were the same as any man and had the same needs as other men.

I didn't have much more hope for the passion or domination of the monsignor as courtly and reserved as he was, but it would aid our working relations greatly if he'd just go ahead and shaft me. My one insistence, though, was that the man who wanted to put his cock inside me had to make the declaration and initiate the coupling. I was quite willing to rise in the church on the strength of sex, but I would not seduce another man to win his favor—nor would I find arousing a man too timid to declare his wishes and to take his pleasure as by right.

Most prominent priests in the Vatican had no trouble taking what they wanted as by right.

* * * *

I was asleep when he whipped the sheets off me and landed on my back. He'd brought restraints and had my wrists bound together and over my head and a gag on me before I was fully awake. He was brutal and cruel. I knew he would be. That's why I'd been keyed up and trembling all the way from Rome.

The restraints weren't necessary. I wanted him covering me. But I understood that they were necessary for Otto. He'd acquired the taste for men when he was in prison and there weren't any women available to meet a man's needs—only other men. And there were two types of men who took cock in prison—those who sought it out and those who were made to take it. Otto was turned on by the latter type of man. And, after all of the furtive, vanilla couplings I'd experienced from other priests at the Vatican, Otto's cruel, take no prisoners fucking was what turned me on too. I fought him valiantly, as I knew he expected, and he overpowered me and took what he wanted from me, as I knew he would.

It was painful, at least at the beginning, when he closed his hands around my throat, forced me up onto my knees, and mounted and covered me from above. I thrashed around, as he wanted me to, fighting for my life because he certainly showed that he would fuck me to within an inch of my life—or beyond if that was his mood. He fucked me dry and raw and until I adjusted to him and we set a rhythm, I was in agony. But he'd taken me like this in a dark corridor of the Vatican too, suddenly throwing me up against a stone wall in a dark corridor, taking the breath out of me, and choking me, lifting me off the floor with the strength of one hand on my throat, while he tore at the buttons of my cassock, pulled my briefs off my legs, hooked my knees on his hips, thrust inside me dry, and fucked me hard.

He'd made no apologies. He just said he wanted it that way—that this was how it was in prison. Little time or opportunity to scratch the burning itch. Overpower and cow the prey and fast in and fast out. Take the risk of being seen as an extra thrill of doing it. Leave the prey curled up on the ground, gasping for air, reamed well open by a massive cock.

It had been exciting then, though—nothing like the tentativeness, delicacy, and guilt plagued half-assed couplings of senior priests I was using to get ahead in the hierarchy. He'd demanded it all, taken it all, and left me sobbing and melted in a puddle at the base of the wall in the dark Vatican corridor, reamed to his specifications. He'd left me wanting it again and again.

And now, the two of us alone in my cell, I was getting it again. I was dancing on the clouds, as he fucked me hard and thick and deep. I flailed against the assault as he forced his thick, throbbing cock inside my unprepared channel. Inside me, the throbbing staff pushed past the resisting sphincter muscle, which, once breached, blossomed open in acknowledgement that I had taken many men before him, Otto held for a few moments, his strong hands on my throat restricting and regulating my breathing. I struggled against him in spurts of ineffectual action. He reared his buttocks back and then thrust forward, giving me all of his cock. I jerked in shock and screamed through the gag. Again he reared back and thrust. And then again and again. He released his chokehold on my throat and, with a gasp and a whimper, I collapsed under him.

I had fought him—without effect, but I had done so—until he had bottomed in me. And then I just went docile. I relaxed and let my channel go slack, and he gained another inch or two. I surrendered all to him, going vulnerable and totally open to his invasion. He gave a low-throated laugh and started pounding my ass in earnest as if we'd be discovered at any moment and he'd have to leave off his victory over me, my total surrender to him. Fulfilling the need he had to take a man by force as he had done in prison.

I denied him nothing. It's doubtful that I could have done so even if I wanted to. But after the furtive half-way fumblings of the old priests in the Vatican, his "take him to hell" approach to sex was intoxicating.

He held and shushed me just as pleasure was outstripping the pain and I was beginning to bang back at him with my pelvis counterpistoning to his thrusting cock. He held me fast in his embrace and stopped thrusting. We were both panting hard, but I caught that he wanted us to go silent.

I heard then what he'd heard. Shuffling outside my door. I had left it unlocked for whoever came to me that night. I had hoped it would be Otto, but I saw the way the young, blond monk looked at him, and I thought that Otto's efforts might go only in that direction. If Scarlotti had come, I would have received him, glad that he'd finally made the commitment. If no one came, I would get a good night's sleep. It wasn't a compulsion of mine—although I would have regretted not being fully fucked by the cruel art thief again. He made me feel alive.

There was enough light coming in from the cell window on the full-moon night to see the door to the cell. We both watched, in suspended fuck, as the footsteps passed back and forth and then stopped. The doorknob turned, but the door didn't open. Otto had locked it behind him when he'd silently entered the room. I wondered if he'd watched me sleeping before he attacked and overpowered me. It gave me a little thrill that he, a connoisseur of art, might do that. That's what many of the priests who had fucked me in the Vatican had said about my body—that I was a work of art worthy of Michelangelo. It would be thrilling to think that Otto thought so as well—and then ravished me anyway.

Ah, I thought, that would be true art—a two-panel painting by a master of a virginal young man, naked, lying posed on a chaise, one the painting of the young man's body before the artist had ravished him. The other afterward.

Lying there underneath him, him deep inside me and throbbing but holding steady, his arms embracing me close, aroused me almost as much as when his shaft was working me hard. All of my thinking went to the sensation of the huge cock inside me, filling me to the limit, throbbing, and I—and he too—felt the muscles of my passage begin to ripple over the hard, buried shaft. He groaned, which cause me to moan, and for him to tighten his grip over my mouth. But I knew both of us were focused on his cock, deep inside me. I knew that when the danger passed, he would nearly kill me with the frenzy of his fucking. I think he knew it too—that he would snuff out my life if he didn't hold himself in check.

I didn't want him to hold himself in check. There was no future. There only was the now—with a monster cock throbbing inside me.

The footsteps receded, and Kepler resumed fucking me hard. His thrusts were so vicious and long that both he and I were bouncing off the cot in the cell, which was groaning and the coils screeching, and I was sure it would collapse. Giving up, sure he would fuck me to death, I lay back, my mouth yawning, my hands dragging the stone floor on either side of the cot, the knuckles being bloodied by bouncing off the stone as he bounced my body in his onslaught. I didn't die, though. After the initial pounding, he regained control and took me in more methodical positions.

He seeded me while fucking me like a dog, and he seeded me in the missionary position, and he seeded me with him on his back and me stretched out on my back on top of him and he trapping my arms over my head in a full Nelson hold and thrusting brutally up inside me. He took me to the depths of hell and, brutal and cruel as it was, I fully understood the enticement of the total taking that hell offered. We flailed our way to a first rush of release and seeding.

He was hard again almost immediately and resumed the onslaught, fucking me interminably to an exhausted sleep.

When I woke to the bells summoning the monks to the morning mass and the first rays of the sun invading the cell, Otto was gone, and I was nearly gone as well—but smiling and humming to myself. Still, I was unable to drag myself to mass and was bowlegged when I managed to drag myself to breakfast with Monsignor Scarlotti. The priest said nothing to me about the night before, but he looked a little sad.

I broke my cardinal rule—recognizing that he had made the effort the previous night. As we were sitting side by side at the table, I let my hand rest on his thigh, and when he turned and gave me a radiant smile, I moved it to his crotch. I thought the man was going to cry, but he maintained his imperial demeanor. When I made to move my hand away, though, he put his hand over mine and held me there. He only did so for a moment, but it was enough to shatter the ice between us. We both now knew we would fuck.

We did so after breakfast, in Scarlotti's room, which was far better appointed than mine was. He proved to be an expert lover, preparing me well, worshipping my body to a point of completely unarming me and begging him to put his long, hard cock inside me. When he did, taking me on my side in a spoons position, we moved with each other like longtime lovers. In less than an hour, he had taken me through four exotic and fully satisfying positions, manipulating my body like a pro and holding off on his ejaculation until he had coaxed mine out of me. In contrast to the brutal battle, conquering, surrender, and ravishment of sex with Otto, Roman and I worked together like one well-oiled sophisticated machine, giving and receiving pleasure, moving in consort like dancers— Roman leading me through intricate steps of every-heightening pleasure and me completely open to him, totally at his mercy and lead, sensitive to the touch of his elegant fingers, long, lean body, and his long, caressing experienced cock.

Surprisingly, Scarlotti proved to be as much an artist in the fuck as Otto was, contrasting Otto's specialty of providing an intense but compulsive hell with a refined working of my body to the slow buildup to and fireworks of an explosive heavenly orgasm—repeated orgasms, one more satisfying than the previous one.

When he left me to dress for the meeting that morning with Otto, I clutched at his body, begging for him to take me to heaven again, and he merely smiled and told me that it was just the beginning for us. We need not approach it like each time was the last.

* * * *

"The bad news is that these are not genuine Bosches, Bruegels, or Fra Angelicos," Brother Kepler said at the morning meeting in his sumptuous office. He stood behind his desk looking smug and satisfied with himself, but he made no reference to having ravished me the night before. Neither did he look like he'd spent all of the night that he wasn't fucking me in researching the paintings. I bet that he knew they weren't genuine as soon as they'd been unwrapped.

"Well, then," Monsignor Scarlotti said, with only minor disappointment. He hadn't had his hopes up. But he had been happy having had the mission outside the Vatican. I hoped he was happy that he'd brought me along for the opportunity for both of us that we fully satisfied each other sexually. I know I was happy we had come—and that we had come for each other.

That didn't mean that I didn't enjoy being worked over so roughly and completely by Brother Kepler.

"But there's good news," Otto continued. "These may not be the work personally of the artists themselves, which means they aren't worth the high millions of euros, but they all are from the immediate school of those artists. All are contemporary to Bosch, Bruegel, and Fra Angelico works of art and are by notable artists in their own right." He then named the artists and pointed out to the monsignor and me on the paintings the markings that led to this judgment. "They still are worth in the high hundreds of thousands and low millions—each."

"Thank you, you've been very helpful," Monsignor Scarlotti said, "and the monastery has been very hospitable."

I looked at him at this point and suddenly realized what he had done the previous night when my door was locked to him. He was looking over at the young, blond monk from the previous day, who was wrapping up the paintings and blushing, with downcast eyes. But his eyes weren't totally downcast. I caught him looking up into Scarlotti's eyes and I couldn't miss the flash of intimacy that went between them. I don't think Brother Kepler missed it either. What he didn't catch, though, was the stab of jealousy that sliced through me. I'd only lain with Scarlotti once and I already was so smitten with him that I resented any interest he showed to another. This was despite my right to have been angry with him, as he had admitted that morning that he had brought me because bringing me and leaving me alone with Kepler had been one of the conditions

Kepler had set for assessing the paintings. Scarlotti had known all along that Kepler would fuck me.

Clearing his throat, Otto proposed, "It's a long drive back down into Flüelen and then on to the airport. I suggest you stay until after lunch."

Scarlotti hesitated. Kepler added, "Perhaps Brother Müeller can help you with these paintings and then show you around our own little art gallery here before the meal. Your assistant can remain here with me."

The monsignor nodded, gave a little smile that seemed to be more for Brother Müeller than either Kepler or me, and the two swept out of the room, Scarlotti placing his hand on the small of the young monk's back.

Otto fucked me on top of the desk, me leaning over it, clutching the far edge of the desktop to hold myself steady as, my cassock gathered up above my bare buttocks and Otto's hands squeezing and releasing, squeezing and releasing my throat, the bull of a man mercilessly and relentlessly pounded my ass in a assault that began brutally in a dry fuck without proper preparation and continued in a "take no prisoners" overpowering.

The fuck was good for me, but not quite up to what he'd done the night before because I couldn't get out of my mind the jealousy of what Monsignor Scarlotti was doing with Brother Müeller in those moments.

Had Scarlotti been dissatisfied with me that morning? Having at last coupled with me, would he not want to do so again?

This was answered that afternoon as soon as we started the long drive back down to the shore of Lake Lucerne from the cliff-top Ettal Monastery. When the driver started to back up and turn around in the forecourt in front the drawbridge, Scarlotti pushed the wrapped painting aside, now worth merely hundreds of thousands of euros rather than hundreds of millions, leaned over and closed the curtains over the glass partition separating us from the driver's compartment, and then put an arm around my shoulders, drawing me to him. He took my mouth with his in a sweet, lingering, increasingly hungry kiss.

As we kissed his free hand was busy unbuttoning my cassock at my crotch, extracting my cock, and stroking it. In turn, I unbuttoned his cassock at the crotch, and, coming out of the kiss, gave a deep sigh of contentment and leaned over, taking him deep into my throat.

One thing I did know, though. Scarlotti was an expert at this. I had thought that, when I'd finally sheathed his cock, I would control him. There was no question now, though, that he was too expert in this for me—he would control me. He would use me for his pleasure but would not deny himself from using other young men as well, and he would give me to other men as it served his ambition, as he had given me to Otto. And I knew that to be under his sway, I would be happy for him to do so.

Jesuit Priests of Goa

"Why Goa? And where is it?"

The question had come from the second row of those few sitting in the dimly lit, voluminous lecture hall at Georgetown University, the venerable Jesuit-founded stone gothic-style campus towering over the Potomac River west of the Washington, D.C., city center. The query was posed to the tall, thin, distinguished-looking professor of religion, Michael Kincaid, standing alone behind a lectern on the wide, raised wooden stage.

"Goa because it was one of the earliest and strongest strongholds in the world of the Jesuit sect, Kevin," the professor responded in sonorous, perfect-diction tones. "It is a former Portuguese enclave on the western coast of India, reached first by Portuguese Jesuits in the sixteenth century and held by the Portuguese—with heavy Jesuit influence—until just fifty years ago, when it reverted to India. It now is the most wealthy district of that vast country."

"But why are we going there for our study of Jesuit history?" I couldn't help but blurt out from the front row. Kincaid turned his handsome face, haloed by curls of platinum-white hair, toward me, and I felt myself sinking back into the wooden theater-style seat. I could feel the professor's eyes bore into me. This was not what I'd wanted. I had been doing everything I could *not* to engage his attention. I hadn't even put in for this long weekend abroad immersion study trip for the Jesuit history course. But somehow when the list came out of those going, my name was on it. It was quite a plum, and only nine students were sent on this all-expenses-paid study trip. I couldn't afford to turn it down, if for no other reason than I couldn't alienate Kincaid. I needed a good grade in this course. But what I didn't need was giving into his obvious advances toward me.

But there was no way of avoiding him. The saving grace would be that we wouldn't all be together the whole weekend. With luck, I wouldn't be any closer to the professor that weekend than I would be here in Georgetown.

"Very good question, Ryan," the professor responded in those measured tones he used. "This is a history course. Nowhere in the world is the historical context of the Jesuits more in play still than it is in Goa. The Jesuit brothers even still practice the martial arts there that marked the sect's foundations as solider priests. Their military skill was so respected at the time that they lived in castles and became the treasure depositories for the nobles with lands around theirs. It's a history course. Nowhere else can we experience the history of the Jesuits as we can in Goa. They have preserved their past there like nowhere else in the world."

And that was that. Kincaid dismissed the other eight students, but, to my consternation, asked me to hang back.

He was turning off the lights in the hall as I slowly, as if going to execution, ascended the stairs to the stage. He beckoned me into the dimly lit wings off the stage and drew me to him.

Lowering his face to mine—he was a good five inches taller than I was—he took my lips in his. I couldn't help myself; I had turned my head up and moved ever so slightly—but move I did—to meet his lips with mine. It wasn't rejection I felt toward him—and certainly not revulsion—it was fear of my own attraction for him. And it was fear of what I wanted in life in a sexual nature. I've never done it before, with either a woman or man, and I feared my tendency to want to do it with men. And Michael Kincaid was all the man I could ever want.

I was just scared; I'd never done it before.

He ran his hand down my body. "Come back to my office with me."

"I can't," I whispered, my voice choked up. "I have another class. I'll barely make it if I leave now."

"Then my apartment—at 8:00 p.m."

"I don't know. I don't think I can—"

"You know you want to do this, Ryan. But I won't force you. When you want to be with me, you'll seek me out."

"But I've never—"

"I know. It makes me want you even more. I'll be good to you . . . gentle . . . the first time."

"The first time" reverberated in my head—not only the fear of that first time but also that he expected other times as well. And he would not be gentle with me then?

I was relieved he was letting me go—but I was conflicted over what he said. I was both scared and elated at the prospect all at once. I wouldn't think about it now, I thought, as I fled the hall to hide out in my dorm room. I had lied to him about having a class to go to.

* * * *

I was the last student left off at my weekend immersion study assignment in Goa. All of the others were assigned in pairs. I was the only one who would be alone—if, indeed, I was going to be alone. I half expected Michael Kincaid to reveal to me after we were wheels up and I couldn't go back that I would be at his mercy in this isolated former Portuguese enclave. I half hoped this was the case—that all responsibility for what I really wanted to do but just couldn't manage yet would be taken from me. I didn't think he had any idea how close to the edge of "yes" I was. I think if he did, I would have lost my virginity to him before now—that he'd be just enough more seductive to take me over the edge.

But this was not the case. He did tell me that my assignment would be the most interesting one, the one that would reveal the ancient ways of the Jesuits more than any of the other students would experience.

"Are we headed to the top of this hill, to what looks like either a monastery or a fortress up there?" I asked as the small bus that had been moving around the area, dispensing a pair of students here and another pair there, turned onto a road that apparently would wind up the hill from the shore of the ocean to a stonework compound at the top, dominated by a church steeple instead of the watch tower that might have been expected.

"Yes," Professor Kincaid answered, "but it's a retreat house—the Francis Xavier Retreat house. That's how the

Jesuit brothers refer to what would otherwise be called monasteries. Originally being soldier priests, in Europe they lived in castles."

I looked up at the compound at the top of the hill. I found it believable that this once was a fortified castle as well as a place of religious retreat. And, prophetically, the thought that it could serve to keep men in as well as keeping men out ran through my mind.

"What are they growing here?" I asked, as we moved higher than the band of palm trees near the ocean coast below to trees with wide, deep-green canopies.

"The coconut palms I'm sure you recognized," Kincaid answered. "These trees we are driving through now are cashew trees. Farther up the hill, just below the retreat house, are the vineyards. All of this goes into the wine the Jesuits produce here to finance themselves."

"Coconuts and cashews made into wine?" I asked. The grapes I could understand.

"Yes, they go into a fortified wine called feni. Separate wines. One is made from the coconut meat and the other kind is made from cashews. It's a strong port-like wine made primarily by the Jesuits, but it's exported throughout Asia and Europe. I haven't seen it in the States yet."

"And this is what I'll be doing for the next two days?" I asked, "helping to make wine?"

Kincaid latched onto my forearm and turned me to where I was looking into his face. "The Jesuits are heavily disciplined and demand total obedience, Ryan. While you are here, you will do whatever they tell you to do. I think you'll find that you're doing more than making wine."

For some reason I took an ominous connotation from that, especially from the intensity with which he was looking at me when he said it, and I involuntarily shuddered.

* * * *

As Professor Kincaid went off to concur with Father Stefan, a towering blond Viking of a German in his forties, a much younger Filipino who had been introduced to me as

Brother Taer shyly touched my forearm and asked me to follow him.

"You will be sleeping in my cell," he said in a melodious, quiet voice as he preceded me along a passage of stone walls, floor, and ceiling that could have been in a medieval castle. He was covered in a simple white cotton shift, with sandals on his feet, which contrasted with the black cassocks that the other brothers I'd been introduced to were wearing.

Taer, small of stature and with facial features that were more feminine than masculine, swayed his body like a dancer as he walked down the passage. His black hair cascaded to his shoulders. From this angle I could have believed he was a young girl.

As we walked, I ran through the names and features of the other brothers I'd been introduced to at the retreat house, knowing that it would be very difficult to remember them all—and only having a hope of doing so because they represented such divergent nationalities. At their head was the German, Stefan, who, of course, I should remember above all else. There was Brother Jacques, the slim, hirsute Frenchman, with dark features and hair and what I thought of as bedroom eyes. He was not more than seven years older than I was, perhaps in his late twenties. The rest were older, ranging from early thirties to the fifties. Not more than the early thirties was a dark-skinned, muscular Goan, Brother Joki, who was the touchy feeling type, slow to take his hand away from me when we were introduced. Those probably in their forties included ruddy haired and complexioned Brother Timothy, who was British, and another dark-skinned Goan, Brother Domingo, who was on the heavy side and whose eyes kept sliding away from me when I looked at him. Brother Benedito, in his fifties, was Portuguese and looked the part of what I was told he had been before coming to the retreat: a rough-and-tumble sailor.

"When you have changed, you will go to the work room to help Brothers Jacques and Timothy," Taer said to me over his shoulder as we walked.

"Changed?" I asked.

"Yes. You will wear a white shift as I am," he answered.

"Not black, like the others?" I asked.

"No. White like me." He didn't elaborate and I let it go, having another question.

"And what work will I do with Jacques and Timothy?"

"Whatever they want you to do," the answer came back. For some reason, because that had sounded ominous when professor Kincaid said it, it sounded a bit ominous coming out of Taer's mouth too. "In the late afternoon military drill will be conducted," he continued. "And that will be the last time that day that any of us will be able to speak. We have a strict vow of silence from sunset to sunrise every day."

"A strict vow?" I asked.

"Yes," he said, stopping at an open door and turning to me. "Very strict. We have military discipline here. This is a fundamental Jesuit sect. We follow the old ways. And there is punishment for not clinging to the vows."

"Even for me?" I asked.

"For anyone who sleeps under our roof," he answered. He continued before I could pursue the point. "Here. This is my cell. Our cell for the next two nights."

I looked in the room. "Cell" certainly was a good word for it. Stone walls, ceiling, and floor, just like the hallway. Small, with just two cot-like beds, a small, rough-wood bureau, and one straight chair, with a seat made from rush. A white cotton shift was laid out on one of the beds, and a pair of plain sandals were on the floor beside the bed.

"The white garment is for me?" I asked. "To wear over my briefs and undershirt."

"As all that you wear," Brother Taer answered. He gave me a shy smile before turning and leaving me alone in the cell to change.

* * * *

I found Brothers Jacques and Timothy in a shed, the tops of their cassocks stripped down and hanging over the sashes around their waists while they worked at cutting the meat of coconuts out of the shells and filling a tub with the white flesh. The milk of the coconuts was being poured off first through a hole bored in the shells into a separate tub set in a large basin of chipped ice.

The shed—more of a cavernous stone-walled area with timbers over two stories overhead—took up nearly one whole side of the fortress-like compound at the top of the hill. It once probably had been for livestock and storage of hay and anything else needing to be under cover, but not inside the living quarters. Now it was the heart of a wine press and fermenting operation.

Timothy hailed me as I stood at the open side of this large area looking into the darkness and picking out the various vats, presses, stacks of wine kegs, and other equipment. The somewhat gawky British redhead was the garrulous one of the two northern European priests at the retreat house. The younger, better-looking dark-complexioned French brother, Jacques, said nothing to me and spoke to and was answered by Timothy in French, so I assumed he didn't speak English. His eyes spoke to me, though, making me feel that I wasn't wearing even the cotton shift and sandals. I tried to think of him as a celibate priest but had difficulty doing so.

The two had muscular, lean torsos, and I learned later how they managed to keep so fit.

It was hot and humid and the air felt close in the shed, but I knew it would be hotter outside on the hillside, where I'd seen the other brothers headed when I came in here, so I assumed I was being assigned duties as light as they came here. Still, it wasn't long before I grew weary of cutting coconut meat out of the shell.

With a smile, Timothy said, "Have you ever tasted coconut milk straight from the coconut?"

I allowed as I had not, and he found a wooden cup and dipped some for me. When I thanked him, he asked me if I'd ever drunk feni made from coconut milk, and I admitted that I hadn't experienced this either.

He said something to Jacques in French, and Jacques leaned over and took the empty cup from my hand, holding my hand for a few beats longer than necessary and giving me a sultry look. I couldn't deny that it affected me and had my loins stirring. He rose, went over to a keg with a spigot in it, and returned with what Timothy told me was feni made from coconuts.

The drink was potent and I could taste the coconut in it. But I knew I couldn't have handled very much of it.

"Wow, that really heats me up," I said. The two brothers were watching me closely. If pressed, I would have had to admit that it heated me up in more than one way. It wasn't just the French priest. These two were giving me looks that I didn't associate with priests either.

"Why don't you take a break and go out on the hillside, where the breezes blow, for a few minutes?" Timothy said. "Take a look at the grapes that the others are beginning to harvest. We make very good wine from those too. The coconuts will still be here when you return."

There was, in fact, a breeze on the hillside, but there also was the beating sun. The Goan brothers and the Portuguese brother, Benedito, all with the tops of their cassocks draped around their waists were harvesting grapes. They, like the northern European brothers in the shed, were muscular. If anything they were more muscular. The sweat from their labors glistened on their torsos.

I could have stood and watched them work with precise, rhythmic motions in the vineyard for some time, taken not only with the beauty of the motion of their bodies but also with their raw sexuality despite being priests, but my attention was drawn to sounds coming from deeper in the vineyard. These were sounds that I'd heard before. Sounds like those from a video Professor Kincaid had once sprung on me in surprise to, he said, put me in the mood.

The sounds were coming from a gazebo-like structure in the middle of the vineyard built of branches covered with vines and most likely there to provide the workers in the field temporary relief from the sun. I drew close enough to be able to see inside it through the breaks in the vines.

At first glance I could see the large-framed blond German priest, Father Stefan, bent over, his body strangely undulating. I thought the sound—huffing and groaning—was coming from him, but then I realized that there was a higher tone of groan and moan mingled with his bass. Looking closer, I could see what he was bent over. It was the small Filipino brother, Taer, naked and on all fours.

I couldn't help remaining there for longer than I should, seeing in real-life dimension what I'd seen on the video Professor Kincaid had play for me once—what he'd told me that he and I could be doing if only I would give in to him. I should have been surprised, I suppose, but at least subconsciously I wasn't. There were signals enough throughout the day—in looks exchanged and touches—that something sexual was going on on this hilltop.

And I had read rumors about Jesuits and other priests having sex among themselves. Kincaid had provided written stories and videos of acts by priests. I had assumed that he wanted the connotation of a black cassock, such as he wore at the university, to become a sexual one in my mind as part of his own campaign to bed me. And it that had been his intent, it had succeeded. Part of the problem with holding him off at the university is that I went hard whenever I saw him gliding around in his black cassock.

Seeing Stefan crouched over Taer and fucking him should have made me fearful—and perhaps the sensation of being trapped and headed someplace dangerous. Stefan was the highest authority and more than one person had assured me that I was at the full mercy of these priests the entire weekend. But, in fact, these sensations aroused me and made me hard.

The arousal continued later in the afternoon when I figured out why the men were all in such tip-top physicality. I hadn't given full thought to having been told that the Jesuits originally were soldier priests and that nowhere were the traditions of the Jesuits being preserved as they were in Goa.

The hour before sunset was devoted to military training—with swords and pikes—in the central courtyard of the fortress, with the six black-cassocked priests, the tops of the cassocks still draped from their waists, pitted off in twos in dances of cut-and-parry thrusts.

Brother Taer stood off to the side, with me, explaining the training routine to me. He obviously had not been elevated

147

to the level of full-blown Jesuit, as he didn't wield a weapon during the practice, although he did help bring them out into the courtyard and then put them away.

At one point, noticing the angry red welts criss-crossed on Brother Timothy's back, I asked Taer how the redheaded Britisher had come to be wounded in this fashion.

"Brother Timothy has trouble holding his tongue," Taer answered. "I told you that we cannot speak—for any reason—from sunset to sunrise. Brother Timothy spoke one day recently."

"And this was his punishment?" I asked, incredulous. "That wouldn't apply to me, would it?"

Taer turned to me and gave me a hard look. "It applies to anyone who is within these walls between sunset and sunrise. And I must say that I think that Father Stefan receives special pleasure from meting out this punishment. I have seen him looking at you. I wouldn't suggest that you give Father Stefan reason to exercise his pleasure in this regard."

"Surely—"

"Let me be clear. I know you saw Father Stefan mounted on me in the vineyard. I must warn you that Father Stefan is built very large and he becomes very aroused when he punishes one of the brothers. The taking of his pleasure extends beyond the whipping. The look I have seen in his eyes when he looks on you is the same look he gives one of the brothers he is going to punish, and punishment for him is an arousal that he often takes beyond the whip with the penitent. You saw him mount me; I assure you that he is built exceedingly large. I hope that is clear enough for you. You'd best not break any rules here."

I snapped my jaw shut, deciding to start my exercising of the vow of silence before the sun set.

* * * *

The evening meal progressed in total silence, and I strained not to let out a peep. When I was given a large cup of coconut feni, I tried to signal that I perhaps should not drink it, but my signaling was to no avail. I had less success—and less intent, considering the potency of the first cup—in trying to turn down the second cup.

Taer had to help guide me to our cell after the dinner. All of my energy was expended in keeping my mouth shut and not uttering a word—and in focusing on the walls and floors, which seemed to be in motion around me.

I wasn't a bit surprised later in the night, lying on my back on my cot, my eyes still open trying to bring the stonework all around me into focus and to a standstill, to hear the wooden door to the cell open in a low screech across the stone floor and the large figure, clothed in his black cassock, of Father Stefan loom over me.

He was in view only briefly at first, but I had no trouble knowing where he had disappeared to. He had grasped my ankles and pulled me down to the foot of the cot. His beefy, calloused hands had run up the sides of my legs, my hips, and my torso inside the cotton shift, bunching the material up under my armpits. And I felt my legs being spread, my left one being raised, a cold tongue at my anus, and a rough hand encircling my cock and beginning to stroke me off.

I knew what was happening and what was going to happen. But I had no capability, only being half there from the effects of the potent feni, nor the will, to stop it. Beyond that, if I were to utter anything, he would feel fully justified to punish me, which could include anything he was doing now.

I also realized I wanted it and had wanted it for some time. I just didn't want the responsibility for it happening. I had even begun to prepare myself in the weeks before taking this trip. I had assumed that Professor Kincaid would take me for the first time while on this trip, and I had accepted that— welcomed it, even—and had begun to prepare for it. I had bought a dildo and had been using it on myself, learning how to take a cock inside me, how to open to it.

I stifled a fearful whimper when I next saw Stefan raise his body over me and gather his cassock up and tuck the folds in the sash at his waist. His lower belly was exposed, and his angry red erection curved cruelly and monstrously up from an unruly, blond bush.

I arched my back, my eyes rolled back in head, and I let out a scream of pain as, hunched over me and holding my legs raised and spread with his fists, Stefan invaded me with his cock—much larger than the dildo I had been practicing with. The thick, throbbing staff slowly moved up inside me, and, when I'd opened sufficiently to him, he set his buttocks in motion and began to pump.

As he fucked me, Stefan brought his face down close to mine so that, even in the darkened cell, he could intimidate me with his glowering expression and he could see in my eyes and the yawning of my mouth the effect of his assault. He was watching me so carefully that I became sure that the communication of my virginity at that point to a man's cock had been exchanged between Stefan and Kincaid and that Kincaid would be receiving some special consideration for having brought me here.

It was only then that I realized that the small cell was crowded with naked men. The other brothers were here. Four of them were watching Stefan fuck me, their dicks in their hands, waiting for their turns, I soon was to find out. The Portuguese, Benedito, was at Taer's cot, holding Taer upside down, the Filipino's shoulders supporting his weight on the floor and his body rising up Benedito's, with Benedito grasping the young Filipino's hips and pile driving his cock down into Taer's hole.

I briefly wondered how this position was manageable, but I learned how it was done before the night was through, as Benedito fucked me later the same way.

When Stefan was finished with me, he was replaced by Jacques, who pulled me back up on the cot, stretched out behind me, and made slow love to me as if we were lovers, covering my cheeks and shoulders with slobbering kisses. At that point, I appreciated the change from Stefan's almost clinical deep, painful thrustings. The size of him was probably more than I should have been subjected to for my first time. I wondered if Kincaid knew what would be happening to me tonight—being fucked by all six of the senior priests in succession, not just Father Stefan—and if he had even

150

arranged it. I certainly was glad I'd thought of starting to prepare myself with the dildo.

That I had started to prepare myself obviated any claim I could make to myself that I didn't want to have sex with men. Well, with a man. I hadn't thought in my wildest dreams that it would be with a succession of men—at least not as a start.

They all were hunky, though, and they all were stripped down now. I looked over to the other cot. Taer was sandwiched between the two Goans, Domingo and Joki, taking them both like he did this every night. And, who knows, maybe he did. The redheaded Brit, Timothy, was prodding Jacques to be done with me and was coming very close to the edge of voicing something. Stefan and Benedito were standing off to the side, the gnarled, but still hard-bodied older men. Both were stroking their cocks and looking from Taer's cot to mine. A full moon was out, sending its beams into the room from a barred window high on the wall. It gave enough light for me to distinctly pick out all of the men—to see the look of lust on each of their faces.

I was afraid the Goans would take me together as they were doing Taer—something that I would have thought to be logistically impossible. It apparently wasn't. But, although they fucked me in a threesome after Timothy, who surprisingly had a long, but not thick cock and who, equally surprisingly, was the most vigorous thruster of the lot, had finished me. Domingo and Joki didn't try to enter me together, they worked each end of me at the same time with their cocks and exchanged places half way through.

It was Brother Benedito's pile driving, with me stretched to the floor, that put me almost over the edge of exhaustion and consciousness, and I felt fortunate that he hadn't come earlier in the parade and caused that soreness in my neck and across my shoulders before the others had been done with me. And before they were done with me, I experienced what Taer had with the two Goans, Domingo and Joki. They put me between them, entered me together, and fucked me with both cocks.

Throughout Father Stefan watched me closely. My impression is that he wanted to catch me speaking so that he could whip as well as fuck me. I did everything I could to hold my tongue, although a sorely wanted to cry out to Professor Kincaid of his cruelty. He doubtless knew exactly what he was doing in sending me here. I had evaded him too long. He wanted to receive me back completely undone.

They left me panting and moaning deeply, flat on my back on the cot, my knees bent, and my legs spread because I couldn't close them. I worried while they were leaving that my moaning would be loud enough to be considered vocalization, and it may have been.

They let me remain prone on the cot in the cell until their martial arts routine started the next afternoon. I wondered throughout this time whether the next night would be the same in the cell as the first one—and, if so, would it become more than I could take.

My last night at the Francis Xavier Retreat House was different from the first, though. I discovered that the fortress had a dungeon when Father Stefan arrived at the cell, pulled me off the cot, threw me over his shoulder, and descended what must have been more than one story down a winding stone staircase.

He bound my wrists and hung me from a hook in the ceiling of the dark and dank chamber he took me to. The whipping must have been mostly to arouse him—but it symbolically might have related to punishment for the loud moaning I couldn't help but engage in the previous night. Although there were faint welts criss-crossing my back the next morning when Professor Kincaid and the rented bus came to collect me, they were too faint to concern him or to bother me when he fucked me in his hotel room bed that night. When Stefan had finished the brief and light lashing of my back, though, his erection was monstrously hard.

He fucked me harder and longer than he had done the night before, but at least there was no gang bang that night.

Regardless, I was completely cowed. I didn't question why there was only one room and one bed for the two of us in the hotel Professor Kincaid took me to after retrieving me from the Goa Jesuits. As far as I know, nothing transpired between him and the Jesuits on what had happened to me while I was in their keeping. I was sure that Kincaid knew—that he had arranged it.

When night came and he was in the bathroom showering after I had done so, I had come from the bathroom naked and went under the sheets on the bed. I was completely tamed, I didn't struggle against the inevitable or pretend it wasn't going to happen. There was no transition between the relationship between me and Professor Kincaid from before to now. I had evaded him at Georgetown University. I had not said "yes" to him, even here. But I said nothing, gave no objection, when he came out of the bathroom, naked and in erection, pulled the sheets up, and climbed into bed.

I was on my back, and when he pulled the sheets up, I spread and bent my legs and he came down on his knees between my thighs. I merely grimaced as he penetrated me with his throbbing erection. I even rolled my pelvis up to aid his entry. Then I turned my cheek to the pillow, watching the moonlight pick out the flower pots on the balcony beyond the French windows, as he worked his way deep inside me and began to pump. I arched my back and gave a little groan as I felt him ejaculate into the bulb of a condom deep inside me. Later he woke me, turned me on my belly, mounted my ass, and fucked me again as I grasped the slats of the headboard above my head to hold myself steady for him.

Thus was my first night in Professor Kincaid's bed. He covered me with kisses. I didn't reciprocate.

* * * *

He fucked me the next morning and he fucked me the next afternoon. By the next night, we were working together in the fuck like long-time lovers. I lay on my belly on the bed in Kincaid's Goa hotel room, my hips raised just a bit, leveraged by pressure on my knees, to give the professor a good angle for stroking his cock inside me. He was covering me close from above, his fists grasping the wrists of my raised and spread arms and his face close to my ear, where I could hear his heavy breathing, panting, and moaning.

His groans had increased as I began to move and rotate my pelvis. His thrusts became more insistent, faster, and deeper. He ejaculated inside me and rolled away from me, jerked the condom off his cock, and dropped it on the floor beside the bed—to join two other spent ones that had been used earlier in the night.

I felt myself being turned onto my side and pulled into his chest. His mouth was at my ear. Until this evening he had spoken nothing about what we were doing. He just took and took and took. Now, when it was obvious I was going to give him whatever he wanted, he seemed to want to discuss our relationship with me.

"Are you sure you'd never done it before then?"

"No, that was my first. Am I responding right, the way you want me to?"

"You are doing it beautifully. I had no idea you would be so good. And you came to me, seeking it tonight, just as I said you would. You were fucked by—?"

"Six of them, in succession." I hadn't come seeking it tonight. He'd just been the first one in the bed tonight. The first one in the only bed in the room—the bed in which he'd been fucking me for a day and a half already.

"It sounds so . . . it sounds. . . . Do you know Sam Holt . . . in the sociology department?"

"You want me to let him fuck me too—while you watch?" I kept my voice flat, to let him know I had no emotional investment in this. He'd let the Jesuits break me, because he wanted me and couldn't wait. This was the reaction I thought a young man he'd caused to be broken for his own pleasure should respond to him. "Or do you want to fuck me with him—both of you together?"

Kincaid didn't answer immediately, but his intake of breath was all I needed to know of what he was thinking. I let my mind wander back to that night, just two nights ago, and how I had felt about that experience—of men standing around me, watching me being fucked and impatiently awaiting their turn. Two of them sharing a turn.

"That's what you want, isn't it? You want to know if I had two of the priests in me at one time. Whether I have experienced and managed that. Yes, I did. Yes, you both can fuck me—together—if you wish," I whispered. "And are there any others you'd like to join in?"

"Oh, fuck," he said, with a groan.

I don't think he got the point.

The Songbird and the Philanthropist

As a child, Monsignor Rainero had always been considered a clever boy, if perhaps a bit more clever than for his own good. He was known to have very inventive and attractive ideas, but he sometimes was known to overembelish them to the point where the scheme collapsed around him. This had played out time and time again and eventually caught up with him. After Rainero had started out in his father's tourist resort business in Umbria and suggested that the visitors at the resort might enjoy the offering of outings to the region's principle economic ventures—which were pig farming and salami production—Rainero's father steered Rainero to a vocation in the church instead.

The newly minted priest, lifted rather high rather fast because of his family's position in the region, became somewhat of a celebrity for his inventive ideas. The latest of these schemes—a populist radio address from Perugia three times a week in which listeners would be enticed to tune in one way or the other and would, in the context of the program, receive a homily from Monsignor Rainero—was thus what brought Monsignor Rainero to the Albergo La Torre café in Castiglione del Lago on the banks of the scenic Lake Trasimeno on this sunny May morning.

He was sitting at the open-air tables just outside the café's wide doors with the patron he wished to reel in to provide financial backing for his radio program, the Count de la Giovani Montefeltro. Both had just immensely enjoyed the singing of Pepo, a young tenor with pure, haunting tones, who had performed for them as he did hourly at this café in the high tourist season. They were a good distance from Perugia, the largest town in the Umbia region, where the parish that Monsignor Rainero now served existed, but Rainero was from the Trasimeno lake region himself and often came down to the small villa he had inherited on the banks of the lake near where

Castiglione del Lago, once the fourth island of the lake, now joined the mainland. For his part, Giovani Montefeltro, who Rainero was now trying to cultivate, was from an ancient noble family of the region.

"This is a pleasant café, is it not?" the monsignor murmured to the patrician nobleman. He had been watching his companion carefully and was gratified that the man's attention had been straying to the corner of the café where Pepo had been singing. Although Rainero lived in Perugia and the count lived in the lake region, Montefeltro habitually came to Rainero in Perugia to give confession. There were a couple of very good reasons for this. The Montefeltros and Rainero's family had been intertwined for centuries, and also what Montefeltro had to confess—which very much had to do with the looks he was giving the young, blond singer at the Albergo La Torre café—was not something the count, married to the daughter of an industrialist who paid the bills for the maintenance of the Montefeltro ancestral estate, wanted to confess to priests in his own parish.

"Yes, quite pleasant indeed," Montefeltro whispered back, without taking his eyes off the young singer, who had finished singing and was chatting with the man at the piano and also with the owner of the café, a big bruiser of a northern Italian named Saladino. The use Saladino was making of his hands at the waist and on the arm of the young singer left little doubt of the nature or extent of his proprietary rights in that quarter.

Herein had been the dilemma that had been set for Monsignor Rainero. The monsignor had first heard the hauntingly beautiful voice of the young tenor the previous month when Rainero had been visiting his family villa, having received permission to air his Perugia entertainment-mixed-with-religion broadcasts but only then realizing all of his plans were just that so far—plans written in a prospectus. He had retreated to Castiglione del Lago to think upon how he could put reality to these plans. He needed money and he needed entertainments that would attract listeners to tune in to his radio program.

Sitting at the Albergo La Torre café one day in deep thought, Rainero's musings had evaporated as soon as Pepo had started to sing. Here, surely, Rainero thought, was one answer to his entertainment needs. He would ask the young Pepo to move to Perugia and sing for him on the radio. The church would pay, of course—or at least some patron would when Rainero solved that piece of the puzzle—but Pepo could also sing just as well—and probably more profitably—in the cafes of the larger city of Perugia as he could here at the lakeside.

As excited as he was about this divinely inspired plan, Rainero rose from his chair in the open-air area of the café and sought out the young singer after he had finished a set. Rainero's progress was arrested, however, at the entrance of the corridor leading from the café's interior dining area to the back of the facility. Just as he was about to enter the shadowed corridor, he sensed motion at the farther end, at an open door at the end of the corridor, into which the sunlight of the day was being filtered.

Two figures were leaning against the wall of the corridor, the larger one encasing the body of the smaller one between him and the wall. Both were men, the singer, Pepo, and the café owner, Saladino. Both were naked from the waist down. Pepo's back was against the rough, white-washed stone of the corridor wall, and his legs were raised and hooked on the thighs of the big brute of a northern Italian, Saladino, whose chest was pushing Pepo's back against the corridor wall and moving it up and down on the rough, white-washed stone, while Saladino's dick thrust up in long strokes inside the young singer's channel.

The café owner must have been nearly fifty, if not beyond. His body was brawny and big boned and his countenance that of a prize fighter past his prime. And yet Pepo was moaning for him and clutching the older man's buttocks closely into him with the digging claws of his hands.

Monsignor Rainero withdrew to plan his line of reasoning with this young man. He could surely do better than the rough and cruel northern Italian café owner in Perugia.

But when Rainero took Pepo aside on his next visit to the café and nudged into his proposition that Pepo come to Perugia to sing on the radio, an offer that surely would be honey to the taste buds of any young man moldering away in the Umbria countryside, he was surprised that Pepo declined, saying that he had a place here that suited him fine. Rainero did what he could to hint that there were better options than the brutish Saladino, but Pepo would not listen to any of this, whether from fear or from fetish for an older, rough lover.

Rainero was amazed at the resistance of the young singer, and this became a conundrum at the back of his mind for the next several weeks. It was even there when next Count Giovani Montefeltro came to Perugia to give confession, and, to Rainero's mind, to place himself in position to be asked to underwrite the costs of Rainero's radio broadcasts. And it was during Giovani's confession that bells started to ring in the back of Rainero's mind.

Giovani was a handsome, refined, older man. He was tall and one might call him thin, but he also was well formed—surely refined and elegant were the best words to describe him. And from his confessions, Rainero couldn't help but discern that the count enjoyed fucking young men. They invariably were stable hands and chauffeurs, though, and just as the monsignor was musing that a noble, refined man like Giovani really deserved a more suitable lover, the thought of Pepo returned to the surface of his mind.

And Monsignor Rainero's mind began to weave an elaborate plan of working his broadcast needs in consort. Thus today and the planned meeting between Rainero and Giovani at the Albergo La Torre café.

"I see you are taken with the café's young singer," Rainero said to Giovani across the café table as he set his coffee cup down and smiled a knowing smile.

Giovani gave the monsignor a shocked look.

"Please," Rainero said in a dismissive tone. "You have brought your confessions to me. Have I ever judged?"

"Yes, yes, I confess I am," the count answered. Then he was caught up short by the repetition of the confession word and its connection to his attraction to the young singer

159

and gave a half distressed look at the monsignor, his confessor. But Rainero just smiled back, clearly signaling that there was no judgment to be seen in his countenance.

"I confess myself," the monsignor whispered, "that I am trying to convince the singer—his name is Pepo—to come to Perugia to sing on the radio program I am trying to interest you in. And you've said you were planning on spending more time at your Perugia residence, did you not?"

Rainero let that linger in the air between them across the café table for several moments, as Giovani gave him a searching look.

Having discerned there was an understanding between them and any shock of what Rainero was working toward had been weathered, the monsignor continued. "I really would like to talk to you more about support for my radio broadcasts, but for now, do you think you and Pepo would like to see my family's small villa here in Castiglione del Lago? It's really quite charming—and very private—and it is nearby."

Giovani looked slightly agitated and then perplexed. "Why are you—?"

"I wish help in convincing the singer to come to Perugia for me. He seems to be under the sway of that brute of a café owner over there. See him? I think young Pepo needs to break from that influence—for his own good. I think he should have more refined friends. Sometimes the priesthood has to work in strange ways to achieve what is best."

Giovani still looked a bit agitated, but Rainero could tell from his change in demeanor that lust and want—and his wish to believe the convenient reasoning he was being given—were winning out.

The count simply curtly nodded his head and looked away toward the lake.

When Rainero sought out Pepo and turned the young singer's attention to the outside table where the count sat, trembling a bit and dreaming of possibilities, the monsignor wasn't altogether unarmed. Other men in Castiglione del Lago had had confessions to make—and although not to Rainero, the brotherhood of priests weren't all pristinely closed mouthed in their discussions with each other. Rainero knew that Pepo would go with a man for a price—that he would more than sing for his supper.

"He won't know there is a price," Rainero whispered to the young singer, as he pressed banknotes in the young man's hand. "He will be more pleased to think of it as a seduction—and you can trust me when I tell you that I have every reason to believe he is good at that."

"Why are you doing this?" Pepo asked. But he had his eyes on Giovani, and Rainero could tell from the slitting of his eyes and the way his tongue was playing on his lips that Pepo needed little convincing to go with Giovani.

"I wish him to be a patron for that radio program I have discussed with you. I only wish for you to help me convince him to invest in that."

Rainero found the seduction of Pepo by Giovani on the balcony of his villa overlooking Lake Trasimeno both touching, and, despite his vocation, arousing.

At first Rainero joined the other two on the balcony, bringing two bottles of wine and three glasses. He stayed with them until all were comfortable and had stripped down to their waists to soak in the sun while watching the boats bob on the waters of the lake. When the second bottle of vino was opened, Rainero faded away into the interior of the villa. The other two didn't even seem to notice he was gone as taken as they were with each other in chit chat and ever-more suggestive looks and exploratory touching.

Giovani had his arm around the back of Pepo's chair, and when he cupped Pepo's bicep in a hand, the younger man leaned into him and sighed.

Rainero saw that the second bottle of wine was empty and he went into the kitchen to get another one. But when he came back, he saw that no more wine was needed—at least on the balcony—as the two men were kissing, and from what the monsignor could see, Giovani's free hand was in Pepo's lap. So, Rainero returned to the kitchen for another wine glass, pulled the cork on the bottle, and sat in a sofa with a full view of the balcony and slowly drank down the third bottle himself.

Pepo disappeared for a while, the view of his kneeling body being blocked by Giovani's back and spread legs. And then a naked Pepo was straddling Giovani's thighs and the two were kissing, with Pepo's hands laced in the well-groomed gray-streaked black hair at the back of Giovani's head. Giovani was gripping Pepo's waist on both sides and moving the youth's body in rhythm to the rocking of the balcony chair they both now occupied and the grunts and groans of the fuck.

When, with a harmonizing tenor and baritone cry of release, the sounds of coupling and the rhythmic movement had ceased and Pepo was sighing and collapsed onto Giovani's body in satisfied exhaustion, the monsignor tiptoed out to the door sill onto the balcony and whispered in Giovani's ear that he had been called away to priestly duties in the village and that the two were free to use the small villa's main bedroom. And then Rainero left. When he returned two hours later, the moans led him to the bedroom, where Pepo was stretched out on his belly on the bed and Giovani was riding his hips like a camel on the desert, crouched over the body of the younger man, his hands covering those of Pepo, their fingers laced together. So intent were they in the pleasure they were giving each other that they had no idea the monsignor had come and then gone.

It was almost morning before the monsignor returned again to find that the villa, at last, was deserted. He barely had time to gather his clothes and motor back to Perugia to be there for the next mass he had promised to give.

Days and then a week and more went by before the monsignor was able to give Pepo and Giovani a thought. Indeed, he didn't think he had to think much about them. He was very pleased with himself and was content in the belief that they both, each working the agenda that Rainero had set for them in exchange for bringing them together, would now come through for his plans for the radio program. It was the radio program that was consuming his time and attention—making all of the preparations for going on air.

At the point where he had to actually provide funds to the radio station, Monsignor Rainero decided it was time for another visit to Castiglione del Lago to settle his two-pronged arrangement with Pepo and Giovani.

At the Albergo La Torre café, the monsignor was met with a sour-faced Saladino, who towered over him, beefy arms crossed, and obviously keyed up and angry.

"Pepo? That worm? He left me, more than a week ago. No notice, no nothing. Not even time to find a replacement, and it's high season."

Backing away from there, and without giving it much thought, Monsignor Rainero drove out to the Count de la Giovani Montefeltro's nearby country estate, where a somewhat surly servant answering the door told him the count wasn't there, and a disheveled countess, appearing at the door as Rainero was opening the door to his car, screamed in distraught tones that the count indeed was gone and a curse on him and all men.

It dawned on Rainero that it was possibly natural that Pepo and Giovani wouldn't be at the Montefeltro villa. Perhaps he should have checked the count's town home in Perugia before he came here. Perhaps they were already set up there. But then, again, perhaps they were at his own small villa here in Castiglione del Lago.

A check there indicated that, no they weren't there— that no one had been there since he had hurriedly left himself. The bed was still unmade and there were two empty wine bottles on the balcony and another one on the floor at the base of the sofa.

As he was leaving the villa, a village priest was walking up the road.

"The count?" the village priest responded to Rainero's query. "You mean Giovani Montefeltro, who fucks young men and thinks others don't all know he does just because he goes to you in Perugia to give his confession? Why, he and that young singer at the Albergo La Torre café ran off to Florence more than a week ago. The word is that neither one is coming back, either."

Monsignor Rainero withdrew back into his villa and sat heavily down onto the sofa. His foot hit the empty wine bottle and he watched it roll away from him.

A radio program to pay for and format within a week and so far he had nothing. Less than nothing, he thought bitterly. He had paid for the first fuck of Montefeltro's from Pepo and he was out three perfectly good bottles of wine. Well, two, he admitted. He'd drunk this one all by himself.

He sat there and thought and thought and thought. Maybe he shouldn't make such elaborate plans all the time. Maybe he should make simpler plans and let them build on their own if that happened naturally. And then he looked at the wine bottle again. It was from the winery of Landolfo Ordelaffi, who lived just outside Perugia and who brought Rainero a bottle of wine from his vineyard each time he came to confession.

Funny that he should think of Ordelaffi, the monsignor was thinking. That man's latest confession was that he had taken the young opera mezzo-soprano Melina Doria for his mistress. "Hmm," Rainero thought. "Ordelaffi has plenty of money to burn and Melina Doria's voice would be simply divine on my radio program."

Ruined Pie

"What a delicious dinner. The cook must be given accolades. I believe, if I'm not mistaken that would be you, Ms. Kathy." The Reverend Father Carl Curtis gave Kathy Fergus a benevolent look where she was sitting at one end of the dining room table in the Fergus's Mobile, Alabama, house, a Victorian cottage on one of the best streets in the historical district. Kathy Fergus wasn't a member of his parish—she wasn't even a Catholic—but her newly married husband, Sam, sitting at the other end of the table from her was, and Kathy had fussed over this meal.

Kathy was a fusser, and Father Curtis, a rather dapper and handsome man in his early forties, who also was somewhat of a fusser, was playing court to her. He could see that she'd been nervy and a little down through the meal.

"A truly fine traditional Thanksgiving meal with all the trimmings. I can hardly wait for the pumpkin pie," he said, patting his belly as if it had filled out, even though he went to great pains to make sure it remained flat.

"Oh, oh," Kathy said in distressed, pushing away from the table. "I'm sorry. Please excuse me. I don't feel at all well." She fled the dining room, leaving a surprised and concerned Catholic priest looking crestfallen. He turned to Sam, who showed a bit of concern but more of reserve.

"I'm sorry," Father Curtis said, "I didn't mean to upset her."

"She already was a bit upset," Sam answered. "And it's certainly not your fault. She ruined two pumpkin pies this afternoon trying to cook a decent one, and that set her on edge. But I think it could be more than that. She could genuinely feel ill."

"From something going around?" Father Curtis asked.

There was a pause, and then Sam seemed to be steeling himself and said, "She's pregnant."

"Ah, I see."

"I meant to tell you before, but I couldn't find the right time."

"How far along is she?"

Sam paused for a moment, and then shrugged, and said, "Four or five months."

"You've only been married for two."

"Yes, only two months," Sam said, he gave Father Curtis a level look. This wasn't going well. The priest was being very direct. There was no give there. Sam had expected that they would be talking around the issue at length, both understanding each other but not being so blunt in saying it.

"I see. Then that's why—"

"Yes, that's why we married on such short notice—in her church—and I didn't discuss it with you beforehand. As I said, I was looking for the right time."

"Who is the father? I don't usually mean to pry, but in this case . . . for her sake as well as yours—"

"Her father is the father of the baby." He gave the priest a moment to absorb that, and, in fact, it did seem to set Father Curtis back on his heels a bit. After a moment, Same continued. "It's a boy. She had DNA testing done to be sure."

"Yes, I see. I suppose I know why then. He paid you to marry her, I suppose. This house is very nice, and you've always liked nice things."

"So have you, Carl," Sam said, his voice a little hard. "Your rectory is as nice as this. You serve a rich parish. You aren't any more ready to give that lifestyle up than I am, I don't think. We've discussed this before. I was willing to make concession on that—if you did."

The priest said nothing in response and Sam continued. "Yes, her father is paying for all of this. He wants what's best for the child and he hasn't been told directly that the baby is his. I imagine he suspects, though, and that's why he's so forthcoming."

"None of it explains why you—"

"The baby *could* have been mine, Carl. The timing works out for me too. I was almost disappointed when I found out it wasn't mine. But it could have been. I would like to be a father. It didn't seem ever to be possible otherwise."

166

"I see," Carl said again. He often used the expression when he wished he wasn't seeing something. "And are you going to cut off all connections, Sam?" he asked. "Will you be changing to Kathy's faith? What is she, by the way? What religion does she follow? And if you're leaving the church why, did you invite me for Thanksgiving?"

"She's Methodist."

"I suppose it could be worse. She could have been a Baptist or a Jehovah's Witness."

Sam gave a slight smile, but then he realized that the priest was being serious. "Yes, but, no, she's willing to convert to Catholicism. Kathy thought it would be a good idea to invite you because she didn't want her father to come this year. She couldn't bear to be with him on Thanksgiving. He dislikes priests, so it was her idea to invite you—partially as a barrier to him coming. But she wanted you to come anyway. She said she could discuss the process of conversion with you. I wanted you just because I wanted you to be here. I thought we could talk. I didn't count on Kathy being so keyed up tonight over a ruined pie."

"But it's not just a ruined pie, is it? It's not that simple."

"No, I suppose not," Sam said. "Would you like some coffee?"

"I think not, at least not now. What I'd like is a walk in your lovely garden, if I may. I've often walked past this house before you acquired it and noticed that it has a fine garden behind it."

"Certainly, if you'd like," Sam said, standing from the table. "Perhaps you could help me clear the table into the kitchen first, though. You could get the dirty dishes by the sink and I'll put the food away."

"You don't think Kathy—?"

"No, I think she's in her bedroom for the night now. She won't be coming back down. I do the dishes anyway."

"Her bedroom?"

"Yes, we're in separate bedrooms for now. Her bedroom is on the front of the house. We're in separate rooms for the duration of the pregnancy, and maybe . . . it was just a one-time fluke, Carl. We didn't . . . I'm not . . . we'd just been to a party and had too much to drink."

"I understand," the priest said in a tone that indicated that he probably didn't understand at all.

When they'd cleared the dishes, they walked out into the garden together. The house was a cottage, but the gardens were extensive, including a fair amount of mature boxwoods, which created private pocket gardens here and there. It was in one of these gardens, well away from the house, that Father Curtis arrested their progress with a hand on Sam's forearm.

"Where does this leave us, Sam?" he asked in a low voice.

"Us? I don't see that it changes anything, Carl—that it should make any difference at all, except that I can stay in Mobile now. Kathy's father has given me a job as well. In time, Kathy will get over the situation with her father. He wants his family near. He'll dote on the baby."

"And Kathy?"

"In time she'll let him dote on the baby. She'll want nice things for the baby."

"That's not what I'm asking, Sam, and I think you know it isn't. This isn't just ruined pumpkin pie, Sam."

"I realize that. But you've seen how Kathy is. In time she will have forgotten even that it was her father."

"I'm not talking about her father either. This isn't just your relationship with Kathy and her father. Or with the baby."

"You've seen that, too, Carl. If she reacts the way she does to screwing up a pie, how do you think she'd react to me telling her that I'm screwing you?"

"I'm afraid, Sam. Hold me."

Sam pulled the priest into his breast, held him close, and the two went into a deep kiss. When the kiss was broken, Carl whispered, "I need to know that you still are going to be screwing me, Sam. I can't just give you up like this."

"You don't have to give me up," Sam answered. He turned the priest around and bent him over, with Carl grasping the arms of a garden bench. He moaned as Sam reached around and unbuckled and then unzipped him and pulled the black trousers down and off his legs.

"Give me a wider stance," he muttered, and, with a groan, Carl set his legs farther apart. He groaned again, deeper, as Sam spread his butt cheeks with the palms of his hands and buried his face in Carl's crack. Within minutes, Sam was standing, crouched over Carl's back, his hands shoved up inside the black shirt with the clerical collar and his fingers working the older man's nipples, while Sam's hard cock invaded up inside Carl's passage.

When Sam began to pump him, Carl, trying hard not to scream it out, gave a muffled exclamation of "Yes, yes. Fuck me. Punish me. Take me to heaven or hell but just fuck me hard."

After he had ejaculated inside the priest's channel and reached around and jerked Carl off with his hand, Sam whispered in the priest's ear. "See, nothing need change. I'll drive you home now."

"Kathy—"

"She knows you were dropped off at the house for dinner and will need a ride home. Kathy isn't a problem."

Father Curtis begged to differ. A new wife—and a skittish one at that—and a baby on the way *were* going to be problems. Now wasn't the time to argue about it, though. Sam was still inside him. He was going flaccid, but he was still inside him.

"She won't expect me back right away. She'll know that we'll be sitting in the car in front of the rectory and talking for a while before you go in."

"But we won't be sitting in the car and talking, will we?" Father Curtis asked, his voice breathy from Sam still inside him, still stroking his nipples with his fingers.

"No, Carl, we won't just be sitting outside the rectory and talking in the car. I'm not finished with you tonight. Not by a long shot."

Debatables

It was like there was some sort of invincible band of fifteen feet surrounding those in the group of three who were sitting, looking somewhat bleary eyed, at a table in the center of the smoky bikers' bar on the edge of the town of Hot Springs. It wasn't the table that provided the isolation, because Paul and Thomas had been given the same wide berth when they had been at one of the pool tables. There had been four of them earlier, with three of them having come in a raucous mood, insistent on having a good and very-well-lubricated time. David Eagleton had gotten his fill early, though, and hadn't stayed around for the pool session—followed by several more rounds of drinks.

The bikers still in the bar at 2:00 a.m. weren't being hostile to this alien party of men who obviously had descended on them from the fancy and very expensive Homestead resort hotel up on the hill above the small Virginia mountain town. Nor were they angered that the men were older than most others in the bar, three of them being in their mid-fifties and the fourth a good twenty years older than that. The aliens were putting the liquor away well, except for the older guy, who was more a sipper and watcher. But he too accepted the drinks that were offered to him, which amazed some of the bikers, although it shouldn't have.

It was more that the bikers were bewildered. None of them could remember ever having seen a man in here in a clerical collar before—and putting beers away hand over fist—let alone accompanied by a second, older man in a dress—in a black cassock, also with clerical collar, to be more exact. Few of the bikers could imagine that an old Jesuit priest could be a boozer. But that was just because none of them had actually come in contact with a Jesuit priest before.

Somewhat pie-eyed and holding a scotch bottle by the neck, the younger priest stopped in the middle of a monologue on pranks played on campus over thirty years earlier and looked around at his companions.

"Somebody check the can to see if David's fallen in?" the younger cleric called out in a slurred voice.

"David left hours ago—before you went off to play pool, Brother Thomas," the silken, well-modulated voice of the older man, Monsignor Sardoni, quietly responded. He leaned over and touched the younger cleric's arm and added, "Perhaps it's time to go back to the hotel. The Debatables aren't on stage until the afternoon tomorrow—or, rather, today—but I have other rounds to put through in the morning."

"I think David was worried about his wife," the third man, Paul Frasier, mumbled. He hiccupped and continued. "Young blonde like that. He probably is worried about her a lot. But if it's because of Chris, I could have told him . . ." His voice trailed off.

"Worried about your Chris, Paul?" Brother Thomas asked, suddenly a bit more sober and with an amused lilt to his voice. "I doubt that's . . ." But his voice too trailed off and he gave a little laugh.

"Drink up; last calls, children," Monsignor Sardoni said. "It's time we be hanging the reminiscing up and facing life as it is."

There was a long sigh of relief and an atmosphere of comfort drifted into the bar as the three men rose, two of them quite unsteadily, from their chairs, and headed for the exit. The monsignor, although two decades older than the other men, seemed the strongest of the group, even despite the uneven distribution of the liquor. He was the tallest, standing ramrod straight, and thinnest—still with handsome Mediterranean features and a full head of steel-gray hair after all his years as a priest. Despite the austere black cassock, Sardoni was fully masculine, fully in control.

The other two, younger, but still in their mid-fifties, were a more comical pair, hanging onto each other for dear life as the monsignor guided them out into the night. It's not that they weren't good looking. On the contrary, both were very well put together. But the other cleric, Brother Thomas, was short and thin, with almost feminine features. His hair was still blond, curly, almost falling in ringlets around his head, with just enough silver running through it to make it sparkle in the light.

And his facial features were more beautiful—thick, pouting lips and startling pale-blue eyes—than handsome. The other man, Paul Frasier, a very successful TV actor, was stereotyped in mobster-type roles. He was large and hulky—not exactly fat, but thick—and was bald as a billiard cue. His black eyebrows were bushy, and when he set them in an intense look, the TV viewer quickly registered "bad boy trouble." None of this denied that he was ruggedly handsome—perhaps more so at fifty-four than he had ever been earlier in his life.

From somewhere in his flowing cassock, the monsignor, ever in control, produced a flashlight, as he preceded his two charges—young college men again in their imaginations—through the short main street of the sleeping Hot Springs toward the winding drive up to the Homestead hotel. Those of the village who were still awake smiled as the small procession passed, though. The song the two friends, hanging on to each other for dear life, were singing was in perfect harmony—Brother Thomas's tenor lilting over the steady baritone of Paul Frasier. It was a ribald drinking song that could only amuse when combined with seeing the clerical garb of one of its singers.

* * * *

"If the subject is abortion, we'll have Amvey—excuse me, Brother Thomas; I understand that you lose the last name when you put on the throat choker—handle the pro argument."

"And if it's corruption in government, you can do the pro honors, Brother David," Brother Thomas countered David Eagleton's little joke.

They were in the Jefferson bar at the Homestead Hotel doing their preliminary drinking earlier in the evening before the Debatables went out carousing in the village at the bottom of the hill. It was an expanded group, minus, for the moment, the monsignor, who was gliding around the hotel's public areas checking on his various teams for tomorrow's events. The three team members, David Eagleton, Paul Frasier, and Brother Thomas, were there, but also huddled around the cocktail table were David's young wife, Amber, and the actor Paul's personal assistant, Chris Cahill.

Amber and Chris, who were lost in a conversation on art while the three Debatables discussed strategy for the next day, were younger than the three mid-fifties team members— by some thirty years each. Amber's husband, David, was studiously not noticing that the two younger people beside him at the cocktail table were getting along famously. Amber was his third wife, a striking blonde, so David had reason ever to be aware of her moods and interests. He was insistent on getting it right this time, even if his circumstances were peculiar, including his life in the public fishbowl. For his part, Chris' employer, Paul, was visibly a bit more concerned that the young people were drifting away from the main discussion.

What the three Debatables had in common was that they were all 1981 graduates of Georgetown University in Washington, D.C., a prestigious university founded by the Jesuits, and that they had constituted the schools collegiate debating team from 1979 to 1981. They were at the ritzy Virginia mountain resort, the Homestead, this weekend, because the university faculty sponsor of all of the school's debating teams from 1980 to the present, Monsignor Sardoni, had developed a debate extravaganza around its premier team of 1980, the team that had won the national championship that year.

Over the weekend the teams of 1980, 1990, 2000, and 2010 would compete against each other in debates on topics of Monsignor Sardoni's choosing. The Debatables—that having been the name they had chosen for themselves—were the centerpiece team in this program not only because they had won a national championship but also because of what two of them had become. Paul Frasier was a well-known actor of television and (minor) movies, and David Eagleton was the U.S. congressman for New York's nineteenth congressional district. For his part, Brother Thomas was important as the glue for the entire program. He had become a Jesuit priest and remained at Georgetown, under Monsignor Sardoni's supervision, and, as an English professor, had trained and sponsored all of the school's debate teams since 1989.

"As the monsignor has selected the topics, though," Brother Thomas continued, "I seriously doubt he would select abortion—and he worked so hard to get David, here, to attend this program that I'm sure he wouldn't include a topic that might embarrass him. I would imagine that at this point in time any political topic would embarrass a sitting U.S. congressmen."

There was a smattering of friendly laughter around the table. The three men had been good-naturedly jabbing at each other all evening with witticisms that came naturally to them."That's debatable," Paul Frasier chimed in. "Sardoni has a surprising streak in him."

"Monsignor Sardoni? That stick in the mud? I don't think he'd do anything at all unseemly." This from David.

Paul and Brother Thomas stole a guarded glance at each other and then both gave a little jerk at what they'd done. Thomas recovered quickly. "Debatable. Did I hear you say 'debatable,' Paul?"

And then all three of the old team members laughed, the use of this word having been one they'd overused and laughed about in "the day."

The shared laugh of old times made David catch his breath, though, as he looked over at his wife talking to Paul's personal assistant as if the three older men weren't even there. Thomas' smile as he had laughed and now Chris Cahill's smile as he leaned into Amber to hear what she had to say struck David by the familiarity it emphasized in the two men, albeit decades apart. Paul's personal assistant today was the near double in appearance and almost feminine, sensual blond beauty that Thomas had been back in 1980. How strange, David thought. And neither one of his friends had appeared to notice that.

"What are you two talking about so seriously, sweetheart?" he leaned over to Amber and asked.

"Chris here is an artist too," she answered. "You know how I was telling you that it's so beautiful in the hills around the hotel that I was sorry I hadn't brought my acrylics? Well, Chris brought his. We were discussing the technique of rendering the light of various times of day in landscapes."

174

"Interesting," David responded, obviously not finding it the least bit interesting. But if Amber was interested in it, he would pretend to keep up. They both did pretense very well.

"We thought that we'd go out and try the late morning light tomorrow," Chris said, turning a young Brother Thomas smile on the New York politician. "We'd be sure to be back for your team's debate tomorrow evening, though," he continued.

"By all means you must catch the late morning light," David responded. He returned the smile, but other emotions were at work as he watched the two younger people talking so enthusiastically about art. The glories of art had escaped him in life, he was afraid.

Amber was looking up at a handsome young waiter who had been very attentive to her all evening and who had brought her a refill of her Margarita nearly as soon as she'd finished the first one. The two exchanged smiles as she handed the empty glass and a napkin back to him.

Amber was fast to flirt with handsome young men, David thought. He wondered how long he'd be able to hold her—although so far their unusual arrangement had held.

"Hold back a bit on the liquor, I would think, young men. It wouldn't do for our best and brightest to be too dull on the morrow."

The five people huddled around the cocktail table looked up to see that the ancient, but well-preserved, prelate who had brought them all here was approaching in a swirl of the folds of the black cassock he had continued to wear long after the Vatican had given dispensation to go more modern. On him, though, the cassock looked good. He was still thin, strong, and upright as steel after all these decades.

After pleasantries were exchanged all round, Amber excused herself, saying she knew the Debatables weren't close to turning in but that she was weary. In her wake, Chris also excused himself to go to the men's room. "And then, after checking for telegrams at reception, on to my room as well, I think," he said. "There's still a lot of Paul's work needing done in TV land this weekend."

All four men watched the younger, beautiful woman and man move off, separately, toward the hotel lobby, each of the older men thinking his own thoughts of the beauty of them and of a lost youth.

"Well, I'm for exploring the village below," declared Paul, standing.

"It's nearly midnight, Paul," Brother Thomas said, with a small laugh. "Everything will be closed in town."

"That's debatable," Paul answered, and there was a memory-dredging laugh all around. "I'm sure something will be open. Are we too old to get blotto as we always did at school the night before the debate? Have we forgotten how that sharpened our wits? Who's with me?"

"If you put it that way, how could I not rise to the challenge," Brother Thomas said.

"And I too, I guess," David said, coming to his feet. "After I visit the john first, of course. There are some aspects of aging a man simply can't escape."

As David walked off to find the men's room, Monsignor Sardoni chimed in in a false morose voice, "I suppose I must accompany you to make sure that my prize guests don't get lost in the mountains."

As the group moved toward the lobby, the waiter started picking up empty glasses and wadded napkins. He was in a bit of a hurry, and he was humming.

* * * *

"What are those over there?"

"The stables, I think. The path up to the hotel is this way, though. Tom. Tom . . ."

Brother Thomas had veered off the path toward the hotel's stables. Paul had moved a few steps in that direction, but he stopped, unsure of going beyond the circle of light shown from the monsignor's flashlight. Monsignor Sardoni was a couple of steps beyond the two inebriated friends who had been stumbling up the hill, supporting each other, but he stopped and turned back when he heard Paul calling for Tom.

"Tom . . . Tom," Paul called out again.

"Tom tom, beat the little drummer boy," Tom's voice rang out. "I want to see the horses. We don't have nearly

176

enough horses in Georgetown." The voice was coming from a bit of a distance away—uphill toward where Paul could see the line of outbuildings against the moonlit skyline.

"I suppose we must indulge him," Monsignor Sardoni said, as he passed Paul, following in the direction in which Brother Thomas had gone.

Paul and the monsignor hadn't gone far, though, before they heard a clatter, a yelp, and an expletive. When they came upon Brother Thomas, who was sitting on the path and holding his ankle, they could see that he had found not only the stables but also a pile of rakes and hoes.

"You OK, Tom?" Paul asked, bending down beside his friend.

"It's my ankle, I think."

"Can you put any weight on it?"

"In his present state, I don't think he should even try," the monsignor said brusquely. "You'd better help him into the stables and settle him comfortably, and I'll go on up to the hotel for a first aid kit and a crutch. A resort specializing in outdoor activities for the lazy rich certainly should have a store of crutches about."

When the monsignor had departed, Paul put his arms around Brother Thomas and started to raise him up.

"Don't bother, I can walk fine," Brother Thomas murmured. "I just wanted to be alone with you for a while."

"Alone with—?"

"Don't talk, Paul. It's been too long." Paul still had his arms around Brother Thomas, and the cleric pulled him further into the clutch and took Paul's lips in his. The two were transported down the years into memories of their relationship at the university.

"Oh, god," Paul croaked. "I've been hard for you all evening. I thought you had forgotten."

"Never," Brother Thomas whispered. "I want you. I can't wait until we can work something out up at the hotel."

"Why do we have to wait until we're up at the hotel?" Paul murmured. Still strong after all these years and the larger of the two, Paul scooped the cleric up from the ground and carried him into the stables. Nearly half of the stalls were empty, and there were bales of hay about, so it took no time at all for Paul to find a stall and lower Brother Thomas' belly on a hay bale. With the cleric's insistence for speed, Paul quickly had the cleric's trousers and briefs around the other man's ankles and was tonguing and fingering his ass open.

"Just like old times," Brother Thomas moaned as Paul hovered over his back, positioned his cock—which indeed had been hard for Brother Thomas all evening—and started working his way into the anal passage.

They both panted and emitted uncontrolled animal sounds as Paul thrust with his cock and Brother Thomas thrust back with his buttocks and the horses in the stalls nearby moved restlessly against their stall walls, disturbed by the strange noises coming from nearby.

Spent, Paul rolled off Brother Thomas' back and sat, his back against the stall wall beside the hay stack. Brother Thomas, in turn, lowered himself from the hay and sat with his back against the stack and his legs draped over Paul's. Instinctively, each man reached for the cock of the other and they sat there, overlapped, each slowly stroking the other, and both breathing hard. What had been easy thirty years ago no longer was, for either of them. But they both had managed as if it had only been yesterday that they had actively been lovers.

"I had almost forgotten," Paul whispered after his breathing became more controlled.

"I never did," Brother Thomas answered. "You always were the best."

"Don't let the monsignor hear you say that," Paul said with a little laugh. "And he'll be back soon."

"Not too soon," Brother Thomas said. "I timed the walk from the hotel down to here when we went down into the town. We probably have another half hour before he can get back, walking in the dark and having to find a first aid kit. And their medical office is closed at night. They'll have to find someone to open that to get a crutch."

"You mean to say you planned this?"

"Would you be upset with me if I did?" Brother Thomas asked.

"Never."

"The way your personal assistant and David's wife were getting along, I half thought he wouldn't be in the way and we could meet in my room tonight. And maybe we still can if they . . ."

"Chris and David's wife?" Paul said it with a snort. "I hardly think so."

"David certainly seemed to think so," Brother Thomas said. "He was nervous and left for the hotel early tonight. He no doubt has his young wife back in line and in his bed by now."

"Oh, you think so? You think David went back for his wife? That's highly debatable. Didn't you see how closely Chris resembles you at that age?"

"I don't know what . . . did you use the word 'debatable' again?"

They both laughed.

"Your assistant, Chris . . ." Brother Thomas now said. "You are fucking him, aren't you?"

"So you noticed," Paul answered.

"That he looks so much like I did back in 1980? Yes. You didn't have to tell me that. When I saw that is when I first believed we might be able to rekindle what we once had."

"And you aren't upset that I kept pursuing the ideal of you beyond the time we spent together?"

"Not in the slightest," Thomas answered in a quiet, hoarse voice.

"We're wasting time, you know," Paul suddenly said. "You said that Sardoni would be back in about—"

"As you said, we're wasting time," Brother Thomas said, as he came up on his knees and covered Paul's mouth with his.

This time, with Brother Thomas lying on the small of his back on the hay bale, and a trouserless Paul hunched between the smaller man's spread and lifted legs, his ankles held in Paul's fists, the two took a bit too long in the fuck. And they failed to anticipate how silently Monsignor Sardoni could move in the night.

He was there, inside the stable, watching them, for several minutes before they became aware of his presence.

When they did, it was after the monsignor had slowly unbuttoned the thirty-three buttons of his cassock and spread the cassock apart, showing not only that he was naked underneath but also that a firm erection jutted out from his gray pubic bush.

Somewhat shocked, but the scenario being too clear for Paul to bother to try to hide it, Paul turned his head to the monsignor. He didn't seem all that surprised that the priest was naked and erect under his cassock. "You didn't have time to get to the hotel and back—and I don't see a first aid kit. Have you been—?"

"I've been watching from the shadows the entire time, yes," Sardoni said. "I figured that Brother Thomas would be at you for this. I didn't buy into his charade of a twisting ankle. And you know what I want now."

It was only after the monsignor had saddled up behind Paul and had thrust inside him and was fucking him from behind while Paul was fucking Brother Thomas missionary style that the mentor and his students of thirty years previously were truly traveling back down memory lane.

* * * *

The three were not exactly missed by those they'd left back at the hotel. David Eagleton, who had carried a crush for Brother Thomas all these years but had suppressed it because Monsignor Sardoni was in control and Paul Frasier had been there first, had been deeply taken with Chris Cahill earlier in the evening. Chris so closely resembled the young Thomas, who David had pined for but had never won, that David was smitten by him. David followed Chris to the men's room from the Jefferson bar and was delighted to find that Chris had no problem with being propositioned by him. Chris wasn't just Paul Frasier's personal assistant; he also was Paul Frasier's boy toy.

While Paul and the clerics were having their memory-lane threesome in the stables, David Eagleton was thoroughly into Chris—in the literal meaning of that word—in Chris's room at the hotel. And David wasn't the least bit worried about where his young wife, Amber, was or what she was doing. They had an arrangement for political reasons.

Amber wasn't being overlooked, however. The message she'd passed to their waiter in the Jefferson bar had had its immediate—and intended—effect. Those two, young, beautiful people were fucking like rabbits in an empty room the waiter had purloined with the help of a friend at the reception desk.

Senegal Surrender

I tried to make sense out of the last several days as the plane began its descent across the eastern Atlantic into the peninsular city of Dakar, capital of Senegal. From there it would be several hours of a dusty ride northeast to the village of Sagata, in Louga Province. I tried hard not to think of this as a banishment, and why it might have been banishment baffled me. The bishop had seduced me. I hadn't been anything but reserved in the monastery until he had lain with me—or, more pointedly until I had agree to lay under him. I was very careful because of my past. But then, of course, Bishop Dominic had known of my past. And with the power that gave him over me, what choice did I have but to lay under him when he commanded that of me?

It was black men—large, muscular black men—who had been my downfall. Bishop Dominic was a large black man. The man sitting next to me in the plane was one too. Big, muscular, a heady musky scent of masculinity about him. Someone who could hold me captive and have his way with me, as men had when I was working the streets of New Orleans—before I was saved, brought into the Catholic Church, and given purpose and a cassock.

I sensed that the man sitting next to me in the plane—most probably a Senegalese businessman—was interested in me. But he hadn't signaled nor did I expect him to. My black cassock now was a barrier to that. I had taken up the priesthood for the barrier it would provide.

It didn't provide a barrier to Bishop Dominic. He'd said that it was a reality of his sect of the Liberal Catholic Church, a progressive, serving church that worked the streets of New Orleans—the soup kitchens and the food pantries, the addiction and AIDS clinics, and the counseling for the downtrodden and social victims. I had been such a victim of society, he told me. I grew up virtually on the street. And being small of stature, more pretty than handsome, and vulnerable, I

182

was able to survive on the streets of New Orleans only by selling my body to men.

That had all changed, of course, with the Liberal Catholic Church took me in, gave me a home and a purpose, and sent me through seminary. Bishop Dominic had guided me the whole way. And when I was under his charge, in his monastery, he explained to me that his was a particularly liberal sect of the Liberal Catholic Church. He said that, although certain things were banned, personal pleasure and physical release weren't—and receiving this from and giving it to other men wasn't irrevocably counted as a sin. Bishop Dominic certainly had his way with walking the edge. There were limits, though, to what would stop short of sin in men having their pleasure with other men. Physical penetration was a sin. These limits didn't prevent him from touching me and kissing me. And it didn't prevent him from coming to my cell in the night, lying beside me, and touching me intimately to evoke physical release and urging me to do the same with him.

Release was good and necessary, he'd said. It wasn't sodomy in his sect's definition of the term. The full meaning of this meant nothing to me at the time. I probably should have asked for specific guidance. Over the weeks the touching led to grasping and stroking with the hand—and providing sexual release, first him masturbating me and this moving into the two of us masturbating each other simultaneously. Eventually, it went to him lying on top of me or stretched out behind me, or the two of us standing, and him holding me close, and masturbating me while I held his cock between my thighs and he stroked it there to an ejaculation.

There was a steady escalation of the need for arousal and release, though, and one night we were breathing hard and writhing against each other, his shaft between my thighs, his hand on my cock, and I begged, "Do it. Take me. Don't tease me anymore. Fuck me."

I was in such a state of arousal, having had men inside me before, that my mind went to all of the black bulls— muscular, powerful men just like the bishop—who had taken me fully. My need and pleading moved his arousal beyond his control, and he brought his thick, hard cock up, entered my ass slowly but deeply, and began to move it increasingly vigorously inside me. I had been fucked—and roughly so—before. There was nothing I was doing with him that I had not experienced with men before. We bucked against each other to a shared ejaculation, his shaft deep inside my channel. He satisfied my need as well as any man had done. I could tell that he had been equally moved and satisfied—at least to the fulfillment of his release.

It then had been as if he'd been struck by lightning, though. He sprang from the bed and ran out of the cell, crying out "Sodomy!" Moments later he reappeared, demanded to take my confession as a tempter, and handed me a hand whip. My penance was painful and self-inflicted. He assured me that his would be too. He stayed around to ensure I used the whip on myself and it seemed to me that he enjoyed watching that.

I didn't see him after that. I was confined to my cell. Two days later I was called into the presence of Father Mark, Bishop Dominic's confessor, and informed that I was leaving imminently for a foreign mission assignment to a Liberal Catholic Church community church and school in Sagata, Senegal. It was, of course, spoken of as a privilege and a progression of my training as a Catholic priest. I had difficulty seeing it that way.

I didn't understand what I had done. I didn't understand the difference between what Bishop Dominic seduced me into doing and what sodomy was—at least how the bishop's sect defined sodomy.

* * * *

The two men, both big, black, muscular brutes, wearing loincloths were wrestling in the center of a crudely marked ring in the dust at the center of the village. Each was trying to take the other down as they locked chests, embraced each other with muscular arms, and danced around in a circle. It aroused me. I knew both of the men, and both of them aroused me even when they weren't pitting muscle against muscle in a dance of control and domination. I was hard inside my black cassock, and I so wanted to touch myself. But there was no way of doing so in the public square without attracting notice.

Idrissa, the rectory's cook and housekeeper, tall, willowy, and dark brown, stood beside me, egging the men on. One of the men in the ring, Malik, was my driver—and Idrissa's lover. The two made little effort to hide their sex play from me. Indeed, when I had been driven from the airport—by Malik—to the bishopric in Dakar, Bishop Jawara, yet another black giant, had alluded to the relationship between the two.

"There is a certain intimacy going on in the rectory of your church and school, Brother Gordon," he said. "I didn't want you to think I didn't know and would worry about telling me, but the men aren't priests and we are a tolerant sect. They are both good men—and are faithful to the church. You will find that life in this part of the world is simpler and more primeval than in most."

The bishop was standing close to me when he said that, touching the sleeve of my cassock, and exuding the same manly musky scent as the man sitting next to me on the plane had done. Because of my past, I had difficulty sometimes determining when a man was being friendly and solicitous and when he wanted to be intimate. This was such a moment.

As we had moved into the aisle when the plane landed, that man on the plane had touched me as well, given me a look of lust, and murmured, "It's a pity you are a priest."

He had stood there momentarily waiting, I am sure, for me to respond that being a priest need not be an impediment. He knew, from having looked in my lap, that I had gone hard on the plane from our arms and thighs brushing. They had come into contact because he was such a massive man that he took up more than his allotted seat space. I think he could smell the arousal on me as I had smelled the musky maleness and sex on him.

But, my back still smarting from the penance I had done for the sin of sodomy—even though I'd been the one penetrated rather than the one doing the penetration—I held myself in check with the man on the airplane.

It was rough, still being hard from the closeness of him, upon seeing my driver, yet another powerfully built black man, holding the sign with my name on it at the arrivals gate.

"Thank you for the guidance, Father," I'd said to Bishop Jawara, willing him to move away from me. The man on the plane had put me in the mood. I was being sorely tempted, first by the man on the plane; then with fantasies of being fucked in the backseat of the church automobile by the driver, Malik; and then thoughts of being laid out on the desk in the bishopric and dominated by Bishop Jawara, who was standing so close to me and touching me in a way that he probably saw as friendliness but that I was receiving as the wish for intimacy.

I knew I had to fight these feelings. I knew that I was here because I hadn't been successful yet in doing so. It helped, though, to know that Malik's sexual interest lay elsewhere, even if under my own roof.

The other wrestler in the ring was someone I knew too—the auto mechanic who kept the church automobile in top shape and a close friend of Malik's—close enough to visit us often. And close enough for Idrissa and Malik openly to scheme also for him to become my lover. It was as if they knew about my struggles, and, increasingly, I came to believe that they did.

Idrissa and Malik did little to hide their intimacy from me. Idrissa slept in the house and Malik in a room over the garage, but in those first few weeks that I was learning my way in this new situation, I saw them together frequently—kissing and touching each other. And Idrissa's door would be open more than a slit when they were on his bed, locked together and rocking back and forth. They did a lot of penile play, stroking each other, Malik stroking their cocks together—much as Bishop Dominic had done with me—but they carried this through to consummation, Malik's shaft inside Idrissa's channel, and Idrissa, the thinner, more willowy of the two, moaning his surrender.

At the height of my frustration of witnessing this, Jakab, the auto mechanic, started visiting the compound. He joined the small church choir I put together, enriching the sound with his silky-smooth deep bass. He was on the front pew for Sunday mass, his hulking presence unavoidable as there rarely were more than a dozen at mass. Suddenly, our ancient Land Rover was needing almost constant attention, and Jakab would be there, stripped to the waist, his muscular torso gleaming with a sheen of sweat as he and Malik worked on the car. Malik occasionally peeked to see if I was watching, which, of course, I was.

Increasingly, Jakab looked up to catch my gaze as well, his look being the familiar look of lust I'd so often seen in the eyes of the men I serviced before taking up the priesthood—and occasionally since then as well. I'd seen it in the eyes of Bishop Dominic and in the eyes of the man on the plane. I'd even seen it in the eyes of Bishop Jawara in Dakar, although at the time I had tried to convince myself that this wasn't so.

I'd only seen it for each other in the eyes of Idrissa and Malik, though, so it was much a relief to me when the day came that Idrissa suggested I accompany them to a swimming lake some ten miles into the bush from Sagata. I went willingly, stripped off my cassock without inhibition just as the two of them stripped down, when we had walked to the side of the lake from the Land Rover, and went immediately into the water. Idrissa and Malik came into the water too, but I remained separated from them, as they were being intimate in their embrace in the water. I stayed in rather longer than they did, swimming out to the middle of the lake and back before I swam back to the shore.

When I came out of the water, I saw that Malik and Idrissa were sitting, naked, barely concealed in a bed of tall ferns at the base of an umbrella tree. Malik was sitting cross-legged with Idrissa in his lap, facing him. The two were totally engrossed in each other and in each other's pleasure as they engaged in the special penile play I'd seen them taken with in the rectory. They were kissing, Idrissa's hand caressing Malik's biceps, as Malik encased their cocks together and stroked them in an act I knew by the term frottage.

I should have gathered my cassock and gone on back to the Land Rover to wait for them to be finished, but instead, infused with arousal and need, I crouched down to where I could watch them enjoying each other's bodies without being in the direct line of sight of either.

I watched, panting quietly and fondling my own cock and balls as Malik repositioned their cocks, docking them, pressing the bulbs together and pulling the foreskin of his thick cock over the longer, slimmer cock of Idrissa. I could hear Idrissa's deep moans as Malik held the two cocks together, the tips of their cock bulbs caressing each other, both covered by Malik's foreskin. He was stroking the two cocks together.

My fingers went to the bulb of my own cut cock, the shaft hard now from the effect of watching the two beautiful naked black Senegalese men making their bodies one, rocking back and forth, and moaning their shared pleasure. As I'd seen Malik doing with Idrissa earlier, I worried the urethra opening of my cock head with the pinky of one hand until it opened for me and gave me penetration. At the same time I spat on the fingers of my other hand, reached under my buttocks, resting on my calves in the crouch, and found my passage opening with the wetted fingers. I was able to open myself up and reach my prostate with my fingertips. I vaguely realized that this was penetration, and thus farther than my sect permitted me to go. It wasn't penile penetration, though, which seemed to be Bishop Dominic's primary concern. I was too aroused for a theological discussion on that, though. My sexual frustration had become overpowering.

Idrissa gave a little cry and Malik pulled his foreskin back off the bulbs of their cocks to reveal that Idrissa had come, slathering their cock bulbs in seminal fluid. Immediately, Malik tipped Idrissa's pelvis back with an arm around the slimmer, smaller man's back, pushed his own hard cock down with the other hand, and pulled Idrissa's hips into his, slowly impaling Idrissa's passage on Malik's thick shaft. The two embraced closely with arms wrapped around the other's torsos and lips possessed by the lips of the other, and Malik sent them into a rocking motion that had his cock moving in Idrissa's passage.

Sodomy, I thought. This was definitely sodomy in my sects' books. But Bishop Jawara had specifically told me that the church servants lived under different restrictions than the village priest did.

Still, I longed to be taken as Idrissa was being taken.

I continued fucking my urethra slit with my pinky and my passage up to my knuckles, reaching and rubbing my prostate. I was about to come when I noticed movement in the foliage off to the right of the obliviously fucking couple. We weren't alone. There weren't just three of us here. I was distressed to see the hulking, muscular body of the Senegalese auto mechanic, Jakab, rise up from behind tall ferns. He was magnificently naked and cupping a gigantic erection with his hand.

I don't know if he had been watching Malik and Idrissa fuck as I had or had been watching me, but it didn't matter. He was looking at me with a lust in his eyes that couldn't be mistaken. And I was in an unmistakably compromised position.

Both fearful and overwhelmed with arousal and an aching need I had to struggle with, I rose, turned, and started walking into the field of four-foot-high elephant grass behind me. I had no conscious idea why I went in that direction rather than toward the safety of the Land Rover, if indeed the Land Rover could have offered sanctuary.

Jakab had signaled his interest in and desire for me in so many ways in the previous few weeks that I couldn't misunderstand his lust and intentions. I heard him behind me, walking carefully, but then increasing speed, as I was doing.

I was running and thrashing through the elephant grass, with Jakab easily narrowing the distance between us, as, panting heavily and whimpering, he caught and tackled me from behind in a wallow by the side of the lake where the grass had been beaten down by wild animals.

There was no preparation, no foreplay, no time for discussion or pleading. Jakab, towering over me and sixty pounds my better in muscular weight and a Senegalese wrestling champion to boot, came down on my back, collapsing me to the ground. His fists grabbed my wrists, forcing my arms above my head.

He growled only one statement, as his knees forced my thighs apart, "Up on your knees; raise your ass to me." Moaning deeply and terrified of the size of him, but needing him so, so badly, I responded as he demanded, raising my buttocks with my knees, presenting myself for his taking. And take me he did, huffing and puffing as I sobbed and writhed in pained response to the difficulty of sheathing his thick cock inside me with no more preparation than the opening I'd done of the channel myself.

But then he was inside me, deep, and began to pump me and I was lost to everything but the feel of the throbbing shaft filling and stretching me, mastering me in glorious pain-pleasure that I had wanted from him for too long.

He didn't torture-pleasure me for long. Just a few minutes of deep stroking and he came inside my channel in a series of explosions. I hadn't had time or opportunity to come myself, imprisoned as I was under him with my wrists trapped over my head. But Jakab proceeded to take care of that himself.

"As you enjoyed watching Malik do to Idrissa," he said for the first time after commanding me to give myself to him, and as he said that, he rolled over into a cross-legged sitting position and pulled me into his lap. He held our cocks together, me still hard, he only half-erect now, but massive in size, and started to stroke our cocks. Exhausted from the fury of his fucking before, I let my torso fall back, shoulder blades pressed into the beaten elephant grass and arms stretched out in surrender and supplication.

When I felt him press the bulbs of the two cocks together, though, and his foreskin stretching over the bulb of my cock, I pulled myself up, grasped his bulging biceps as Idrissa had down with Malik, and pressed the top of my head between his pectorals. My eyes were downcast, watching Jakab caressing the bulbs of our cocks against each other inside his covering foreskin as he stroked the two shafts together. I was panting and so was he, both of us building up in intensity, his cock engorging again.

Building quickly up to a climax, I cried out and came inside the fusing of our docked cocks. He pulled his foreskin back to let my cum burble over the heads of both cocks. As Malik had done with Idrissa, though, he gave me no time to respond in any way, although my impulse was to go into an intimate and closely embracing kiss.

He tipped me back, pulled my passage onto his cock, deep, grasped my hips with his hands, and began to pull me on and off his reinvigorated shaft.

"No, no, we can't. I can't," I cried out. "I can't go this far." But he laughed and proved that he could and that I could. I gave up the struggle and gave into lust when he was several inches inside me. Once again, I allowed my torso to fall back onto the beaten elephant grass, spread my arms out wide, and totally surrendered to the mastery of his fuck.

I could have escaped him after he fucked me that first time, although it wouldn't mitigate my sin no matter how many times he fucked me here now. When he was finished seeding me again, he rose, ran to the water, and dove in. He spent a good twenty minutes playing in the water. As soon as he had entered it and come up again for air, he let out a war whoop of victory—which, I'm ashamed to say, made me grin—and made like a dolphin playing in the lake. At any time, I could have gotten up, returned to where I had come out of the lake myself, retrieved my cassock, and returned to the Land Rover. But I didn't do this. I also didn't join Jakab in the lake. I was torn between joining him and begging him to fuck me again in the water and my duty to fight my baser desires and escape the situation.

I was still struggling with myself when he came out of the water, flopped down beside me, and reached for my cock. Turning all thoughts off from what I should do, I lay there, stretched out, beside him, taking his cock in my hand as well, and we masturbated each other to a mutually timed ejaculation, managed by the two of us whispering to each other about the pleasure each was giving to the other and how close we were to releasing. After we had released, he rolled over on top of me, taking my breath away as he pinned me to the elephant grass matting under me, and, for the first time, covered me with kisses, as I reciprocated.

As he regained his vigor, which didn't take the young, virile bull long, he stood, bringing me up with him, draped my body in front of his, facing away from him, his cock up my ass channel, holding me in a bear hug, with me wrapping my legs around his thighs and digging my ankles into his calves, as he fucked me to another of his ejaculations.

He was on top of me, between my bent legs, kissing me on the mouth, and fucking me deep in a missionary position, when darkness overtook us and, at last, I realized that this glorious day was over—a day that I would have to put out of my mind; a day that I would have to scourge myself raw for in seeking penance.

I pulled out from underneath him then and stumbled back to the Land Rover, riddled with guilt, no less than because I was totally satiated with having been repeatedly sodomized anally in the eyes of my church. Jakab, thankfully, didn't follow me. Somehow we both would need to forget that this happened, I thought, and I would need to seek penance.

Malik and Idrissa were waiting beside the Land Rover, knowing what Jakab and I had been doing, probably very pleased with themselves for having brokered that.

I wouldn't forget it anytime soon, though, I knew as I climbed into my bed that night. My back was raw from my having knelt in front of the altar in my bedroom, murmured my sins, and struck myself on the back again and again with the many-strands hand whip with the knotted ends. I moaned as I turned to my side, unable to sleep on my back.

And I knew I could not forget what had happened, when I heard and felt the springs of the bed complain as the massive naked body of Jakab stretched out, facing me, and, as his lips went to mine, his hand docked our cocks, his foreskin pulled over my bulb, the tips of the two bulbs caressing, as he stroked me to a burbling flow with the sheath of his foreskin.

"Please, please, I want you to fuck me, but I can't, I just can't. My faith, I—"

"I've already fucked you, and I'm going to do it again," Jakab responded. "I've made you come; I've given you release. I am not sodomizing you tonight, though. Isn't that what the bishops have been telling you not to do? I did it this afternoon, as my reward and as a humbling concession to your need for you, and I feel that your back is raw from your penance for that. We are at a new beginning. I will take you in other ways but sodomy now and you can make peace with yourself while still finding release."

I sighed as he drew us closer, forcing his long, thick cock between my closed thighs and beginning to stroke, as he reached between us, fisted my cock, and masturbated me.

"Like this, nearly every night," he murmured. "No penetration. No sodomy. But repeated release."

"But how long can you——?"

"Until you come to peace with yourself. Until you realize that you cannot live without having me inside you. Other priests have come to terms with it. I think you will too. I can wait—for the reward of someday being inside you again."

* * * *

"Yes, I know your sin," Bishop Jawara said when I visited him for confession and consultation in his office the next day. I stood just inside the French window out onto a balcony, not able to be seen from the outside but looking at seminary students walking across a quad. I found I was unable to face the bishop. "Yes, I sent Jakab to you, Brother Gordon—just as Bishop Dominic sent you to me."

"Sent me to you?"

"Yes. Am I making myself clear?"

"I . . . I don't know," I stammered.

"I think I *am* making myself clear. We are a liberal sect, taking a literal interpretation of sodomy, but you wanted your bishop to cross that line. You have had to learn the difference between sodomy and pleasurable release of tension. Jakab has been a means for showing that to you. When you were sodomized by him—by one-time dispensation—you rightly saw that as sin, and your self-punishment penance for that was proper. What Jakab said he did with you last night is within acceptable bounds—there was no penetration yet I think you found that there was sufficient release. I'm afraid Jakab has fallen for you and wants to go further, though. Bishop

Dominic and I are asking you to just not take it farther than Jakab did last night. Do you understand?"

"I'm beginning to," I answered. And I was. I didn't flinch as I felt his presence now close behind me.

"I feel I must withdraw Jakab from you now, as he is losing the sense of restraint with you. But he will be replaced by someone who does know the limits and will keep within them while still giving you the pleasure you desire."

He was reaching around and gathering my cassock up around my waist. As he pushed my briefs down, and I stepped out of them, I realized that he was naked, his hard cock pressing at the base of my spine. I whimpered at the thought of what was happening.

"And do you understand that I am asking you to do that with me now and then with Bishop Dominic when you return to New Orleans? Far enough for pleasure and release, but no farther?"

"Ah."

"Fear not," he whispered. "There will be no penetration. No sodomy by our sect's interpretation. Penetration is not required to give either of us release and peace." One of his hands went to my cock and the other one to my chin, cupping it pulling my head back and turning it so that we could kiss.

His hard cock slipped into my crack, between my buttocks, the underside against my entrance, rubbing up and down inside the crack. I understood that it would continue to do so until the bishop ejaculated and that his stroking of my cock with his hand—coupled with the arousal his attentions brought—would bring me to completion too. I was to stand here, in his embrace, until we both had had our pleasure and release. And I now understood that there would be no penetration, that, according to the unrecorded tenets of my sect what the bishop did with me would not be sodomy, and therefore, I would not have to do penance for what I now was enjoying.

I would try, and I hoped it would be enough. But I'd had more from men—so much more. My thoughts went to Jakab. I was losing care for these fine edges the priests of this sect were trying to adhere to in what form of sodomy was a sin and what wasn't. I thought that perhaps—just perhaps—I would live with Bishop Jawara's boundaries when I was with him and keep my own counsel from now on when I was with Jakab.

Fitting In

"But you don't have classes today, do you?"

I was sitting in the dean's office, steeped in the Gothic architecture and trappings, including the imposing stained-glass window behind where he sat, of the older buildings on the Georgetown University campus. Georgetown was the premier Jesuit educational institution in the United States, sitting on the heights beside the Potomac River just to the south of the government center of Washington, D.C. It was a real privilege for me to be able to teach there. It was hard not to say yes to anything the monsignor requested in this setting. This was especially so, since I was a Jesuit priest myself and charged to obey.

I must say that it also was because I deeply admired the monsignor and considered him my principle guide in life.

"No, Monsignor," I answered, but it was not a welcome task. "But I was planning to catch up on grading essays and a test—and in visiting the shelter and clinic up on P street." I was an assistant professor of American literature at the university but we all had duties in the Washington, D.C., community as well. Mine were at the P Street gay men's shelter and clinic, where I counseled the homeless and otherwise lost. I had been lost myself once and had been found by the Jesuits.

"As you know, Father Ormand, from Paris, is joining our faculty to teach French literature for a semester," the monsignor continued, not responding immediately to my weak attempt to beg off. "As he is in your department, I had thought you would help him fit in . . . starting with giving him a tour of the university today. But if you . . ."

"No, that's fine. I can certainly do that," I answered. There goes all of my plans for today—and possibly for days to come, I thought. "Is he—?"

"He should be along in a few minutes. Thank you for doing this, Mark. It will be a help to him for fitting in, and I think it will be a help to you, as well."

"I help to me?" I asked. I no longer bridled at his use of my given name to address me. It initially had seemed too familiar when I was struggling not to be too familiar with the church leader. Georgetown wasn't exactly liberal church, where now some Catholic institutions were dropping all use of titles altogether and even not dressing in clerical dress, but it had come half way. The monsignor could use given names for those lower in the order, and those on the same level could use given names with each other—but the old ways held for addressing a superior. And, although we didn't wear cassocks here except on formal occasions, we did dress in black and wear the clerical collar.

I was relieved that the monsignor wore the clerical collar. It was a constant reminder to me of the limits to our relationship.

"You seem to have had your own difficulties fitting in here, Mark. You seem like an affable chap by nature, but you are withdrawn here. You hold yourself in isolation. I think it would be good for you to spend more time with others. Having Father Ormand to show around should give you more contact with others. I'm not asking you to do this entirely for his benefit. You would benefit from more contact with your colleagues too. I know there was that business at the seminary before coming to us, but you mustn't punish yourself forever. I think—"

"Yes, Monsignor. I understand. Thank you for thinking of me." I couldn't stand the thought of him bringing up the seminary and what had happened there. In reality, I couldn't really understand him knowing about it at all—or the Sword of Damocles that hovered over my head continually from that period in my life. I hadn't thought of doing anything in life other than being a Jesuit priest and scholar. I couldn't imagine being forced to be anything else. The monsignor didn't seem to understand. My reticence and isolation were the penance I had sought to be able to continue as a priest—and were a self-imposed barrier to unclean thoughts of others, including the monsignor himself.

"Ah, there he is now," Baum said, standing and looking to the door to the outer corridor, a smile of welcome on his face.

Following the monsignor's line of sight, I swiveled my head and simultaneously went hot and cold and felt a stirring in my groin. He was gorgeous. Dark and sultry, his lips full and sensuous. Despite the dark, wavy hair, his eyes were a pale blue. His smile went into his eyes, scrunching up at the corners in honest laugh lines. He must be in his forties, I thought—his early forties, maybe. Just like Philip. His effect on me was just like what Philip had had. He was solidly built, muscular, on the rugby player form. I counted my blessings for the barrier of the clerical color he and I both wore.

His eyes went directly to the monsignor but then slid off his figure to me. Did I detect the smile becoming warmer then? Back to the monsignor, but almost immediately back to me before taking the proper stance of looking directly at the monsignor, walking toward him, and going down on his knee.

"Come now, none of that formality, Christophe," Baum said, pleasure clearly showing in his face. Despite the disclaimer of the old-style bending of the knee to a far superior, the monsignor put out his hand for the priest to kiss before putting a hand on his shoulder and bidding him to rise.

In the meantime, I was hyperventilating and madly trying to come up with reasons why I, in fact, was too busy today to show the French priest around. This was disaster. It was the devil's work.

"Christophe, I want you to meet our Mark Redmond. He teaches in the literature department too—American literature—and has gracefully volunteered to show you around today—to help you fit in at Georgetown."

"Father Redmond," the Frenchman said, turning his mesmerizing blue eyes on me. He took my hand, and for a second I thought he'd lift it to those sensuous lips of his and kiss it. But he didn't. "I thank you for taking the time to show me around. I know you must be a busy young man."

"No problem. My pleasure . . . Father Ormand," I managed to squeak out. He was denoting the difference in our ages, but treating me as a superior. I could do no less than return the title of respect.

"Come now, it should be Christophe and Mark between you," the monsignor said in a jolly voice. "You two are, I'm sure, going to become close friends here."

My heart was beating fast. I'd already had a close friend like Christophe and it had nearly destroyed my life.

* * * *

The tour of the Georgetown campus had moved out from the academic buildings to the student centers and arrived, eventually, at the Ginsburg Sports Center.

"You must be worn out from all of the walking," I said, half hoping that Father Ormand indeed was tired and ready to go back to the visiting priest faculty residence. Having to turn to him every few minutes and see that glorious smile and the pale blue eyes to be lost in was getting to be much too disconcerting for me. This was what I was trying to escape, deny myself to.

"Not at all," Christophe answered. "In fact, I wish I had my sports gear here. This facility looks great and I really need to get the kinks out. What I wouldn't give for a game of racquetball just now." They were standing across the glass wall from what was an empty racquetball court. "Do you play racquetball?"

"Yes, I do," I admitted. It was one of the fastest ways to keep one's body in trim.

"That would be just what I could use right now to top off my day."

So, if he got in a game they could wrap this up and the torture would stop, I wondered. "I have my gear in a locker here," I said. "And I have extra shorts, T-shirts, and jocks . . . if you really want to play. I see that the court is free for a couple of hours yet." I half hoped it wasn't.

"That would be great. I feel sluggish from the lack of exercise. And the shorts and jock will be sufficient. These sneakers should be good enough too."

I almost hyperventilated at the thought he wanted to go skins. But we just walked for over an hour and a half, I thought. Just how full of energy is he?

Quite full, it turned out, as we had an active game in which Christophe, looking magnificent playing skins, his chest and arms covered in silky black down, danced circles around me, making me feel like I was the sluggish one. For such a solidly built man—not fat, by any means, but with a hard body that was thick and muscular—the Frenchmen moved quickly and gracefully.

We both got a good workout, though, raising a sheen of healthy sweat on our bodies. I had pulled off my athletic T toward the end of the game as well to try to get cooler and to equalize the field of play. Christophe patted me on the back and butt as we walked, close beside each other, to the locker room and the communal shower. I got a charge out of it, but reasoned that he probably was just being French.

Christophe was completely uninhibited in the shower, contrasted to my own efforts at more modesty. He frankly looked directly at me, turning three quarters toward me, as I turned three quarters from Christophe to soap up. I made every attempt to hide my half hard, cut cock. Christophe didn't. He was uncut and horse hung. Whereas I drew my body in as I showered and was the last one in the shower and the first one to leave, Christophe proudly stretched his body out, having every right to be proud of his hard body, and covered all crevices and curves with the soaped sponge. He spent considerable time soaping up his groin.

I almost hyperventilated again when, stealing a glance at Christophe that I couldn't help from doing frequently, I saw Christophe pull his foreskin back to soap up and rinse his bulb, revealing that it was pierced and had a gold ball near the tip of it.

Rinsing off as quickly as I could, I was out of the shower and into my briefs and trousers, hiding a full hard on and having a bit of trouble fitting it into the crotch of my pants, when, naked and walking proud and with a half hard on, Christophe strutted out of the shower. He put a hand on my bare back as he passed me to reach the guest locker assigned to him. I almost moaned and could feel the burn of the palm of the man's palm on my back after Christophe had cleared past me.

It was the devil's work. I was being tempted, I knew. It was a good thing that Father Ormand wasn't "like that." He was so open and unconcerned about our nakedness that my plight and temptation couldn't have entered his mind. There was the half hard monster cock, of course, but he had handled it at length while soaping off—he'd thoroughly worked his entire body with the soap and sponge. I had almost embarrassed myself from not being able to stop stealing glances. At least the ordeal was about over, I thought. I'd take him to the visiting residence facility now and try to forget him.

"I'd like to see more of Georgetown," Christophe said as he pulled on his briefs. "I understand that it was a town before the capital grew up around it. I feel like having a drink now. I've heard of a place up on P Street that I'd like to try. Do you have time to join me . . . and help guide me how to P Street? I'll buy."

"Sure, I'd be happy to," I responded. Oh, shit, I thought. When will the agony of this temptation end?

* * * *

I was surprised as we moved into Georgetown and Christophe told me what bar he was looking for. But I didn't know how to tell him about the bar and why Christophe might not want to go there after all. So, in my weakness and cowardice I said nothing and led Christophe into the bar, which was just down the street from the clinic and homeless shelter where I did volunteer work.

Still, when the bartender hailed me with a "Hi, Father Redmond. Haven't seen you around for a while," I felt my cheeks begin to burn and ready to shrivel up into a ball. I hastily ushered Christophe to a table near the back. It's true I hadn't been in here for more than a month. I only came in here when I was looking for someone who hadn't made his appointment for counseling at the clinic and I could be fairly certain the man would be in here.

"What made you pick this bar?" I asked as we settled at a downstairs table at The Fireplace on P Street.

"Monsignor Baum told me you volunteered time at a clinic in this neighborhood. I had hoped that your showing me around would include that—maybe it would be something I could help with too. I studied to be a doctor before entering the priesthood. I have a nursing degree. From the States even—Colombia in New York."

"Ah, I wondered by your English was impeccable," I said. "Did the monsignor tell you what sort of clinic it is?"

"Yes, of course," Christophe answered. "Does it embarrass you for it to be known that you work with gay men?"

"No, I suppose not. They need the support and succor of the church as anyone else," I answered. Did Christophe know, though, that the bar he had sought out was also gay friendly? I could have told that by looking around at who was in here. But Christophe wasn't looking around much. He was devoting his attention to me—almost to an embarrassing degree.

"Well, I'm relieved to hear that," he said, as he looked up and smiled at the bartender who had brought mugs of beer over to them. The bartender grinned back, which made me cringe a bit. Donny, the barman, was obviously gay and on the make. And we obviously were on friendly terms. Even the priests collars wasn't seen as a barrier to him if the man looked macho. And Christophe quite definitely looked macho. "I'm relieved to hear that because I don't want there to be any discomfort between us," Christophe said as he turned his attention back to me.

"Discomfort?" I asked, taking a big swig of my beer, setting up a barrier between me and any serious conversation with this man who was driving me wild in an arena that I was fighting mightily to stay out of.

"Yes, I want to fit in here at the university—and I want to fit in with you, in particular."

"Oh, well," I said, at a loss for words. I took another gulp of my beer. But I knew this wasn't a good idea either. It wouldn't be good to lose control to the booze. I'd let that happen before, with tragic results—although it certainly didn't seem that way as long as that ride lasted. I looked up into Christophe's face. He was taking a long draw on his beer too, but his eyes were boring into me from above the rim of the mug.

"Yes, I'm heartened that you work with the gays of the community and accept them. Acceptance is important with me—especially when it has to live in a world of secret where it suppresses and puts a man in isolation. I understand you are a counselor at this clinic of yours. You must counsel men who have this problem—although I would ascribe the problem not to the men you counsel but to those who condemn them."

"Yes, of course," I answered. I feared that the response sounded strained. I could hardly breathe.

"And what do you counsel these men to do, Mark? Do you tell them not to have the urges and preferences they have?"

"No, of course not."

"Do you tell them they must withdraw into themselves and try to deny their feelings and desires even to themselves?"

"No. I tell them . . ." I couldn't say it.

"You tell them accept the feelings and inclinations they have and to try to find someone special . . . someone they can be comfortable with, can fit in with, don't you?"

"Yes." It came out in a whisper. How did he know so precisely what I told them? And, no, what he was saying—through what I myself counseled men in the same position I was in—wasn't lost on me.

"Look at me, Mark."

I looked up into Christophe's eyes. Christophe reached across the table and took my hand and held it in his. Panicked and trapped, I looked around the bar, but everyone else was absorbed in someone else. Everyone here was here with someone. Even Donny, the bartender, was engrossed in an intimate conversation with a big bruiser at the bar.

"It's hard for a Jesuit priest," Christophe said. "It's hard for a Jesuit priest to be gay and to exist within the church—to do what he knows what his purpose is in being a priest without being able to fully and openly be himself . . . true

203

to himself. We are lucky, you and I, that we are in an order that takes a very forgiving and supportive view of all of this."

"You don't understand. . . you just couldn't . . ." Again I couldn't say it; couldn't bring myself out of the depths.

"Yes, I do know it, Mark. I'm gay. I'm a gay Jesuit priest. But I worked my way through it and came to a reconciliation of who I am—and what I do in the church. I was like you at the beginning, in the seminary. No, don't pull away from me. You are gay too. We both know it. And we both know that you are attracted to me as I am attracted to you. I'm a dominant and you are a submissive. We are a fit. You want to lie with me; I've seen it in your eyes. I saw it in the shower. I want to cover you as much as you want me to. I can help you become reconciled to what you must do to maneuver in the church and still be comforted and you can make my time in Georgetown complete."

"I . . . I can't."

"Yes you can. You are drowning here. I am offering you a lifeline. Let me bed you, make you complete. I can satisfy you, drain you of your tension and anxieties and make you so much more effective at your work. I assure you that I'm very good with a submissive man."

Of course I knew it. If I hadn't realized it before, I knew it in the showers in the Ginsburg Sports Center the way Christophe was with his body—the gold ball pierced in his cock glans. The brush of his hand on my back in passing me in the locker room. I knew overtures from one man to another when I experienced them. And I had experienced them before—and given into them as well. The mutual attraction had been obvious too. But, it was wrong. The church wouldn't condone it—even though neither of us had a parish; we were both academics. There could be no harm done to anyone's souls other than our own.

"I have vows. Monsignor Baum is strict and knows everything that—"

"Yes, Monsignor Baum knows everything," Christophe said. "He's the one who sent for me. He's the one who brought me to reconciliation when I was in seminary in New York. He knows what I can do for you. He told me to do it.

He's the one who will comfort and guide you when I'm gone—if you let him. Do you understand what I'm saying?"

I didn't answer "yes," but I didn't answer "no" either. The revelation hit me like a ton of bricks. It wasn't just admiration I felt for the monsignor. It was something deeper. And I sensed it in him, because it was really there. And now the instances flew through my mind of when he had been signaling that as well.

"Do you live alone, Mark?"

"I'm a resident counselor at the Gewirz Student Center, across from the law school. It's mainly for law students, but single faculty members have rooms there and provide counsel to the students."

"Do you have an apartment there—just for you alone?"

"Yes. It's an efficiency, though. Just a room and a bathroom and a kitchenette."

"But you live alone there?"

"Yes."

"It has a bed, doesn't it?"

I couldn't respond to that. But I didn't say no. I wasn't saying no to anything, and he knew it.

"Drink up your beer, Mark . . . and take me to this room—this bed—of yours."

* * * *

The lights were off, but there was enough light coming in through the single window from the street light on the walkway between academic buildings outside the Gewirz Student Center for us to savor the deepening pleasure of both of us as our arousal built and we each came closer to release. I was backed up against the wall just inside the door into my efficiency. One foot was on the floor. my other leg was hooked on Christophe's hip and the Frenchmen pressed me into the wall. I was trembling from the compromising position, the ease with which I surrendered, and the anticipation of what I hoped—not that I had surrendered to it—of what was to come. Both of us were still wearing our cleric shirts, but they

205

no longer were a barrier to anything. Our trousers and briefs were puddled on the floor at our feet.

I cupped Christophe's head, my fingers digging into the curly black hair of the Frenchmen, in both hands. We were locked in a kiss, Christophe dominating, his tongue swabbing the inside of my cheek. I had never been as fully possessed as this before. Christophe was dominating in all. He was pressing me against the wall. He was rhythmically pressing and releasing against my body. He was holding me in place and in thrall just with one hand on his waist. He was grasping both of our cocks in a hand and relentlessly frotting them. I was completely lost to his control, the total submissive to his masterful domination.

I was moaning deeply, panting, breathing heavily. In complete charge, Christophe was forceful and in command. Both of us were hard, but I was the one who was writhing, belabored, under Christophe's determined control.

The kiss was broken, and I whispered, with a whimper, "Please. I'll come if you don't—"

"Do it. Come for me. Release. Give in. Allow yourself to come for me. There will be more later. We have all night. There will be much more later."

With a deep sigh, I did so, relaxing to the overpowering control of him, coming in his hand, and Christophe took possession of my lips again.

Pulling out of the kiss again, but maintaining control of our frotted cocks, Christophe said. "I didn't see a bed when we came in. You must have one."

"It's just a single," I answered in a breathy voice.

"That's enough for us."

Once I'd come that first time, all resistance was gone from me. The sin could not be compounded at this point. I didn't actively initiate any part of coupling that night, but both I and Christophe knew that would come in time. When Christophe pulled away from me at the wall and held me up when I almost collapsed there, I permitted Christophe to take my hand, gestured where the bed was in the room, and docilely permitted Christophe, who was carrying his own trousers over his arm, to guide me to the bed and pull my clerical shirt over his head.

What I had come to think was my protective barrier to my sinful lusts proved all too easy to desert me.

I surrender was complete. Both naked now, on the bed, in front of the window, the moonlight making our bodies silvery, Christophe knelt on bent knees, his knees pressed under my buttocks, as, facing Christophe, I sat on the Frenchman's knees, with my legs wrapped around Christophe's hips. I had one hand wrapped around the neck of the Frenchman and the fingers of the other hand were brushing through the matting of black, curly hair on the Frenchman's arms, chest, and belly.

Christopher held my body to him—as much psychologically as physically—with one hand on my waist, with the other one frotting our cocks once again. I gasped as Christophe cupped my cock in his hand and moved his pinky finger to the urethra opening of my cock bulb and started to worry the hole, encouraging it to open for him, which it did. The bulb was still moist from my coming earlier, and he swirled this around my cock head and used it as a lubricant to aid the opening of my urethra to his pinkie finger. I had never been worked so wantonly before. All of my defenses, my theological protections, were being brushed aside by another priest as if they meant nothing in the reality of being who I was. That they changed nothing in my worth. And perhaps that was the message I he was giving me in how fully he was seducing me.

I was breathing heavily and moaning softly. No one had ever done this to me before, and it was incredibly arousing. I leaned forward, pressing my forehead against Christophe's as the Frenchman worked his pinky finger into the urethra opening.

"Oh, fuck," I murmured as Christophe pressed the pinky inside the opening and then releasing, pressing in, releasing. Fucking the slit with his pinky. Precum formed as I moaned more loudly and deeply, and Christophe swirled his finger tips around on the cock head.

"You shouldn't. We shouldn't . . ." I murmured.

"Do you hear a stone curtain being rent asunder?" he asked.

"No."

"Then we can and will. That's the point. It isn't a taboo unless you hear the stone screen being rent asunder. Have you ever been sounded?" Christophe whispered.

"Oh, shit no," I answered, not knowing what it was. When the Frenchman told me what that was, I shuddered and moved ineffectually within his grip.

"In time," Christophe murmured and I shuddered and groaned. "I time we will do it all. This for now." He moved the beaded tip of his cock against my bulb. I began to tremble more uncontrollably and pull away as the bead was pressed inside my urethra opening, but Christophe moved his free hand to the small of my back and held me in thrall. Physically I could have broken away. Emotionally I was totally captive to him.

"Oh, god, oh, god, oh shit," I whimpered as Christophe pressed down on his cock, causing the foreskin of his uncut cock to envelop the bulb of my cut shaft. He held the two cocks together, docking them, slow fucking my urethra slit with the bead of his cock head.

Moaning, I slowly arched my back toward the surface of the bed, allowing my head to fall over the foot of the bed, and letting my arms go slack straight out from my body. My body was in a cruciform attitude and in total submission, all of my senses focused on the docked cock and the gold bead pressing inside my piss slit and releasing. In and out, fucking my cock.

With a shudder, both of us came, our cum mingling and burbling out of the docking foreskin of Christophe' cock.

"That was good," Christophe murmured.

"Yes," I whispered, remaining stretched back, my body slightly twitching in after spasms. "Glorious."

"You are mine now."

"Yes."

"We are a fit. We can make this work."

"Yes."

"The monsignor knows and approves."

No response; that was too overwhelming for me to respond to without much thought.

"He too wishes . . ."

"Yes."

"He was a good lover. Very attentive. Discreet. He will totally dominate and satisfy you."

Christophe had released my cock and now was slowly rubbing the underside of his still hard cock inside my buttocks crack, across the rim of my opening. Again and again. I was sighing and groaning.

"When I have fully recovered, do you want—?"

"Yes," I interrupted.

I sensed Christophe fumbling around in the pocket of the trousers he'd brought over to the bed and heard the snap of the condom being smoothed into place on Christophe's shaft. I jerked and gasped as the cock entered my channel, but I settled into sighs and groans as the shaft started to move deep inside me. After he had established that he could and would and set a rhythm that I moaned to in harmony, he stopped, holding long, thick, and hard in me to the hilt.

"Do it yourself," he whispered. "Fuck yourself on it."

And, all inhibitions erased, I did.

Banishment

I was seated at the high table, but just barely. Newly minted Bishop McLeod—Andy to me in moments of privacy—was four seats to my right, at the center of the table. I couldn't have achieved eye contact with him, if I'd wanted to. I wondered if Crandel, seated to the bishop's right, the dean of the college, had arranged that seating that on purpose. Crandel was the organizer of Belmont Abby College here in Charlotte, North Carolina, as well as its eyes and ears. I wonder if he had divined the relationship I shared with the bishop and even now, when Andy had been elevated and changes were inevitable, was intervening.

I tried the words, "Bishop McLeod," out again, silently, on my tongue, and the man next to me turned and smiled, saying, "I know. Such a privilege for the college to have provided a bishop." I just smiled back wanly, not realizing I'd said it out loud, and pretended that I saw the honor in this elevation as well. The title "bishop" still seemed strange. It had been barely a month since his elevation, and this was his celebration banquet. We were sending him off to Charleston to ascend to the bishopric of the Charleston Diocese. Until then he had been Monsignor McLeod, president of Belmont Abby College, and I had been simply Father Blackwood, the lowest-ranked assistant professor of English at the school, in my first, trial year here.

Everyone was having such a jolly time at the banquet and my jaw was getting tired from the false smiles I had to set to pretend that everything was all right—better than all right. James Crandel had been named earlier today as the school's new president. Everything was so "all right" about that that I thought I might be sick. I started to tell the head of the English department, sitting next to me, that I felt slightly ill and thought I'd take my leave early, but Dixon's attention was completely devoted up table, where he was prepared to laugh at the joke that Crandel was making, no matter what the punch line was. The ranks were already falling into line behind the new president.

I slipped out of the banquet room, with no one noticing, I thought, until I looked back at high table and saw Crandel's eyes on me. He was telling a joke and his mouth was set in a sly, I'm-so-clever smile, but the smile didn't extend to his eyes. The joke was for the table, but I knew that the eyes were for me.

I went to my apartment at the top of one of the resident halls, using the back stairs so that none of the students would realize I had returned and took advantage of that to come to me with one of their petty concerns. As junior faculty, I was a resident counselor as well as an instructor. I stripped out of my black cassock—trying to draw my thoughts where they should be by thinking on the Savior as I released the thirty-three buttons, each button representing a year in Jesus's life, although only being able to conjure up the image of the last time the buttons had been undone by someone other than me. I showered and lay down on the bed in the nude. The image of the kiss and having my cassock unbuttoned and of what came afterward when it was revealed I wore nothing underneath it caused my hand to move to my crotch, for me to moan, and for me to arch my back.

I had to think. I couldn't stay here after Andy had gone. Crandel hated me—and suspected me, I was sure. In fact, he probably knew. There were other possibilities. But I was in orders and chained to the Charleston Diocese. Andy was walking into a position where he had complete control of my life and could reassign me at his will. Would he take me to Charleston with him? These last two weeks he'd been referring to the elevation to bishop as the opportunity of a new life, of dedicating himself even more closely to God's work and a pure life.

"I will be the first black Bishop of Charleston," he had said. "Can you have any idea what an opportunity that provides to be a leader for tomorrow, Matt?"

I could certainly see that the elevation had changed him—that he no longer was just Andy, to me, or even Monsignor McLeod, the president of the first college I was teaching at. He was a bishop, and not just any bishop. He was the bishop of the order I was married to. Our relationship inevitably was changed.

I heard the door to the back stairs landing open, and there he was, in his new trappings, the black cassock, with the red trim and red sash. I rose from the bed, erect and lightly panting, and walked to him. He had seen me leave the banquet hall after all. And he had left earlier than he needed to, as well, and had come to me. He was in the middle of the celebration of his elevation, but he had broken off from that and come to me.

We embraced and our lips met. I untied his red sash as we stood close together, clinging to each other, me trembling and he towering over me. His hand was on my shaft, stroking it, as I unbuttoned his cassock, flared it open, and went down on my knees to him. He lifted his hand, and I kissed his ring, ever the signal between us of my total submission to him.

He was erect even before I took him in my hand and stroked him as I kissed the crease where his lower belly transitioned into the top of his left thigh. He was a bull of a man, both in size and musculature, but also in equipment. He was a black bull, the first black bishop of the Charleston Diocese, his balls meaty and hanging low and his cock hard as steel, thick, long, proudly protruding. When I took it into my mouth and he lay his hands on the back of my head to guide me, I gagged in the unsuccessful attempt to take it all inside me.

I was able to take it all inside me later, though, as I lay on my belly on the bed, raised on my knees, my pelvis elevated a bit to him, and he covered me close from above, one hand grasping my wrist over my head, and the other arm encasing my heaving belly, holding me in his total control, as he fucked me in long, thick, deep strokes. No man dominated me as this black bull did. No man satisfied me as Andy could. I opened completely to him, becoming soft and vulnerable inside, in the core of me, totally trusting he would be good to me, when, if he lost control, or became cruel, he could rip me to shreds inside with the monstrous club between his thighs. But he took me slow and easy, giving me time to open as much as I could

212

to him, moving slowly inside me, gently going deeper rather than thrusting, and coming in a prodigious, peaceful flow rather than as a conqueror in pain.

As he was standing beside the bed, me collapsed on the bed on my belly, an arm draped over the side, knuckles dragging on the carpet, and me watching him rebutton the thirty-three buttons of his cassock in a worshipful daze, he said, "Come to my office at 9:00 in the morning. We must discuss your future."

The next morning, at 9:00, I was standing in front of the bishop's desk, behind which he was sitting, toying with a feather pin in his hands and framed by photographs of him with the pope and joking with the Archbishop of Atlanta. Already he no longer was Andy to me, or Monsignor McLeod. He wasn't the man who covered me close from above and possessed me deep with his monster cock as recently as the previous night. He was my bishop. He had told me where I was to go. There was no questioning his judgment or decision. But . . .

"Where is this Daufuskie Island? How many Catholics are there? You say I'll be the only priest?"

"Some would think the island is remote—it's off the South Carolina coast and is serviced by a ferry—but Hilton Head is just to the north of it and Savannah just to the south, so it is a restful place between activity," the bishop answered. He was looking at the feather he was spinning between his fingers. He wasn't looking up at me. "It doesn't matter how many Catholics are there now. You are being sent to build the church up. The church is St. Mary's. I understand it's in a bit of disarray. You are interested in working with your hands. I'm sure you will find it just the challenge you need."

Banishment was the word that went through my brain. He is sending me away to someplace so remote I'll never be heard from again. This is what his new life entailed. I should have heeded the feeling that last night, the most intense of our couplings, had been a farewell fuck. But, that hadn't proved to be the case.

"Yes, Reverend Father," I said and turned to leave.

"Matthew," I heard him mumble in a voice that sounded strange. I turned back. "Lock the door and come here, son," he murmured.

He pulled his chair back from the desk, took my hand when I came to the side of the desk, and pulled me around, facing him, between him and the desk. "Kneel to me, son," he whispered. I went down on my knees in front of him. He presented the ring on one of his hands, and I kissed it, as he unbuttoned his cassock with the other. He was naked underneath and in erection. I took his shaft in my mouth and he guided my head, making me take him to the root this time. He lifted me when he had engorged, unbuttoned and flared, my cassock. I stepped out of my briefs as he pulled them down my legs. It was my turn to moan and hold his head between my hands and luxuriate in his attentions as he took me in his mouth and gave suck.

"One last time," he murmured as he pulled away from me and nudged me onto his lap, holding his cock erect with one hand, guiding me with the other hand on the small of my back, as I positioned myself on the cock head and descended on the shaft. He leaned forward, burying his head into my sternum and grasped and separated my buttocks with his hands as, using the leverage of my feet on the floor on either side of his thighs, I raised and lowered my passage on his steel hard, black bull cock. He sucked the aureole of one of my nipples into his mouth, in its entirety, and flicked the nipple with his tongue as he sucked it. I moaned for that and then again when he did the same with the other nipple.

I tried to show him I no longer was as open to him as before—as I had been the previous night when I'd gone soft and spongy for him and opened for him to go deeper into the vulnerability of me than he'd ever sunk before—but my own needs defeated me. My passage opened right up for the thickness of him as he went deeper with each downward pull, controlled by the bishop now with hands gripping my hips.

My passage muscles rippled over the throbbing cock, blossoming open, stretching for him, coaxing him deeper and deeper inside me. I started to cry out in ecstasy, but sensing that, he gripped my face with a large, brown paw, forcing a thumb inside my mouth, which I sucked on as I rose and fell on the cock with muted sounds of groans and moans.

He turned me around on the cock, lowering my chest to the surface of the desk. My arms shot above my head, scattering framed photographs aside. I gripped the edge of the far side of the desk, as he crouched over me from behind, one hand grasping my mouth, the other hand gripping my waist. There was no peaceful end to this now. He was pounding my ass, deep and hard, fucking me with a fury as he'd never done before. I was gasping and groaning and moaning under his control, being fucked hard as he'd never done before. Being taken higher and higher. Gasping for breath, every ounce of my attention going to that huge cock battering at me deep inside, finding that I could take it. I could be soft deep inside again and still take his relentless pounding. Discovering that this was what I wanted from him, albeit having learned that too late.

We achieved a near-simultaneous ejaculation, the first time we'd managed it. The last time we'd try, we both knew.

We didn't look at each other or say anything while we stood half an office away from each other and rebuttoned and adjusted our cassocks. He wouldn't look at me directly as he restored his treasured photographs on his desk to their original positions—supplanting me with them for the ultimate time. Sometime in the next week they would be packed up and sent to Charleston. Sometime in the next week, I'd be packed out and sent to a remote island off the coast.

It was over and we both knew it. We also both knew that no matter how much closer to divinity McLeod's elevations would take him, he wasn't going to fundamentally change. Neither would I. We'd both try, but I wouldn't fool myself that it would work. I'm not sure he could fool himself either, but I wasn't going to be the one he discovered that with now. He might fool himself now, but his needs were insatiable. There would be some other young priest to be known biblically and used by him in the near future.

As I left the office, I encountered Crandel in the reception office, waiting to go in for his turn at submission to the bishop in an entirely different way. He smirked at me, no doubt knowing where my next parish assignment was. He'd probably even been the one to come up with the location. I was too sad to say to him all that I felt in my heart and so would have loved to say, but I would leave it to someone else to take that smirk off his face. I was too heartsick to take on that assignment.

* * * *

"Don't you find it a little too hot to be wearing a choke collar like that?"

I would have laughed if I hadn't been so hot from wearing this choking clerical collar when I stepped off the ferry at Daufuskie Island and into . . . what exactly? I had expected a town of some sort, not just a small collection of time-worn buildings on the wooded land running up from the public dock. There was a small marina next to the dock, but this looked more like a private home compound than the center of island life. It wasn't just the collar that chaffed; I was in a shirt and trousers rather than a cassock, but they were black. Black most certainly wasn't a color to be wearing on the South Carolina coast on a summer's day.

"It's a clerical collar. It identifies me as a priest," I answered. "You wouldn't be Frank Chisolm, would you, or know where I can find him?"

"Yes, that's me. Frank. You must be Mr. . . . . Father Blackwood. The minister of my church wears a T-shirt and shorts in this weather. I figure you could do the same."

"Your minister? So you aren't Catholic?"

"We don't have any Catholics on the island, as far as I know—well, until you arrived just now—unless it be some those fancy people in the enclaves along the coast, who don't come further onto the island—just boat themselves over to Hilton Head or Savannah as they wish. Don't know what religion any of them are; we don't mix with them. This is a Gullah island and we're all Baptists here. Freewill Baptists back to the time when we were slaves."

216

"Well, you do have a Catholic now. A Catholic priest. And this, apparently, is Saint Mary's parish of the Charleston Diocese."

"Yes, I was told that when I was hired to meet you and help you get set up. That was news around here, I've gotta say. We had a good laugh at that. All this time we've been a Catholic parish, and we didn't know it. You could have seen me almost bend over laughing when I found out that the building our women had been using as a bingo hall is actually a Catholic church owned by the church. The ladies have been good about moving out, though. They even helped dig out the brush around it so you can get to it more easily. You've got a good line of credit to put the building to rights—and the house that goes with it."

That was the one good thing Andy had done for me. He'd set up a generous line of credit. I'd been told I'd need it too. And he'd had someone hired to help me get established here. I don't know if he realized that the man who was hired, this Frank Chisolm, was a hunk and a half. He was black, but of a mix with white. On him the mix looked good. He wasn't any older than I was, from the look of him, and muscular, but not overly developed. He was lanky and walked with grace. His hair was black and straight and came down to his shoulders when he didn't have it pulled back in a ponytail to keep it out of the way and him cooler, which he often did when he was working.

His smile was languid, sexy, his amusement contagious. The first thing he'd said to me coming off the ferry had been criticism of my dress—but he had said it in such a way that it hadn't offended me a bit. It also had signaled to me that saying the Catholic community here was inactive would be a gross understatement. My parish may not have anyone to serve but me. Of course, my sins were so numerous and deep, that I might be as much as the Lord could handle on this island.

I was surprised that our conversation was so easy as we walked up into the small group of buildings at the public dock, one of which was a combined grocery store and pharmacy, not much more than a convenience store and the other a larger souvenir shop. Frank told me that tourists coming over from

Hilton Head provided most of the money that came into the island. Beyond that it was mostly subsistence farming among the Gullah community, the ancestors of the freed blacks from the Civil War who had remained in scattered communities across the Carolina coasts. The culture was no stronger anywhere than right here on Daufuskie Island, which had remained remote.

I could tell from Frank's drawl and the loose, but manly way he walked—more of a saunter—that the lifestyle of the island was laid back and slow moving. It also was easy going. It was clear from his response—the response of a Baptist, whose sect pretty much dominated the island—to a Catholic priest that he was accepting and unshockable. I wondered if he'd be shocked to know that I'd been sent here to hide away the sexual sin of a bishop. Well, to be fair, it was my sin too, and making the best of being banished to the edge of civilization here was a penance that I had decided to accept as no more than what I deserved to serve. I would be as celibate from henceforth, I had declared to myself, as the bishop no doubt believed—falsely—that he would be.

Still, that was hard to resolve as I followed the young Gullah half breed up the rise to the community buildings and watched the roll of his steel-like buns under the loose material of his shorts. He was wearing white cargo shorts and a very loose T-shirt. On his feet were skimpy rope sandals covering strong-looking feet with long, plump toes. He exuded sex, and, although I knew what he was wearing must have been cheap, I was equally sure that he could have been photographed for a yacht ad in a glossy magazine and been a sensation of style, grace, and sensuality.

"What are these?" I asked as we approached the souvenir shop building.

"Golf carts—or modified ones," Frank answered. "There are no cars on the island. We move in these. You'll want to buy one for your church and your own use. I could help you locate a used on in good condition. It isn't far from anywhere to anywhere on Daufuskie Island or any hurry to get there, so much of the transport is by foot. But transfers from elsewhere like you and the day tourists need these carts. And your luggage requires the use of one, of course."

It was only now that he seemed to notice that I was lugging two heavy suitcases. He hadn't offered to carry one or both for me. I actually had found that satisfying—that he didn't give me the impression of being subservient. In fact, if I were to guess, I would take him as a dominant—which was quite all right with me. Not that I assumed he was attracted to men, of course.

The cart ride wasn't long. The road—more like a narrow, shell-paved drive—entering the island from the public dock area was called Haig Point Road. Taking this for about a half mile to the Melrose Plantation area on the central-east shore of the island, one of eleven original plantations that covered the island at the time of the Civil War, we came to an intersection with the Avenue of the Oaks, which led into Melrose. Saint Mary's Church and rectory were located on the Avenue of the Oaks near this intersection. The landscape was almost all scrub, with scrawny pine trees. The few building in sight were weather-beaten and in an advanced stage of melting back into the scrub.

I stood, almost in disbelief, and looked at the two run-down buildings, both of weathered wood that once had been white, but no more. Both were small. The church appeared to be leaning, although Frank assured me that that was an optical illusion caused by the lack of balance of the foliage engulfing it. It hit me how hard this penance was going to be to fulfill.

Standing at my side and looking at the same buildings I was, Frank said, "You're lucky. The buildings are in better condition than most that the Gullah live in on the island. The walled vacation estates of the millionaires along the island's coast, are, of course, a stark contrast to these. But if you want any of the Gullah to be attending your church, I suggest you do little more than repair the window and door frames and put on a coat of paint. We are one with the earth here. We aren't much for putting on airs."

Somehow, this bucked me up—and even more so when he added, "Tom and I will be here tomorrow to start helping you with the repairs."

I wasn't going to have to do this alone. He added, though, "Which should we start with first? The church building or the house you will live in?"

"The church, I think," I piously said. "God's work first."

He laughed. "Maybe you shouldn't answer that until you've seen the inside of the house."

He was right. We started with the house first. Somehow it didn't matter that much. It was just a joy to have him there, working with me—in fact, doing most of the work. I could not have done it without him. I would not want to try.

The downside is that, although my determination to remain celibate in fact remained intact, any determination I might have had of not fantasizing in the moments of lying on my bed at night and drifting off to sleep of a man like Frank covering and moving inside me did not hold.

* * * *

The black shirt and trousers and clerical collar lasted all of two days. I found that Frank had dressed up to meet me at the ferry and wore even less than that when he was working on the church buildings. When he appeared for work Monday afternoon, after saying he'd be there bright and early on Monday, he was wearing gym shorts that dipped to show a curl of black pubic hair in front and the crease of the curve of his lower, flat belly into his upper thighs, as well as the start of a separation of the buttocks in back. He was wearing the rope sandals as well, though. Anyone thinking of calling him Droopy Drawers would be arrested by the reality of how sexy he looked that way. Tom, a younger and smaller man, fully Gullah, who accompanied him, was similarly attired, except his cotton trousers were longer. But men were well-worked muscular, and both worked hard, but in sporadic spurts.

I was to learn, from brief conversations with the two, that they both picked up work as they could, that this was the way of the Gullah of Daufuskie Island, and that it carried them through. Most of their subsistence—the subsistence of most here—came off the working of the land, which was taken care

220

of mostly by the Gullah women and that was close to communal in both effort and sharing. It apparently worked for them. I didn't meet a single Gullah on the island who wasn't smiling and moving at his or her own languid pace. In addition to the stipend Frank now had and shared with Tom to work on Saint Mary's church and my house and to help me get established here, he was a backup golf cart tour guide of the island for tourists coming over by ferry from Hilton Head for a brief visit to the island, and he ran a fishing boat out of the marina by the public dock. I gathered that he lived in the fishing boat as well.

By day two, I was in a T-shirt, shorts, and sneakers, with socks, and by day four, only the shorts and sneakers, without socks. I was growing brown as a berry from working on the outside of the buildings while Frank and Tom mostly worked on the insides, miraculously bringing the standards of the house to almost civilized and the interior of the church, with four pews recovered, that being more than enough, back to order and cleanliness. I also was hardening up. I'd been in good shape before, but now I was getting toned. Frank remarked on this, which embarrassed, but also pleased, me.

The two men worked a sporadic schedule, not showing up when there were other odd jobs to be had or when Frank heard that fish were running down off the mouth of the Savannah River. Even when they were on the job, they took long breaks whenever they took the notion, often leaning against trees and smoking despite my "friendly" lectures on the dangers of cigarettes. I was piqued at first at their half-hearted approach to work, even though when they were working they were productive and efficient, but Frank would just smile at me and say that there wasn't anything that had to be done today that couldn't be done just as well tomorrow, and I slowly fell into the rhythm of the island.

Sometimes the two disappeared for a half hour or more on one of their frequent breaks. They were working with me for only a week before I found out where they went and how they took their breaks. It also provided an answer to my wondering what Frank's living arrangements were. The Gullah seemed to be one large family, even though they lived in scattered family units around the island. More often than not they congregated to eat and party and, in one of their major revenue projects, work together in weaving intricately designed sweetgrass baskets that sold for big bucks in the Charleston and Savannah markets. They worked the fields together communally and one afternoon when I took a long walk, I discovered that the men were casual about covering the women in the fields and that the women could be casual about letting more than one man cover her.

I wondered if Frank, an unusually handsome and well-formed man, satisfied his needs by casually covering Gullah women in the fields. He may, as far as I knew, do that, but one afternoon when I went looking for him and Tom when one of their breaks dragged on and I needed advice on how to replace a board on the side of my cottage, I found out at least one way that Frank satisfied his sexual needs.

Both men were naked, both of them had beautiful bodies, the beauty of which was enhanced in how they were working together as one unit. Ebony-skinned Tom was bowed over, feet and hands buried in the ferns under a creeping-rooted Cypress tree next to a bog, his tail held high. Taller, milk-chocolate-skinned Frank was plastered to his back, draped over him. Frank's feet were planted beside and outside of Tom's feet, and his fists were gripping Tom's wrists. His chest was pressed into Tom's shoulder blades, his face into the hollow of Tom's throat. He was fucking Tom's ass in long, slow slides. Tom's eyes were set in a glassy stare, showing the pain-pleasure of what I could see was a long, thick, jet-black cock working his passage. His mouth was slack open in an expression of sheer pleasure and submission.

I watched for a moment, lost in the beauty of the tableau—what I'd been determined, when I came here, to understand as a sin that I was to shake in my own life and that I was enduring penance here for having indulged. The natural, primeval way these two men were engaged in it, though, and in a simple, honest setting such as this challenged both the ideology-based prejudices I was attempting to acquire to be right with my church and my resolve. I was particularly mesmerized by seeing that, although of light-chocolate skin tone from his mixed heritage, Frank's hung cock was jet black.

I couldn't help but shudder in arousing pleasure as I watched the huge shaft move in and out of Tom's hole.

Thoughts of sex with men—sex with Andrew McLeod—that I had been trying to suppress for weeks came flooding in and I turned and stumbled back to and into the cottage. There had been so much I had wanted to write about—to put into a novel—in thinking of these past several weeks. I hadn't been able to do so, as the electricity to the two buildings hadn't been connected until the previous day, and, more important, I was trying to convince myself that it was a sin to write about my feelings let alone think on them.

When Frank and Tom returned to work, Frank stuck his head into the front door of the cottage, finding me pounding away on my computer on the desk.

"There you are," he said, "You asked me a question about replacing a board in the siding before I went off on break. Would you like to come out here and show me where—"

"It can wait," I answered. "There's nothing that has to be done today that can't just as well be done tomorrow." And I turned, blushing, from looking at him, as I now couldn't see him without imagining him naked with that big jet-black cock hanging down between his legs.

The buildings quickly became usable—they'd never be full presentable—and I moved forward to holding my first mass, digging around and finding my black cassock, which, when nothing was worn under it, proved cooler than the collared black shirt and black trousers I'd brought to wear on the island.

My first mass was attended by two squirrels, a cat, and, outside the door, a bleating goat. There were three Gullahs, an old crone in addition to Frank and Tom, at the second mass. A half dozen showed up to the third one, attending, Frank assured me, out of curiosity and flexibility. They would attend their regular three-hour-long services at the Baptist church that afternoon. They were interested in what Catholics did in their services. Thereafter I put on a real show of full-blown formal ritual, and they loved it, filling the church. It wasn't too hopeful, but it was a start—and I was fulfilling my end of the bargain with the church.

At least I was fulfilling my duties in that regard. I also increasingly was lusting after Frank, dreaming of him lying between my thighs, mining me deep with that jet-black cock of his. With Andy, and now Frank, I obviously had an obsession with black bull cock. I tried working off my frustrations by banging away on my computer on a novel draft. That helped, but it only served to hold me in check, not to decrease my desire or sexual frustration.

I took to taking long walks in the evening and, on more than one occasion, I passed gatherings in one clearing or the other where a few of the Gullah shacks were gathered of a festival party going on, with communal basket weaving moving into picnicking off a common table, music on primitive instruments, dancing, and raucous laughter. More than once someone from the group would wave me to come join them, and the smiles turned on me assured me I would be welcome, but I had nothing to share, so I would politely demure and continue with my walks.

I noticed that they wore clothes of colorful cotton for these festivities and I ordered a few bolts of material from Savannah, figuring I'd find some occasion of giving them in the community to symbolize my wish to fit in here. The opportunity presented itself when I asked Frank about the parties one evening.

"You should attend them. You'd be welcome," Frank said. "It would help you become part of the community. Many of the Gullah have told me that they enjoy the entertainment you put on at your church. They would be happy to include you in their celebrations. We celebrate life here. Often when we weave the baskets together we celebrate the beauty of them—and of what we've been given here—and the friendship of each other in our gatherings."

I couldn't think of anything better that I could be preaching to these people than they already had—and that I was aching to have as well.

"Until now, I've had nothing to contribute," I said. "But I've ordered this material from Savannah and I know they like to dress in colorful clothes for their festivities. Do you think—?"

"That you've taken an interest in the people of the island—that you aren't just vacationing in a walled compound at the water's edge and raising huge piles of rocks to live in—is enough for the Gullah here. We accept all kinds, and we do not judge. I know you have talked of being banished here for some sin or other, but we don't judge here."

"I am a priest, Frank, and I've taken a vow of celibacy. I am here to do penance for that, which includes not falling into the pit again. I haven't just sinned against the vow of celibacy, but I've done it with a man." I don't know how that escaped me, but it had been bottled up inside me too long. Well, that was a lie. I knew why I did it. I'd seen him fucking a man. As much as it scared me, I wanted him to know I was a man who had let a man fuck me. I wanted him to know that we were closer connected that he thought. I couldn't look at him, but when he spoke, I could clearly hear him.

"This is a world of our own on the island, Matt," he said—using my Christian name for the first time and laying his fingers gently on my forearm. "We banish the guilt of sin from here. You can be what you want here, and you can be a priest to the people here. They have room in their hearts and lives for all manner of spiritual nurture and lifestyle. If you have sinned with being with a man for sex, you are no worse than I am. I have been with a man for sex too."

"Yes, I've seen you," I murmured. I couldn't look at him to see how this registered.

"I know where there will be a gathering tonight," he said after a moment of silence. "I will come for you in a cart at 8:00 p.m. Will you go to the party with me?"

"And afterward?" I asked, not being able to help myself. I was open and vulnerable to him, as good as lying down in front of him and open my legs for him. I did lift my eyes to his now, but I couldn't gauge his reaction. He must have known that I was offering myself to him—begging him to take me.

He merely repeated, "Will you go to the party with me?"

"Yes," I said, still not being able to look at him.

He turned to walk away and then turned back and said, "You've been honest with me about the nature of this sin you say you are fighting. I'll be as honest with you. I was told of your desires and needs. And I was told I was hired because I lay men and that I was to make sure you were happy and satisfied—if you wanted to be. When and if you wish it, I will be pleased to lay you too. We aren't much about being coy on the island. If I didn't want to lay you I wouldn't tell you this. Since I do, I see no reason not to be open about it. I understand if being a priest means something to you in a man being with a man, but it doesn't mean anything to me. Sorry, but I just see you as a man I'd like to fuck. Now, I guess I should ask again with all my cards on the table. Do you want to go to the party with me? It doesn't mean that we ever have to get it on, depending on what you want. But if you want me to fuck you after the party, I will."

And then he, as I blushed and stammered that, yes, I still wanted to go to the party, turned and left.

I also said, "and lay me afterward," but by then he was gone.

The party was a delight, everything I could have hoped for it to be. From the time we arrived and a group of women took me in hand to laugh at my crude attempts to weave sweetgrass into a basket and Frank went off with the men cooking sausages on a grill and smoking their cigarettes, I was welcomed with smiles and friendly conversation.

I sat with the group, cross-legged on the ground through a shared meal, and listened to the harmonica and strange string-instrument music. I even participated in the dancing, in which there were no partners, just everyone moving about in a circle under strings of colored lights. And when the home-brewed booze was passed around, I imbibed in that—fully.

Perhaps too fully. All inhibitions flowed away from me. I became one with the Gullah of Daufuskie Island.

I woke to a rocking sensation and staring into Frank's eyes, which were open and watching me. We were in the cramped cabin of his fishing boat, lying stretched out against each other, both naked. He had shown me his fishing boat before and I'd been in this cabin. I'd seen where he slept, and I had dreamed. It was like I was in a dream now—except that I wasn't. I was lying on my back, one of his arms under me and the other laying across my chest. My legs were spread and bent, the soles of my feet flat on the mattress. I could feel his erection laying on my thigh. I was open and feeling the sensation of rippling inside my passage. I had been fucked—I certainly knew the feeling of having been fucked. In fact, my rim, gaping open from the feel of it, was still puckering and releasing. I'd been fucked within the last several minutes. My passage was sore. I hadn't just been fucked; I'd been reamed.

"I'm sorry," he murmured. "It was the booze. I never would have taken the liberty otherwise. I know I said I wanted to fuck you, but I said I'd wait for you to say you wanted it. I'm afraid I might not have waited. The booze did it for both of us—erased the inhibitions. I'm sorry. If it's not what you wanted or were ready for, I'll never—?"

"You've fucked me?" I asked, putting a mock edge on my voice.

"Oh, yes, I fucked you. More than once, I'm pretty sure. I'm still hard from the last time. Again I'm—"

"Shhh," I whispered, raising a finger to his lips. "I did tell you last night I wanted it; you just weren't still there when I said it. I'm just sorry I wasn't conscious for it. I wish—"

"You want—?"

"Yes, please," I whispered.

He rolled on top of me, between my open thighs. I arched my back, gave a little cry, and dug my fingernails into his shoulder blades, as he slowly, relentlessly entered me with that big, jet-black cock of his. He been there before—often enough that I had been reamed to accept him. The muscles of my passage walls responded as in joy, clutching at the throbbing cock as it moved deeper inside me, rippling over the steel-hard shaft, pulling it inside me. His lips found mine as he started to stroke me in long, hard, deep, slow, possessing slides. My pelvis went into motion of its own volition and we were going with the lapping of the waves under the boat, joined in the coordinated rhythm of the deep fuck. Fifteen minutes later he came—again—in a peaceful flow deep inside me and a harmonious shared sigh—his a deep baritone, mine a low tenor. I had already given up my seed up his flat belly, moments before.

I drifted off to a light sleep. When I opened my eyes, he was watching me with his eyes again—but from across the cabin, where he was perched on a cabinet, smoking a cigarette, and looking pensive. My eyes went to his crotch, mesmerized again by that big jet-black cock, half hard now, protruding from a thatch of curly black pubic hair and standing out in stark contrast to the milk chocolate tone of the rest of his body. His free hand went down to stroking his cock and I took mine in hand as well. We stroked ourselves hard, me lying there on his bunk and him just a few feet away, crouched on a cabinet. We said nothing, letting our eyes, electric with arousal, say it all.

He turned and flicked his still-smoldering cigarette into a small sink in the cabinet and, with an animalistic grunt, covered the space between us in two strides. He turned me on my belly and whipped an arm around my midsection, bringing me up on my knees, with my chest flat on the mattress, in one swift movement of covering me. I cried out as he thrust hard and deep inside me. His fists went to my wrists over my head, trapping them. He buried his face in the hollow of my neck and I felt his teeth latching onto me, painfully, there. I groaned and moaned and whimpered as, breathing heavily, he took me hard, vigorously, almost cruelly, showing no mercy, giving no quarter.

We fucked like dogs in heat, him pounding my ass, me crying out my need and my want and churning my pelvis against his onslaught, wanting him to take me fully and totally, which he did. I was as wanton as he was, as much in high heat as he was, fucking him as hard as he was fucking me. Both of us animals in full rut. We both ejaculated joyously and prodigiously and he lay on top of me, collapsed to the mattress now, and chewed lightly on my ear lobe and played inside my ear with his tongue.

He was young and virile. It wasn't long—we were still calming our breathing—when he was hard again. He turned us, he on his back on the mattress and me on my back on top of him. He wrapped his arms under my armpits and forced my arms up in a captive full Nelson position. I raised my pelvis, placing my feet on the mattress on either side of his thighs to elevate me and give me leverage, positioned his cock head at my hole, descended on the cock, and raised and lowered my passage on his cock in a smooth, slow slide that eventually resulted in a long sigh from each of us and him releasing his seed inside me again.

Once again I drifted off into an exhausted sleep. When I woke, I was alone in the cabin.

I returned to my little church on the Avenue of Oaks, working on the buildings by myself for two days and holding a mass on Sunday that neither Frank nor Tom attended. Monday morning I drove my cart down to the public docks. Frank's boat was gone.

That afternoon Tom showed up by himself, to work.

"Where's Frank?" I asked.

"He's taken his boat to Savannah," Tom answered. He wasn't looking me in the eye.

"When will he be back?"

"I'm not sure he's coming back," Tom answered. Was there a mild rebuff in the tone of his answer I wondered—or was it just me, worrying that Frank had felt guilty about causing me to forsake my vows, and understanding how important vows were—or should be—to a Catholic priest?

* * * *

I heard a familiar voice coming from the dock as I was sitting in the cabin of Frank's boat, tapping away on the draft of my novel. I rose and moved to the hatch leading up on deck where Frank was, washing down the boat, but I didn't go topside.

"Father Blackwood, you say?" I heard Frank respond to the question Crandel was asking. "No I don't think we have a priest here on the island. Everyone I know on Daufuskie Island is Baptist. Most of us are Gullah and have been here since before the Civil War."

"I've been to Saint Mary's church. That's where the priest was supposed to be. The place is a wreck," Crandel said.

I wanted cry out in objection, "You should have seen it when I first saw it," but I didn't want him to know I was here.

"Do tell," Frank said, his voice a study in innocence. "The unhappy truth is that island is hard on man-made structures," he said. "If there once was a Catholic church here, it's probably long past returning to the soil. I hear tell them Catholics are sticklers about sin, and we sin pretty regular here on Daufuskie. Fact is, visitors tend to get bitten by the sin bug as soon as they step foot on the island. Best not linger here if you don't want to be bit by the sin bug."

Crandel, sounding a bit snippy, said, "A mutual friend of ours asked that I check on him. He hasn't heard from Father Blackwood for some time. He's a bishop and is particularly worried about his friend."

Andy—the Bishop of Charleston—having pangs of guilt and wanting to know why I hadn't answered his letters, I thought. And he sent James Crandel, possibly the only other person who knew about us. Still protecting himself.

"As I said, I wouldn't know about that. Don't know about there being an active priest on the island," Frank answered, his tone friendly and only half interested. "Sorry I couldn't have helped more. Maybe Daufuskie life was found as not being for a Catholic priest. Maybe your friend went somewhere else or changed into someone else. Maybe he doesn't want to be found. But there, that's the 'last call' sound for the ferry. Your last chance to get back to Hilton Head today—unless you want to spend the night on the island."

Fat chance of that, I thought. And then I thanked Frank again for covering for me—for covering me like he did—for believing me when I tracked him down in Savannah and declared that I wanted life with him and the lifestyle of

230

Daufuskie Island and the Gullah more than I wanted or needed the Catholic Church.

I turned and went back to my computer, resuming the writing of my novel draft. It would be somewhat of a clearing of my soul and a revelation of the state of some matters inside the church. I had already decided to title it "The Bishop's Lover."

Frank came into the cabin, his gym shorts hanging low on his slim hips. "You heard?" he asked.

"Yes, I heard," I answered, drawing him over to between me and the computer, facing me.

"Do you have regrets? I can call him back."

"Not a single one other than how long it took me to accept my nature," I said, pushing the shorts down off his hips, pulling him to me, opening my mouth over his jet-black dick, and starting to suck him off.

~

About the Author

Habu is one of the pen names of a former supersonic spy jet pilot, intelligence agent, male model, movie actor, and diplomat. A wild youth in Southeast Asia was spent enjoying whatever sexual opportunities came his way, and much of his gay male writing is about recalling incidents from those days and inventing ones he'd perhaps have liked to experience. He now leads a very quiet and ordinary happily married family life.

An American, he is a published mainstream novelist and short story writer under another name and in another dimension of his life. He has written or cowritten (with Sabb) approaching 1,000 published short stories and over 100 published erotica e-books, primarily of gay fiction but also memoir, straight fiction and ménage fiction. His hand and creative writing can be seen in stories and books by habu, sr71plt, Dirk Hessian, Shabbu, and Stephen Kessel—among unrevealed others that might surprise readers. The fictionalized GM memoir *Flying High, Diving Deep* is loosely based on his life experiences. He can be found at the adults only gay male site www.BarbarianSpy.com, which he shares with Sabb and Dirk Hessian.

Our authors always like to receive feedback, and appreciate it when readers post reviews at distributors and other sites.

BarbarianSpy

FOR LITERARY HEAT

BarbarianSpy Books

Not all books listed below may currently be on release.
* indicates the book is available in paperback and e-book.
BOOKS BY CHRIS CROSS
Multisexual Adult Romance
Pulaski Square
Chocolate in Vanilla (MF)2
Christmas with Chris (MMF) (MM) (MF)
BOOKS BY ALEX LOCKHEED
Transgender Romance
Meeting Jenna
Transgender Other
Being Sarah
BOOKS BY DIRK HESSIAN
Xtreme Historical Erotica
Dirk's Ancient Times Collection (Print only Bundle)*
The King's Men
Shores of Tripoli*
Prophecy of Noto
Pretender's Fate
General Historical Erotic Romance
Dirk's America's Founding Collection (Print only Bundle)*
Soldier,Spy
Ridden West
Deliver a Virgin
Clouds and Rain
Confederate Gold
Puttin on the Ritz
To the Hessian Hills
Fire Down the Valley*
Constantinople*
The Beautiful Way*
Blue and Gray
Colonel's Treasure
Beginning of Time
Labyrinth
BOOKS BY HABU
Gay Erotica

Memoir Faction
Flying High, Diving Deep*
Xtreme Erotica
Fist of Gold
Liaisons
Chain Gang Banged (Short Story)
Tramp Steaming*
Escape to Girne
Silas' Choice*
Last Call
Choke Hold
Apyko: The Greek Pimp
Visits of the Schlange
Second Coming: Emile La Cour Unleashed*
Vortex: Sacrificed by Curiosity*
Dark Angel Sounding *(in e-book & included in Sounding:Ultimate Control paperback)**
Sounding: Ultimate Control *(Print Only)**
Sounding Five *(in e-book & included in Sounding:Ultimate Control paperback)**
Romance
The Aviators
Poison Pen
Need to be Needed
Key Westing (short)
Finding a New Sam
Bangkok Summer Seduction
The Photograph
Inevitable Case
Turn to Love
Rain Check
Built for Pleasure (Sci Fi)
Danny's Choice*
Pull of the Groove
Sugar n Spice Christmas
Friday Nights with Lenny (Christmas Romance)
Snowy, Snowy Nights (Christmas Romance)
Tank n Bull
Sail to the Sun
War Letters
Ravens Roost
Caribbean Cruise Top to Bottom
Arena Stage
Trading Partners (Valentine's Day)
Four Coins
Lower Than the Heart (Valentine's Day)

Brambleton
Finding Amnad
Platres Conclave
Other Novels/Novellas
Also Want to Thank
Ranger Guided
Key Westing
Syrian Ram
Temptation's Clutches*
Descent into Chaos
Escape to Girne
Journey Through Abilene
Harmony and Dissonance
Stallion Station
Racing With the Devil (espionage suspense)
Prepared in Cape Verdi
Gilded Cage
House on Park*
Anything for Ambition
Dance of the Ravishers
Hard Knocks U*
My Neighbor's Spa*
Man's Man: Tales of a High Priced Gay Hooker*
Trip Money
The Indian Doctor
Sailorboy
Home to Fire Island
Murder Mysteries
Retribution (Hardesty)
Snitches (Hardesty
Gotta Keep Trying (Hardesty)
All Fools Day Foolery (Mike Kavanagh)
Inevitable Case (Mike Kavanagh)
Vanishing Laura
Death on a Ping Pong Table
Clint Folsom Mysteries Compendium Volume 1*
Death to Blonds - Stolen Judgment (Clint Folsom Mystery)*
Clint Folsom Mysteries Compendium Volume 2*
Gay Erotica Anthologies
Earth Cry*
Shunga
Habu's Christmas Balls
Eight in D*
DevilMENt
Silas' Choices*
Stallion Station (A Novella in Parts)

Eleven to the Dogs*
Fifty Seventy*
Spy Tails 001*
Spy Tails 002*
Doubled*
Doubled Again*
Tails in the Tropics*
Tails in the Med*
Tails in the West*
Rough Riders*
Grab Bag 1*
Grab Bag 2*
Grab Bag 3*
Grab Bag 4*
Grab Bag 5*
Grab Bag 6*
Grab Bag 7*
Grab Bag 8*
Grab Bag 9*
Grab Bag 10*
Grab Bag 11*
Beyond the Beaded Curtain*
The Sporting Life*
Fetish Galore!*
Literary Gay Erotica
Cairo Surrender*
The Handyman*
Homeward Bound
Journey to Mirage*
Bisexual/Menage/Multisexual Erotica
And Eat it Too
Two Men, One Woman*
Every Which Way
Summer of Denial
Death on a Ping Pong Table
Cruising Gigolo
13 Ways for Halloween
Luther*
The Indian Prince*
BOOKS BY SABB
Driver Reliever
Hiring in Hollywood
The Legend of Holleystone Grange
Surprise Encounters*
She is He
Wrong Man

Loyal to his King
Barbarian Tales - Book One - Traveler's Tales*
Barbarian Tales - Book Two - Journeys Begin*
Barbarian Tales - Book Three - The Inheritance*
Barbarian Tales - Book Four - Road to Persepolis*

BOOKS BY SHABBU
A Season in Galicia*
Blind Dates*
Velvet Interrogation
Finding Jason
Dirty Pool
Operation Black Jade
Cigars!*
Angel in the Barn
Gayly Complicated*
Despoiling David
The Tree of Idleness*
I Met a Man
Rough Road to Happiness
BOOKS BY STEPHEN KESSEL
Gay Romance
The Forever Man
Two Chances
BOOKS BY KIM BLACK
Lesbian Romance
Transfixed on Tammie (F/T lesbian)
~

www.ingramcontent.com/pod-product-compliance
Lightning Source LLC
Chambersburg PA
CBHW031133210626
46816CB00014B/693